INTRODUCING
Sonika
EILIS FLYNN

An Ellora's Cave Publication

www.ellorascave.com

Introducing Sonika

ISBN 9781419964411
ALL RIGHTS RESERVED.
Introducing Sonika Copyright © 2007 Eilis Flynn
Edited by Shannon Combs.
Cover artist Syneca.

Electronic book publication December 2007
Trade paperback publication 2011

With the exception of quotes used in reviews, this book may not be reproduced or used in whole or in part by any means existing without written permission from the publisher, Ellora's Cave Publishing, Inc.® 1056 Home Avenue, Akron OH 44310-3502.

Warning: The unauthorized reproduction or distribution of this copyrighted work is illegal. Criminal copyright infringement, including infringement without monetary gain, is investigated by the FBI and is punishable by up to 5 years in federal prison and a fine of $250,000.
(http://www.fbi.gov/ipr/)

This book is a work of fiction and any resemblance to persons, living or dead, or places, events or locales is purely coincidental. The characters are productions of the author's imagination and used fictitiously.

INRODUCING SONIKA
ಐ

Dedication

This is for Interlac members in the past and in memoriam; for Rover the cat, who more or less consented to being a character herein when she demanded to be petted; and for Mike, whose book this always was.

Trademarks Acknowledgement
୨෮

The author acknowledges the trademarked status and trademark owners of the following wordmarks mentioned in this work of fiction:

Band-Aid: Johnson & Johnson Corporation
BMW: Bayerische Motoren Werke Aktiengesellschaft
Boy Scouts: Boy Scouts of America Corporation
Diet Pepsi: PepsiCo, Inc.
Doc Martens: Dr. Martens International Trading GmbH
Enfield: BAE Systems plc
Kryptonite: DC Comics
Lexus: Toyota Motor Corporation
Marriott: Marriott International Inc.
MIT: Massachusetts Institute of Technology Corporation
Mustang: Ford Motor Company
Saint John: St. John Knits, Inc.
Salvation Army: Salvation Army, The Corporation
Saran Wrap: S. C. Johnson Home Storage, Inc.
Science: American Association for the Advancement of Science
Sharpie: Sanford, L.P. Newell Operating Company
Spider-Man: Cadence Industries Corporation
Supergirl: DC Comics
Superman: DC Comics
Starbucks: Starbucks Coffee Company
The Three Stooges: Comedy III Entertainment, Inc. Corporation

Tiffany: Tiffany (NJ) Inc.
Time: Time Inc.
Twinkie: Interstate Bakeries Corporation
USA Today: Media West, GSI Inc. Corporation
Weight Watchers: Weight Watchers International, Inc.
Wonder Woman: DC Comics
Yugo: Zavodi Crvena Zastava

Prologue

"Velocity!"

"Sounder, it's no use," his wife whispered, voice cracking, her faint words bouncing around the rough walls of the cavern. Catching her unawares, the rockslide had knocked her down, and now her legs and most of her upper body were buried under immovable stone. The irony wasn't lost on him — she was the fastest woman in the world, and she couldn't move. "I can't get out from under this rubble and you can't use your voice to help me—"

He gritted his teeth. *No.* It couldn't end like this! "You can't give up, Vel. We'll find a way," he insisted.

But even as he said it, he knew.

They had no way out of this. Sounder knew it and so did Velocity. And so did the cause of it all, Gentleman Geoffrey.

"All three of us are stuck, Sounder. And she's trapped," the tall, thin man shouted across the crevice, a sneer distorting his face. Smudges of dirt nearly obscured his features, the monocle for which he was infamous nowhere in sight, probably shattered during the struggle with Sounder and Velocity. The ledge he was clinging from was barely large enough to hold him. "You could get the rock off her with your voice-song, but then we would very likely die, because this area of the old mines is geologically unstable and that would trigger another rockslide. Velocity could vibrate to get the rubble off herself, but that would still bring the cave down on us. This ledge won't hold me forever, and there's nothing close enough for me to jump to. We're all screwed. Nice to have known you!"

Geoffrey started to laugh, a thin edge of hysteria cutting through his words. "You won't be taking me into custody, not this time, Sounder. What do you think? Care to make a wager?"

"Damn you, Geoffrey," Velocity said, her voice barely audible. She took a breath—and coughed. Sounder winced. That didn't sound good. Broken ribs, maybe a punctured lung. "We're not going to let you get away, not this time. I'm going to make sure you go down!"

The sound that followed was unmistakable, that high-pitched, whirring noise that filled the space in an instant. The second Sounder heard it, he knew. "No, Velocity! Don't!" he shouted, but it was too late. She began to blur as she vibrated, knocking the rubble off her. And just as Geoffrey had predicted, the cave started to tremble and dust filled the air. The walls of rock began to collapse on them.

"No, Velocity!" Sounder shouted.

"We have to try, Sounder!"

He could hear the tears in her voice.

"I love you..."

* * * * *

Sonya Penn woke up, her eyes wet. The same nightmare, every year. "I'm so sorry, Mom. I'm so sorry, Dad," she whispered.

Introducing Sonika

Chapter One

The words on the gravestones had been etched over a decade before, but for Sonya, it might as well have been yesterday. She touched their names, the way she did at the beginning of her visit every anniversary—SAMUEL PENN. VICTORIA PENN.

She had considered having something else engraved—"defenders of the defenseless," perhaps, destroying the anonymity by which they had led their lives—but decided against it. They had lived in secret, so they should rest in secret. She had settled on "Beloved father and mother".

And that was as true now as it was then.

"It's been twelve years, Mom and Dad," she whispered, blinking away the tears. "I haven't done what you hoped I'd do, but I still help people."

Wiping her eyes, she laid a bouquet of daffodils between their plots before turning away. She walked to her battered, red SUV and started the ignition, flinching when the radio blared to life. She moved to switch it off, but paused when she heard the topic and she listened as she drove.

"You remember Sounder and Velocity, Ron?"

"Sure do, Mike. Today's a day to mourn."

"For those of you out there too young to remember, twelve years ago today our local superheroes gave their lives protecting us from organized crime figure Gentleman Geoffrey, who also died in that confrontation. There's going to be a candlelight vigil tonight in Morrissey Park and if you plan to attend, go in groups. We're told the police will be around but it's still not safe out there."

"You said it, Mike. In related news, the current crime wave has the city council calling for more police—"

Sonya turned off the radio as she exited the freeway. She wasn't going to think about it, not right now. The crime rates had been going up for the past twelve years and that wasn't going to stop anytime soon. Right now, she had other things to worry about.

Like finding her way in the suburbs.

She slowed as she approached the cul-de-sac, glancing left and right, looking for addresses. Surrounding her were large, sprawling, older homes from the days of gracious living—estates protected from public view by high fences and high gates. Locked gates.

This one had to be the place. Sonya double-checked the address as she turned off the engine. "Wow," she muttered.

It's a big house, the physical therapist originally assigned to this client had told her. *You can't miss it.*

"Margie, you were wrong," Sonya said aloud. "This isn't a big house. This sucker's a fortress!"

And if her newest client could afford to live here, he was going to be her ticket out of crushing, lingering debt, at long, freakin' last.

But she had to find him first, and that meant getting onto the estate.

Sonya hunted for an intercom, found it half-buried in ivy. She pressed the button. In the distance, with her sensitive hearing, she could hear the blare of the buzzer echo through the main house. No answer. "Someone's got to be home," she muttered, frowning. She pressed again. Nope.

She peered through the bars of the gates, calculating. Was the guy out of the house? Or was he peeking around the drapes?

For a moment, she was tempted to get back into her car and leave. There had to be some other way to pay off her aunt's hospital bills. And besides, it was her birthday. She deserved a day off.

She was tempted. But no. "Oh, hell," she muttered.

We help those who need help, her parents had told her.

Sonya took a deep breath. With a quick look around—there were only a few security cameras around the perimeter of the property, smashed and hanging useless, which surprised her in this tony neighborhood—she stepped back from the gates and stared at them, assessing. They weren't that tall. She could do it.

She looked around. No cops, nobody.

Sonya took a running leap, scrambling for a foothold. She missed a crossbar and nearly fell, her boot making a solid *thunk* against the strong metal before she recovered her balance.

"Shoot," she whispered, panting. She hadn't scaled a gate in years, and at that moment, she keenly felt the lack of practice. Pick the lock or jump over?

The sound of an automobile approaching made her decide fast. She clambered to the top and straddled the gate. Right before the car came into view, she jumped down inside the property and secreted herself in the dense ivy that covered the stone walls.

The car—a black-and-white police vehicle, she noted as she peered around the corner—idled for a few seconds before it went on its way. Sonya waited until the sound of the engine died away before she headed up the long, curving driveway, moving quickly and quietly, looking around as she did.

Once she was at the house, she knocked on the heavy mahogany front door. "Anybody home?" she shouted. She waited a minute, then pounded some more. Still no answer.

Grumbling, she reached into her satchel and pulled out the notes she had inherited from Margie, her predecessor, about her newest client…provided, of course, she tracked him down.

"Who are you, John Arlen?" Sonya whispered. Five cards clipped together, scribbled with notes about her newest client—that was all the information she had about the guy, as opposed to the usual several dozen. "Who are you? All I know about you from these cards is that you won't open the door for your appointments."

At least he was consistent. According to Margie's notes, John Arlen was a "difficult" client. And even when he did allow the physical therapist in for their sessions, he was short-tempered and moody. His last therapist had given up on him, which was how Sonya had inherited him. So why, if he was willing to pay for the in-home therapy, wouldn't he answer the door to get it?

Well, she was here to find out. He would be her client—provided, of course, she tracked him down and sweet-talked him into it. "Mr. Arlen?" she shouted. She shoved the cards back into her satchel.

No answer. She glanced up the side of the mansion. Three floors, not counting the basement. And some of the drapes were open.

It wouldn't be that hard to climb up and peer in, just to see if anyone was home. After a quick look around—no cameras at all inside the property? Weren't rich people supposed to be security-conscious?—Sonya shinnied up the drainpipe. She got to the second floor and edged her way over to the nearest window.

Damn. No light, no sign of life, nothin'.

Disappointed, Sonya made her way back to the drainpipe and slid down. She started to jump off the porch when she did something she hadn't done very often since her parents died.

She stopped and, for the lack of a better word, she listened.

Sonya heard the boiler rumble deep within the house as it heated the rooms. She listened a little harder and heard the hum of electricity, zillions of electrons moving at the speed of light through the wiring, powering the house—she could hear it all.

And she heard something else.

A heartbeat and a high-pitched whine, in the same part of the house. Bingo.

Sonya cocked her head, listening. *You could* look *for the noise,* she told herself. *The old-fashioned way.*

But this way is so much quicker.

Glancing one last time over her shoulder, the way her mother had taught her, she stretched out her hand and focused.

A thin stream of light burst from her fingertips and traveled in a straight line along the side of the house. She followed the luminous flow as it zeroed in on a small window, low to the ground. *Jackpot!*

The glass was too dusty for her to see through, but she could hear the screech of a belting device and the heartbeat as well. She rapped on the glass.

The high-pitched whine crackled and died. She heard a muffled curse, then something being dragged across the floor—a rubber-soled walking shoe?—before a face appeared.

It was a man, and he didn't look happy. "Mr. John Arlen?" Sonya asked. She smiled—looking friendly was half the battle, she figured.

"Yes," he said, growling. He glared behind his tortoise-shelled glasses, but that also might have had something to do with his white-knuckled grip on the crutches tucked under his arms. "Who are you? How did you get past the gates?"

"I'm Sonya Penn," she said, offering him her business card. "Your new physical therapist? We had an appointment."

"I have an appointment on Thursday. How did you get past the security system?"

"Today's Thursday," she said helpfully.

He groaned. "Listen, can you come back later? I'm in the middle of something important." He glanced over his shoulder, at something Sonya couldn't see.

"Sorry, I've got a whole day of appointments lined up," she lied through her teeth. "Should I come in through the front door, or would you like me to come in through this window?"

He snorted. "Go ahead and try."

"Don't mind if I do," she said, considering the space. The window was small and narrow, but that was no problem. Sonya grasped the edge of the casement and slipped in without effort, pulling in her satchel after her. "Hello again," she said cheerfully. "Shall we get started?"

He stared at the window, then at her. He shook his head. "I could have sworn it was too small. I—"

"Gymnastics when I was a kid," she cut in. "Comes in handy when I have to wiggle in and out of tight spaces." She smiled again, trying her best to look harmless. "How 'bout it?"

He glanced at her before he looked over his shoulder again. This time she looked too.

In the dim light, she couldn't see much—concrete walls, concrete floor and something metal in the far corner. She couldn't see it, but that wasn't her concern right now. "So how 'bout it?" she repeated. "Shall we get started?"

"Right." He blinked. "I guess."

She noticed his eyes—gray and bloodshot. He hadn't shaved in the recent past either, which only accentuated his features—hawk-like and grim. He was also sweating, his hair standing up in tufts. And his T-shirt was grubby.

He stared up at the window again, then looked at her, as though she were an alien. If she hadn't been dressed for work—a plaid woolen shirt, jeans and Doc Martens boots, her curly fair hair plaited into one fat efficient braid—she might have been insulted. But she also knew her clothing was in sharp contrast to her face—round face, rosy cheeks, big, blue eyes and most damning of all, dimples. No matter what, she looked too angelic to appear tough. Damn it.

"You say you rang the bell?"

He didn't ask again about how she'd gotten past the gates. That was good. "I knocked too," she added. "You probably couldn't hear me from down here, considering how loud that contraption is—"

"What are you talking about?" he demanded. "You can't even see it from here. It's—"

Shoot! "I could hear it." That much was true. "I heard something and I thought it was coming from the basement. That's how I tracked you down."

He closed his eyes. "Too noisy. I'll have to work on that."

"Do that after your physical therapy session."

He groaned. "Can't you come back? I'm really busy."

"No, I can't."

Finally, he shrugged, his gaze straying to the corner again. "I was busy," he mumbled. "I *am* busy." He shifted from one leg to the other, keeping a grip on his crutches.

At one point, he had to have been athletic. His arms were sinewy, with a hint of the grace he must have had. Despite the silver streaking his dark hair and the lines lining his face, he was still a young man.

Enough. "Mr. Arlen, if you ever want to walk without those crutches again, you've got to have therapy on that leg and that shoulder. You're too young to be hobbling."

He groaned again. "If I say yes, will you go away after the session?"

Yes! She smiled as sweetly as she could. "You bet." She stifled the urge to do a happy dance. Instead, she gestured toward the staircase. "Shall we? Or do you want to do your exercises down here?"

He sighed. "Upstairs. Let me just turn off—uh, my contraption."

Sonya stepped toward the staircase, then turned back. "Don't forget to close..."

She gaped. The metallic "contraption" in the corner... She hadn't seen one in years, and this was a lot more sophisticated than the one she'd seen as a kid, but there was no question what it was. "What are you doing with an antigrav propulsion unit? That's what it is, isn't it?"

He stopped dead. "How do you know what it is?"

Would she ever learn to shut up? "I've seen pictures of the ones the scientists at MIT came up with," she said after a pause. A little lame, and not quite the truth, but it was close enough.

His eyes narrowed. "Let me see your ID."

Without a word she flipped open her wallet. He peered at her driver's license. "The weight's not right," she said helpfully.

"How do you know what an antigrav device looks like? They're not exactly the most common device around."

Sonya shrugged. "I studied recent patents and their possible applications when I was a kid," she added. "My parents insisted. I don't even know if MIT's made any progress with the device. The last thing I read was that methane power was being considered."

He was openly skeptical. "Do your parents still insist?"

She smiled, wistful. "They died years ago. It was a wild guess."

"It was a good one." But he still looked at her suspiciously.

Sonya held her breath, hoping he wouldn't ask anything else. She climbed the stairs and waited at the top as he followed, one step at a time. Once or twice she nearly reached out to help him, afraid he would lose his balance. Finally he made it upstairs, though by then he was on his knees.

"The last physical therapist suggested the library for these sessions," he gasped, sweat pouring down his face.

She almost felt guilty for being able to stand. "So you go up and down these stairs every day?"

He braced his body against the wall and pushed up. His teeth were clenched. "No. I spend most of my time downstairs." He paused, his legs visibly wobbling, almost fully standing straight. He took a deep breath.

She couldn't stand it anymore. "Do you need help?"

He glared at her. "Get away from me."

Good. She preferred patients who were cranky. "You know, with a little therapy—"

He snorted. He was finally on his feet, crutches in place again. "Spare me. You've convinced me the only way you're going to leave is if I do what you want, but that doesn't mean I'm going to listen to a lot of bullshit."

Sonya shrugged. "Fine. The sooner we get to the living room to do your therapy, the sooner—"

"Don't have one." He closed his eyes for a second before he looked at her. "No living room. This is not a house meant to be lived in," he added, with a flash of humor.

Sonya liked that. "So where—"

"Follow me," he said, sighing. He started down the corridor, pausing on occasion to adjust his grip on the crutches.

Sonya took advantage of his slow pace to gawk. The house was even bigger on the inside than it looked on the outside. The halls, high-ceilinged and broad, were lined with rich, brocaded wallpaper and old-fashioned landscapes, with crystal chandeliers and sconces lighting the way.

Finally, he pushed open a set of doors, carved of ornate bird's-eye walnut. "There's enough space in here."

She stepped into the library and *really* stopped to gawk. "You're probably right," she conceded. "Nice place."

Lined with filled bookcases and traditional landscapes, the room had to be the size of her entire apartment. It should have looked warm and cozy but somehow it wasn't. At the flip of a switch, a fire started to crackle in the gas fireplace, but that didn't seem to cast any heat. The room didn't inspire anyone to care, only be impressed.

She noticed some framed photographs on the marble mantel—the most inviting, most personal items in the room. "What's that?" she asked, curious. She checked it out.

An older couple, both wearing thick, round spectacles, were in the photographs, the twinkle in their eyes endearing. Picking up one of the photos, she glanced at Arlen. "Your folks?"

"Yeah," he said after a pause. "Be careful with that. It's the best picture I have of them."

"Sorry," she said as she replaced it. "They don't like having their pictures taken?"

"They're dead too."

Sonya winced. "I'm sorry."

She got down to business, sitting him down into position—and nearly recoiled. His shoulders felt like stone.

"If you don't like taking the stairs to the basement, how about those steps leading up to the front door?" she asked as she started to massage his shoulders. Good grief, he was tense. "They're steep."

"There's a door out the basement. But I don't go out much."

That she knew. Near-recluse, Margie's cards noted. Sonya passed her hands over his back, which was ramrod straight, and then she touched his right leg. He twitched. "Bend your leg. Does that hurt?" she asked, rotating his ankle slightly.

"No." But his breath caught.

"Are you eating? Tilt your foot up."

"What the hell does eating have to do with therapy?"

Feeling the tension sweep his muscles again, she bent his leg a little more.

His breath caught again—not good. "It didn't hurt until you did that," he accused.

Sonya stifled a laugh. "You live on pizza and beer, right?"

"Not beer. Well, once in a while," he amended. "Mostly pizza. I get that delivered, and I don't have to stop working."

She worked his leg, gently manipulating it as she watched him. The circles of exhaustion that ringed his eyes worried her. "When's the last time you slept, Mr. Arlen?"

"I sleep plenty."

"You've got a cot down in the basement, don't you?" When he didn't answer, she added, "You're not doing yourself any favors. Now let's bend the other leg."

"I know what I'm doing," he insisted, but a tremor ran through his words. "I'm fine."

"Are you? Bend your leg and hold it. Then why are you trying to kill yourself by overworking?"

She watched his reaction as first the exercise and then the accusation took their toll. "I've got work to do," he insisted. A fine sheen of perspiration beaded his neck. His heart beat faster—she could hear it practically tripping in its haste. "I don't have time. Damn it, that hurts!"

"Of course it hurts. You should have been working this leg and your shoulder since you left the hospital. How's your arm?"

"That's been a problem," he admitted.

She stopped working his leg for a moment. "You're admitting to a problem? You?"

"It hurts." He turned over, favoring his right shoulder. From Margie's notes, Sonya knew his left leg had five steel pins keeping it together, his right arm had limited mobility and he needed extensive therapy on his shoulder. It didn't help that he had to use crutches, but he refused to use a wheelchair.

Sonya would have felt sorrier for him if he'd been more cooperative. "Sit up and raise your arm, please." She slipped her arm behind him to help.

He sat up. His face was ashen but he managed to raise his hand halfway to his head. "That's as far as I've been able to get it." But he didn't lower his hand, he kept it there, quivering. It must have hurt like hell.

All right, she'd cut him a break. "Do you want to be able to raise your hand above your head ever again?"

His gaze met hers. Even bloodshot, his eyes were expressive. "You know I do."

"Then you're going to do what I tell you."

Sighing, he lowered his arm until his hand rested against the mat. "How long is it going to take?"

Under her touch, she felt him relax. "As long as it takes."

Sonya closed her eyes for a moment. "My notes say you were assaulted in a family dispute," she said. "So what happened?"

Sonya didn't count on his reaction.

"Time's up," he snapped, struggling to sit up. "I want you gone. You can come back tomorrow."

"I'm sorry, what did I say?"

"You heard me. Go." Leaning on a side table and breathing hard, he pushed himself up. "Sorry about the misunderstanding."

Mystified, she sat back. "What did I do?"

Arlen didn't answer, instead working himself into a stand.

Fine, if that was the way he wanted to play it. "If you need any help with that antigrav device, give me a call," she said as she rolled up her mat.

"Thanks. I can manage."

She tried again. "Do you live alone?"

He didn't answer. He slipped his crutches under his arms, then gestured for her to follow him. She guessed he was making sure she left.

She gave it one last shot when they arrived at the foyer. "Do you live alone?"

He stopped, still facing the door. "Why, are you planning on robbing me?"

She stifled a smile. "So you go up and down those basement stairs you're not comfortable with everyday? You only eat when you can't avoid it? You know you're cruising for trouble."

He bristled. "That's none of your business."

"The possibility of you getting seriously hurt is my business."

He turned, eyes blazing. "Let me tell you about getting seriously hurt, lady. I was in the hospital for half a year, but at least I'm alive. My dad was murdered. And I'm going to get the son of a bitch responsible, with or without you!"

Shit. Sonya stepped back. "I'm sorry," she whispered. "I just want you to get better."

Sighing, he slumped against the door. "It's been a bad day."

"Just a day?"

"A bad year," he admitted. "Now, if you would—" he turned, starting to open the door.

"You know what, Mr. Arlen?" She touched his shoulder again.

Warm. He was finally warm—the exercise helped—and she could feel his muscles shift through the thin T-shirt.

Last-ditch effort. He needed the help and that was her job. "I think you're tired and hungry. I shouldn't do this, but do you want to go eat? I noticed a coffee shop a couple miles down the road."

Even before she had finished speaking, he was shaking his head. "Adelaide's. Thanks anyway."

"So the food's bad?"

"Not at all. I used to go there—"

"I'll drive," she suggested. "So how about it?"

"No. But thanks for the offer, Miss…"

He'd forgotten her name already. She wished she could feel insulted, but she couldn't. "Sonya Penn. I hate to eat alone," she wheedled.

"I've got too much to do."

Last chance. "Oh, c'mon. It's my birthday and I don't have anyone to celebrate it with." She could feel her face flush. But it was the truth, sad as it was.

He stared at her. She thought she had lost but then he said, "Happy birthday. Will you leave me alone if I say yes?"

She smiled but she couldn't meet his eyes. "Sure."

"Fine." He opened the door and stepped out, covering his eyes against the weak winter sunlight. "Let's go."

"Don't you need a jacket? That T-shirt—"

"No. Let's go."

John Arlen made his way down the driveway just fine on those crutches, she observed. Even given the long curving driveway had a slight slope leading down to the street, she had to hop once in a while to keep up.

They stopped at the end of the drive. Puzzled, he turned to her. "Where'd you park?"

The question had finally come and this time she couldn't duck it. Sonya met his questioning gaze. "Outside the gates."

He looked up the winding driveway. There was a question but he wasn't asking it. *How did you get past the gates?*

She sighed and answered it anyway. "I climbed over them."

"Those gates are ten feet tall."

She shrugged. "Fence is about twelve feet. And there was a police car coming down the street, so I had to get over fast."

"I didn't answer the intercom, I didn't answer the door and you climbed the fence anyway? There's a door next to the gate. Why didn't you try to come in that way? You know, force the door, pick the lock."

"I was in a hurry."

He stared at her again and she thought maybe she shouldn't volunteer any more information.

It was a quick trip down to the shopping center. He didn't offer any small talk—he was probably wondering if she was a lunatic. She didn't blame him for that, either. She turned on the radio.

That was a mistake. The same radio commentators were on. "What about this current crime spree in town, Ron? Did you hear about the police commissioner being mugged?"

"I sure did, Mike. Lowell Zilber, the police commissioner for the city of Morrissey, was—"

Sonya groaned. "I don't need to hear this," she muttered. She reached out to shut it off but his hand shot out and grabbed hers.

"Leave it on. Sorry," he said after the news item ended. He switched the radio off. "The police in this town are incompetent. We're all too dependent on superheroes to protect us. And we don't have any, not anymore."

Sonya was aware of her own heart pounding. He was a bundle of surprises—she wasn't expecting that grip. The light turned green. She tapped the gas pedal, jerking the car forward. "The cops have a lot of work to do," she said, amid her own bemusement.

The coffee shop was cozy, white-painted brick on the outside and cracked red vinyl booths on the inside. John Arlen made a beeline for the window booth closest to the door, looking out at the street. She liked how he looked sitting there—almost relaxed. "So what's good?" she asked as she slid in across from him and opened the plastic-covered menu.

"It's all good."

He could talk more. She was sure of it. "So tell me about John Arlen," she said after they ordered.

His only response was a tight smile. He would have been relatively attractive if he hadn't looked like a very tired mad scientist. "Not much to tell." He pushed his glasses up. "I've lived here all my life, except college. My dad was a physicist, so I wanted to be one too."

"Of course." Sonya snapped her fingers. "Arlen Labs. I should have realized." The basement lab should have been a dead giveaway but she was out of practice in jumping to conclusions.

"That's me. I did some work I was proud of," he went on. "I met you. The end."

And she prided herself on being taciturn? He had her beat by a mile. "Spend all your time working?"

"Mostly."

"No hobbies?"

"No. Well, I used to play the piano."

"Were you any good?" she persisted.

"No."

Sonya snorted. "You don't kid yourself, do you?" She tried to think of something to say, anything to keep the conversation going. "I spent most of my time studying and practicing gymnastics," she offered, though he hadn't asked.

"Sounds like you worked too hard when you were a kid." He glanced out the window. "Didn't you do anything fun? Reading?"

He was making idle chitchat, but she'd go along with it. "Do professional journals count?"

At that he stared at her. "When you were a kid? Sports?"

She shrugged. "The gymnastics thing."

"Music?"

"Butterfingers," she said sadly. She waved her fingers.

"Gardening?"

"Hay fever." And that was all true.

To her surprise, he reached over and touched her hand. "You couldn't wear a ring like that if you gardened, anyway."

The simple ring sat high on her finger, etched with an intricate swirl of a monogram. It glinted in the dim daylight and it reminded her of all sorts of things she tried to forget. "It was my mother's." Her voice quivered. Damn.

But he didn't seem to notice. All he said was, "I'm sorry. How—" he stopped.

This was why she shouldn't talk about the past. "Car accident," she lied, her voice getting stronger as she added, "My parents were in the wrong place at the wrong time."

"I'm sorry." He was still looking at her hand. "Your ring looks familiar. I don't know why."

"It's a pretty common style," she lied with a smile. She was a pro. She was trained to lie. "The look was popular ten, twenty years ago. You remember Sounder and Velocity?"

He smiled, really smiled, for the first time since she'd met him. She liked it. "The superheroes? Sure. Sounder was my hero when I was a kid."

"Mine too," she said, smiling back. "He and Velocity were every local kid's heroes."

"It hit me like a ton of bricks when they died." He got quiet when the waitress arrived with their orders and they started to eat. "There's a reason I have an antigrav device in my basement," he said after a while.

She nodded. "I wasn't going to ask."

"That's why I figured I'd tell you. The Engineer killed my father and he crippled me."

Her stomach twisted. The name of the criminal currently terrorizing the city was painfully familiar. "I'm so sorry," she ground out. All of a sudden, the scrambled eggs she had been eating tasted like ash. "Why?"

"Dad and I were working on something the Engineer wanted and we wouldn't give it up. So he killed my dad and told me I'd be next if I didn't give it to him."

"And you did?"

He took a deep breath. "No. I told him he had murdered the only person who had it. That's when he beat me into a pulp."

Sonya winced. "I'm so sorry. So...why the antigrav unit?"

His face was set. "I know the odds. I could still end up in a wheelchair. If I could perfect the antigrav device, I can retain enough mobility. I'm not going to avenge my father from a wheelchair."

She flinched. She wanted to walk away—away from this man who so obviously had so many issues it made her own look like a trifle. But then she could hear what her mother would have said. *We help those who need help, Sonya. It's why we're here.*

It's been twelve years, Mom. I don't know what to do.

But Sonya had no choice, not if she ever wanted to feel clean again.

She took a deep breath. "Mr. Arlen." She covered his hand with hers. "John. I can help you."

He stared at her for a second. Clearly, he didn't understand. Why would he? His goal was simple revenge. Hers was fulfilling a dream lost over a decade ago. "Physical therapy's going to help me only so much."

"I wasn't talking about PT. I want to help you get the Engineer."

Just saying it made her stomach churn.

She could hear the blood start to roar through his veins. "What are you suggesting?"

"I know physical therapy." She ignored the knot in her stomach. She had thought—maybe even hoped—this was all behind her. But no. "I know self-defense. I even know the antigrav device you're working on. You need my help."

His eyes narrowed. "Who are you?"

"I told you who I am."

"Why?"

Sonya breathed deep and stepped off into the abyss. "Because the Engineer's father killed mine."

Chapter Two

Sonya held her breath as John Arlen stared at her. "I thought you said it was an accident." He shoved away his plate.

She felt sorry for him. He wasn't having a good day. First he managed to short-circuit his antigrav device—of that she had no doubt, considering his aggravated mood—and then he managed to tune out the sound of the doorbell, gate buzzer and her pounding at the door. And now, he had just told her what he was planning. He might as well have taken an ad out in *The Morrissey Herald*.

Well, he hadn't told her *everything*. But he'd probably told her more than he had told anyone else since his hospital stay.

"I thought you said your father died in a car accident," he repeated. His eyes narrowed.

She looked down at her coffee, milk swirling. "It was an accident set up by the Engineer's father, Gentleman Geoffrey. My father tried to stand up to him."

"How old were you?"

"Sixteen." She heard her voice break again. Damn it, she promised herself she wasn't going to do this, not today!

Sonya cleared her throat, twisting her ring. "My mom died a while afterward."

"How do I know you're not working for the Engineer?"

"You don't."

John looked at her. She met his gaze. "Screw it. Fine," he said. "It's a deal, Miss—"

"Call me Sonya."

He looked at his mostly empty plate, littered with scraps of congealing egg. "If you aren't who you say you are," he said without looking up, his voice crackling with tension, "I could be in a shitload of trouble."

Despite the situation, she had to laugh. "Or I could be, for agreeing to help you. Life's a crapshoot, Mr. Arlen. I could be signing my death warrant going up against a master criminal." Even as she said it, the qualms rose. Maybe she should leave well enough alone. After all, Gentleman Geoffrey was dead. But—

He snorted. "Right now, I couldn't kill a fly." He slapped his hand down on the table, startling her. "Let's go."

Considering she had just told him she would help him hunt down a known killer, it was ludicrous she had to help him get up. To confront a supervillain in the making, they needed a superhero, and the city was short a couple. It had been for over a decade and that wasn't about to change.

"This is insane, you know that," he warned.

She snorted as she handed him his crutches. "Tell me about it. I don't know if I want to help someone crazy enough to fight a fight like this."

"Then why did you say you would?"

She grinned. "I like a challenge."

His face lit up. He slipped the crutches under his arms. "Glad to give you one."

John glanced at her and hesitated. *What now?* Sonya wondered. What else was he not telling her? For all she knew, he was going to take over Gentleman Geoffrey's old crime syndicate after he got the Engineer.

"I don't have my wallet on me," he said finally.

She sighed in relief. He couldn't pay for his meal. That she could handle. "You bet. I did invite you."

They left the restaurant, Sonya slightly behind John Arlen. He had to trust her. He had to. "We must both be insane," she whispered. He was in no shape to be doing any of this and neither was she. But she could feel for him and his determination.

She bet he had changed the locks more than once since he had gotten home from the hospital, but she had to bet it hadn't made him feel any safer. Worst of all was the sensation of not knowing if someone who turned up on his doorstep was going to kill him too. She knew. She remembered.

"Thank you for making me leave the house," he said when they were on their way back. "I...really needed that."

She shook her head. "I know what it's like to be consumed by something. I know what it can do." *I know what it's like to be frightened,* she wanted to say, but she didn't.

"What about you?"

She shrugged. "I've gone on with my life. Geoffrey is dead. The caves in the Wasserman mines collapsed, taking any chance of his body being recovered. It's not the ending I wanted but it's the one that happened."

"Your parents would have been proud of the way you grew up."

She laughed. "No, they wouldn't. I haven't done a tenth of what they expected of me."

They arrived in front of Arlen Manor in a matter of minutes, passing another black-and-white police vehicle and a private security car along the way. If nothing else, the people who lived in these ritzy homes seemed to have a lot of protection.

Except John Arlen, she realized, recalling the smashed perimeter cameras. Why was that? She frowned and turned to ask. "Why—"

"Why don't you think I'm nuts?" he interrupted.

"Actually, I do."

"But you're not calling for the butterfly nets. Why not?"

"I know what you're going through."

"It's one thing to sympathize, it's another to actively encourage my lunacy."

"You're not going against the Engineer on crutches, Mr. Arlen. It's not going to happen."

He reached out and clasped her hand. "Thank you."

Once more she was surprised. If she wasn't careful, she could get to like that. "You're welcome." She turned away. "Should I drive onto the property, or will out front do?"

"Driveway. Let me open the gates." As Sonya watched, John twisted the band of his wristwatch and tapped a link. The security gates—tall, heavy, forbidding—slid open.

"Very nice," she said. "Attached to your watchband?"

He nodded and suddenly she realized he looked uneasy.

She knew why. To hell with it. "You're still worried I'm connected with the Engineer and microcircuitry like that might be something he would be interested in," she guessed as she parked and helped him out.

He jerked. "Of course not."

She grinned. "Sure you are. If you weren't, you wouldn't have a prayer of defeating him. It's a good start."

"So paranoia and suspicion are good things?"

"Trusting someone always means it might backfire on you."

Sonya let Arlen chew on that. He opened the front door cautiously—he had forgotten his wallet, but he had his keys with him, apparently—when he stopped.

Was he hesitating because he didn't want to go back into his own home, or was it something else? "There's no time like the present to start, Mr. Arlen," she said, prodding him.

"You're absolutely right." Still, he seemed unsure. She watched as he entered his own home slowly, looking around.

She did too. Nothing looked out of the ordinary, but with his reaction, something had to be.

John Arlen continued to look around as she unrolled her mat again. "Are you sure you're not just humoring me to make sure I get my exercises in?" His face was set despite his light tone. Something was definitely wrong.

She laughed, but not too much. The hairs at the back of her neck bristled. "Stick with me and you're going to learn all the paranoid basics of being a superhero." Way, way too close to the truth.

He snorted. "A superhero? I can barely walk."

Some of the best superheroes couldn't walk, fighting crime despite it, but she didn't tell him that. "It takes a superhero to go after a supervillain."

"Sounds good, doesn't it?" He sounded wishful as he settled on the mat again. Sonya guessed the idea appealed to the little boy within him, the one who had grown up worshipping Sounder and Superman and Spider-Man.

But first, John Arlen had to be able to stand on his own. He was right, the antigrav unit was a far-distant option.

By the time the hour she had allotted for his therapy ended, he was sweating and she knew he was going to have trouble getting up the next morning.

That didn't matter. "No. Keep going," he gasped when she tried to stop.

"Overdoing it isn't going to help." She pressed on his shoulder. Sure enough, his muscles were twisted into harder knots than before. "You won't be able to move tomorrow if you do too much."

He reached out and grabbed her arm. "Please."

She flinched again, but she didn't pull away. "Okay, but not much more. As it is, you're not going to feel like getting up tomorrow morning," she warned.

"I haven't felt like getting up in months. I do it anyway."

Sonya could hear his heart thundering by the time she stopped, his breaths shallow. He rolled over and sat up slowly.

"No more," she said. She patted his knee—he was almost too hot to touch—and she stood.

"I'm good for more," John insisted, panting.

"Nope. Rule One, know when to quit," she said, stretching. She linked her hands and raised her arms above her head. She had to go work out herself. She was almost as stiff as he was.

"Tomorrow?"

"Same bat time, same bat channel." She rolled up her mat. "Just an hour tomorrow," she added, remembering her schedule. "I've got other clients—"

"Whatever they're paying you, I'll double it. In fact, just cancel your other clients. I'll need your full attention."

She halted. Bingo! Little dollar signs flashed in front of her eyes, along with an image of stamping "paid" on her last bill, but she restrained herself. "That's going to cost you."

"I can afford it."

This just seemed too easy. She had a feeling she was going to pay for it, one way or another. "Okay, I'll take care of it. I'll see you tomorrow, Mr. Arlen."

"Call me John. Just one question."

She stopped at the door. "Name it."

"Is it really your birthday?"

She laughed. That one she could answer. She pulled out her wallet, flipping it open to her driver's license again.

He leaned forward, swiping at his hair that fell in front of his glasses. He probably hadn't been to the barber anytime recently, either. "Happy twenty-eighth birthday."

"No, thank *you*. For eating with me." She flipped her wallet closed. "I didn't want to eat alone, not on my birthday," she added when he looked at her, puzzled.

Sonya left after that but she could feel him watching as she made her way down to her SUV. She could still feel his gaze as she got in and drove away.

It was time to do a little research.

To do that, she had to hit her friendly neighborhood library and make use of the public computers. She didn't want to use her own computer for research like this, just in case. She remained hunched over a terminal for the rest of the evening, checking any and every reference she could think of. But Arlen, John, was a mystery.

"C'mon, there has to be something," she whispered. The therapy assignment had come from Arlen Industries—at least the corporation existed. It was privately held so there wasn't much public information, but still…

"He had parents," she muttered aloud. She brightened when the screen refreshed—yes! Here was something! Then she frowned.

It was a community paper mention, not even in one of the city's major newspapers. It was a simple obituary about the death of John's father, Jonathan. His late wife Lorraine—John's mother—was mentioned, but nothing about his son. The article mentioned Arlen Industries and that was it. There wasn't even anything to indicate the family and company donated to charity, which meant they were either amazingly cheap or very, very private. She bet it was the latter.

By the time the librarian shooed her out, Sonya knew little more than she had when she came in. But she did know one thing—there was more to John Arlen than met the eye.

"He's as bad as I am," she muttered as she walked home, huddled in her jacket against the evening chill. She had had it drilled into her to keep a low profile, but he probably paid to make sure no one could find a trace of him.

But with some research, she knew she would show up. An only child, she had been orphaned at the age of sixteen—that would be in any article related to the deaths of her parents. Sonya Penn had gone to college, majored in criminology of all things, but earned a doctorate in music theory—that would show up too. Then, because a doctorate in music theory limited her job prospects, she had become a physical therapist. It never failed to amaze her where a mention of her would show up. She just tried to make sure it was at a minimum.

The only puzzle for anyone looking her up would be the way in which her father had died. For years after their deaths, Sonya would randomly try an Internet search to make sure there was little. Then as now, she could only find two references to Samuel Penn's death and neither mentioned a confrontation with Gentleman Geoffrey. In fact, there was a discrepancy in manner of death. One document said car accident. The other, a newspaper article, said mining accident. The more confusion the better. Her mother died less than a year later from injuries related to the same accident. Other than a notice in one of the local papers, there had been nothing else.

Otherwise, Sonya Penn was everything she claimed to be.

More or less.

Was she doing the right thing, agreeing to help John Arlen? She didn't know. But if she didn't offer to help, her mom and dad would haunt her dreams.

Too troubled to rest immediately, Sonya worked out at her all-night gym until she was tired enough to sleep. The next morning she called the clinic.

"I'm returning the favor," she told Margie after she filled in the other woman about what had happened the day before. "My appointments are now yours for the duration. He wants to make sure he regains mobility, so I have to make sure I'm available—"

"I'm amazed you got inside," Margie said.

Sonya could hear the wonder in her voice and chewed on her lip. "Maybe you should have climbed over the gates."

Margie laughed. "You're such a kidder. You'll be okay, right? You're sure he's not a nutcase?"

Sonya nearly choked. *No, I'm not sure of that at all,* she wanted to say. Instead, she said, "He's getting over a death in the family." Which was absolutely true.

That was always the part of the superhero life she never liked—the lies. But without the lies neither her parents, nor she, would ever have had a life.

Could she do this? Train someone to do something she herself had only been partially trained to do, against overwhelming odds? Was it such a bright idea?

No, but she had to help him anyway.

The question of how, beyond physical therapy and advice, occupied her thoughts as she ran her errands. She stopped by the supermarket not far from the Arlen estate, intent on picking up some groceries for him—he probably didn't have anything in his refrigerator, and pizza was not going to be on the menu for him for a while if she had anything to say about it—when she spotted, in the distance, a familiar figure.

What the hell was John Arlen, a borderline recluse, doing out of his house?

She left her SUV at the ritzy supermarket's parking lot, down the block from the coffee shop she and Arlen had gone to the day before. A cold drizzle started to fall as she watched from beneath the overhang in front of a Starbucks, far enough away she wouldn't be noticed, as her newest client hobbled into Adelaide's once again.

Sonya relaxed a little as she blew into her cupped hands. He was hungry, that was all. And today, he was willing to leave the house to eat—a good sign.

He had parked almost directly in front of the coffee shop. As she watched, he took the same window booth they had been in the day before—either he liked it, or the booth held some meaning for him, since it was clear he was familiar with the place.

She lingered some more, just to make sure he was all right. Buying a latté, she took it outside to drink, keeping an eye on her client. She gauged the distance between them—a few hundred yards, ambient noise of the traffic interfering—and adjusted her hearing so she could do more than watch.

"Johnny! I haven't seen you in ages! How you doin'?"

"Addy, it's good to see you. I'm doing better."

Sonya could see a gray-haired woman, with shrewd dark eyes and a smile, approach Arlen's booth. She had to be the owner of the coffee shop. *"My nephew said he saw you in here yesterday with a lady – serves me right for taking the day off."*

"My physical therapist."

"I hear she's pretty but she dresses sort of plain."

Sonya snorted. "I don't dress to impress my clients, lady," she muttered. She sipped at her hot drink. Her fingers were starting to tingle from the heat, much to her discomfort.

"I wasn't paying much attention to her looks, Addy. I'm much more interested in her skills."

"I may take that personally one of these days, Mr. Arlen," Sonya muttered. A couple who had just walked out of the Starbucks glanced at her, startled, before hurrying away.

Sonya heard Addy laugh. *"Keep tellin' yourself that, John. Now what's for breakfast?"*

"Coffee, please," he ordered. *"Regular. Two eggs scrambled, bacon, rye toast. Orange juice. And maybe a banana split."*

Sonya grimaced. For a while there he was doing so well—but a banana split for breakfast? He was *so* not going to do that, even if she had to walk in there.

"No, you're not," the older woman ordered, apparently agreeing with Sonya's assessment. "Donna, one egg poached, vegetarian sausage patty, whole-wheat toast, and OJ for Johnny-boy here."

Addy had to have known John Arlen for a long time. Or maybe she was just pushy. *"Thanks a lot, Addy."*

"Your father couldn't be here so I'm just doing what he would have, John," the woman said, adding, "You haven't been back here since—"

"No, I haven't," he said, cutting her off. "I couldn't—I practically grew up in here."

"I remember when you were a little boy, John," the woman said gently. "I remember the time you and your father came in here and you were talking about physics or something—"

"When weren't we?" John asked, laughing. "That's what we talked about. My dad taught me the basics of physics right here, using coffee shop materials to illustrate his point. I must have been three when he started."

"And I remember you teaching your dad how to balance a spoon on his nose," Addy said.

Sonya took another scalding sip and remembered her own father. Unlike John, she hadn't learned physics at her dad's knee. Instead, she had learned the lessons of crimefighting, among which had been to observe without being seen.

Speaking of which, she had been loitering in front of the Starbucks long enough. She decided to walk down the street, meandering slowly back to her car, stopping every so often to stare into whatever storefront window caught her eye. The fact that the ones she stopped in front of happened to have a clear reflection of the coffee shop across the street was sheer coincidence, of course.

Once in a while, she turned around to confirm he was still in the booth. He looked up at one point, forcing her to sink to her knees—fortunately, in front of a *USA Today* newspaper dispenser. She pretended to read the headlines, keeping a wary eye on Arlen as he finished his breakfast.

She was starting to feel hungry. Even the idea of a vegetarian sausage patty sounded good right now.

"Just buy a copy, why don't you," a passerby murmured, sotto voce. Most people would never have heard the rude comment under his breath, but of course Sonya did.

"Fine, I will," she muttered. She rummaged through her pockets and came up with the proper change. She pulled out a copy of the newspaper from the dispenser just as John Arlen came out of the coffee shop. She tensed when she saw him look across the street, but not in her direction.

The shops. He was going shopping?

Sonya groaned as she shoved the newspaper back in. What was down the street? Frantically, she tried to remember without standing up to check…a bookshop, and—that dusty little music store.

Whichever he was headed for, it didn't matter, because he wasn't bothering to use the crosswalk. "Don't do it," she muttered under her breath. "Use the crosswalk, damn it!"

Damn it, he wasn't going to! He was going to jaywalk, across speeding traffic. The cars were going too fast, despite the posted ten-mile-an-hour zone. She watched, her teeth gritted, as he narrowly dodged a BMW that wasn't even speeding. Then he stumbled out of the way with his crutches, veering to the side of a Lexus SUV that slowed down—barely—for him, horn blaring.

She started to breathe again after he managed to cross the street. There was only one slightly alarming episode involving not a car but an overly friendly Great Dane and its owner, a tiny, fur-trimmed woman who kept fussing, "No, Duke! Bad dog!"

Sonya assumed the dog took the lady for walks.

Arlen peered at the window display of the music store. The music store? She hadn't figured him for that. She tried to recall what was in the display—she remembered sheet music, faded by the sun, some dusty-looking guitars, two violins, a flute, a triangle, a set of maracas and an accordion.

Well, he did admit to having played the piano. Maybe it was a secret vice. Otherwise, she couldn't imagine him playing any of those instruments.

And she was the one with the doctorate in music theory. Fat lot of good it was doing her.

Sonya glanced at her watch. She'd have to take off soon for his place, but it would be pointless if he weren't there. She walked down the street, getting closer to the music store, but not so close Arlen would notice her. Concentrating, she could hear inside the little shop. She heard someone shuffling around, probably the proprietor. She heard the soft click as he flicked on the lights, the harsh sound of the rattan blinds being drawn up on the door, and finally, the rattle of the door as he unlocked the deadbolts.

Sonya found herself staring into the bakery next to the music shop as she listened to what was happening next door. She could hear Arlen moving around on his crutches. His breathing was regular, not too fast, his pulse regular—that was good.

She heard a querulous voice inquire, "May I help you, sir?"

"Yes. I'd like to buy a triangle. You know, those things you ding—"

"Yes, the triangle. One moment, sir."

A triangle? Why the hell was he buying a triangle?

Sonya watched him—forget the covert observation, she decided, since he obviously wasn't paying any attention—as he stood at the edge of the sidewalk after he had paid, the packet with the triangle firmly in hand. Again she held her breath as he looked both ways at the traffic—with the ten-mile-an-hour speed limit apparently ignored by one and all—and down the street at the crosswalk, then at his car.

Sonya knew what he was considering. His car was directly across the street from him. If he went for the crosswalk, he'd end up walking a block out of his way, half a block down to the crosswalk and then half a block back up to his car. And he was probably tired after his adventure in the real world, even if it was only breakfast out. "To hell with it," she heard him mutter. He stepped out into the street.

She saw the oncoming car, heading straight toward him, before he did. "John! No!" she screamed before she realized what she was doing. She heard the squeal of tires, then—

Chapter Three

ಬ

No!

Even if John noticed the car, he wouldn't be able to react fast enough. The car—sky-blue Mustang, late model, dent on driver's side door, crack in right side of windshield, Sonya noted frantically, her instincts snapping into place—was weaving. An out-of-control driver on rain-slick streets, or was he aiming? And Arlen? An easy target on crutches, crossing against traffic, helpless to jump out of the way.

What could she do?

She decided the instant the screech of the Mustang's tires against the wet concrete cut through the little shopping area, when she saw John realized what was about to happen and he froze, bracing for impact—

The squeal of the tires was enough for her to grab onto, in a way she had not allowed herself to since the death of her parents. In front of her eyes, the rest of the world seemed to slow down as she reacted to that single, all-encompassing screech of the car's tires.

She reached out and clenched her fists. *Now!*

The raindrops shimmered and solidified, the soft sounds of the rain and the shriek of the skidding tires coming together to form a giant, translucent net, almost directly above John Arlen, who was still frozen in that split second.

Yes! Twelve years without practice and she could still do it!

Eight seconds.

She didn't have much time. Swiftly, she stepped forward and caught the edge of the net, yanking it down. It floated into her hands as if it were gossamer, wisps caressing her skin, and she wrapped the stuff around her fists.

Six seconds.

With a cursory yank, she wrapped the net around John Arlen and cocooned him in it, gliding the wispy substance with him in it across the street. His left hand slipped out and scraped along the ground before she noticed and tucked it back in. His glasses had fallen off—folding them, she slipped them into his pocket.

Four seconds.

The net started to dissipate—the short time it existed hadn't changed since the last time she had done this. Sonya arranged Arlen into a sitting position on the curb, letting the net fall around him, and watched as the net crumbled away into the chilly rain. Right at that moment her own hyperworld and the regular world met and merged, the harsh meeting of the two making her stomach roil as it always did.

And then—nothing. None of the pedestrians had noticed.

Sonya winced. She was starving. That hadn't changed since the last time she'd done this, either.

She watched as John, shaking his head, came to and stared at the bleeding gash on his knuckles. He was dazed. Good.

Fighting her nausea, she knelt beside him. "Can you walk?" she asked, her voice soft.

He blinked and looked at her. "Sonya. I-I think I was in a car accident," he stammered. Then, "Why can't I see?"

His glasses. Sonya slipped them out of his pocket, wiped the lenses against the fabric of his shirt and slipped them on his nose. "Is that better?"

He looked up at her, blinking. "Yes…but there's something wrong with them." He unhooked his glasses from around his ears to examine them.

Oh, crap. One of the lenses had cracked, probably in her haste to wrap him up. She hadn't noticed the hairline fracture.

He stared at it. "When did this happen?"

When someone tried to run you over, she wanted to say, but instead, she tried to scold. "You can't run across the street when you're on crutches. Can you stand up?" She touched his cheek.

He shook his head. "I'm still a little dizzy." Together, they watched as the blood welled across the skin of his knuckles. It wasn't a bad scrape, but it had to smart. "I remember checking to make sure the street was clear and then that Mustang came out of nowhere and— What happened?"

She chewed on her lip. He remembered more than she thought he would, considering. She didn't know whether that was good or bad. "Did you hit your head? What are you doing here, anyway?" She placed her hand across his forehead.

His skin was moist and cool. Probably a little shock, she decided. "I decided to get breakfast at Adelaide's," he mumbled. "I don't think I hit my head. I don't know how I hurt my hand or broke my glasses, though."

Sonya glanced up at the sound of rapid footsteps. "What happened out here?" Addy exclaimed, hurrying out of the coffee shop. "Johnny, what are you doing down there?"

The rain was coming down in earnest now. Blinking, he looked up at her. "Addy? How did I end up on this side of the street? I started off on the other side. I was at the music store. Where's the triangle?"

Damn it, he was coming out of it too fast. If she wasn't careful, he might actually remember something she couldn't afford for him to remember. "You're still holding it," she said, tapping the little paper bag clutched in his hand. "It was almost a hit-and-run," Sonya explained to Addy as she stood up and introduced herself. "I was running some errands when I saw Mr. Arlen crossing the street. There was a car going way too fast—I don't think the driver even realized what happened." That fit what happened—she wasn't sure it was true, but it would explain why the Mustang was nowhere in sight.

Of course, in her haste to make sure she had John out of harm's way, she had neglected to take note of the car's license plate. If she hadn't been so happy Arlen was more or less intact, she would have been furious at herself.

Just then she heard him repeat, "How did I end up on this side of the street?"

At least he didn't remember how. She knelt again. "We'll figure it out, but let's fix your hand up first. Do you think you can stand now?"

"I think so." He grabbed his crutch, then stopped. "Where's my other crutch?"

Sonya looked across the street, where a single crutch lay on the sidewalk in front of the music store. He saw it too.

Damn it.

"Let me get that for you," she said abruptly. She scampered across the street, picked up the errant crutch and ran back.

The activities of the past five minutes had caught up with her. She wasn't out of breath, but she was perspiring, and she knew her skin was getting clammy—other reactions to using her abilities, reactions she'd apparently never outgrown. "I'll drive you home," she said. "I'll pick up your car later." She slid his other crutch under his arm.

She helped him to his feet. He looked all right—no visible injury other than scraped knuckles and the cracked lens. By this time, he probably was wondering if he had hit his head.

"Good to see you again," John said to her vaguely as she helped him to her SUV. "Thanks for coming by."

Nearly killed but still polite. Too bad she couldn't be. "Next time, try the crosswalk," she snapped.

"I know that now. Small mistake."

"You nearly got yourself creamed back there, Arlen," she told him as she started her car. "Avoid the small mistakes, because the big ones are enough to get you killed. Got it?"

"Sorry."

She could hear her pulse start to race. "You idiot, it's not for *me*. It's for you! Rule Two, avoid the small mistakes."

She sighed. Getting him ticked and stubborn wasn't going to help him. "Never mind," she muttered. She slowed as they approached the gates to Arlen Manor. A police car passed by.

"I'm starting to think you need a bodyguard," she grumbled as she pulled up at his gates. "You also need to get those security cameras fixed around your property."

He shrugged, still listless. "The cameras keep getting broken. Don't know why, because the other homes around here haven't had that problem. At least we have cops passing by regularly. It's the least they could do. And the security firm does keep replacing the cameras." He touched his watchband. The gates swung open.

His indifference was starting to get on her nerves. His heart rate wasn't even elevated. "Find another security firm," she said, her teeth gritted as they pulled into the driveway and the gates closed behind them. "Otherwise, you're a sitting duck."

"I keep the house locked up—"

"That's not enough," Sonya interrupted. She got out, slammed the car door and he followed suit. She looked at him. He didn't look so good.

Apparently he returned the sentiment. He looked at her. "Are you coming down with something? You look kind of gray."

I'm nauseated and starving, thanks to you, she wanted to shout. But she didn't. Instead, she took a deep breath. "I'm fine. You just gave me a shock." She leaned against her SUV. "I brought a cot today, so you're not going to be on the mat," she said, changing the subject. "And I didn't have breakfast, so I'm going to have a bite before we start." She struggled to get the cot out of the car. She hated feeling weak, but she'd feel better soon.

"Here, let me—" he began, grabbing onto the cot.

Sonya shook her head. "No. I bought some groceries that have to go into the refrigerator. Take one of the bags in, please, if you can." She closed her eyes. *C'mon, get out of here.*

She waited until he went inside before she pulled at the cot. A task she could ordinarily do with ease would be less so for a while after she did her thing. "Gotta remember to keep a Twinkie or jerky or something in the car," she muttered, wiping the sweat from her face. And practice. She needed something sweet for the fast energy and she needed lots of practice.

Her nausea had diminished by the time she got the cot out of the SUV. By the time she dragged it up to the front door, she almost felt like herself again. But she still wanted to eat.

He met her in the library, his jaw set. "Someone was here."

Thoughts of food vanished. "How long were you gone?"

"Two hours, no more." He hesitated. "I left a layer of flour in front of the windows and the library door."

"You got footprints?" she said, brightening. That would help.

He shook his head. "Vacuumed," he spat. "Whoever was here vacuumed, the son of a bitch."

Weirder and weirder. "Stay here. I'm looking around."

"I'll look around the main floor and the basement."

"I said stay here. If I'm not back in ten minutes, call the cops."

"I'm not letting you go alone!"

She rolled her eyes. Heaven protect her from chivalry. "Arlen—John. Unless you can fight with a crutch, you're safer here." She lowered her voice. "I'll be fine. Really."

Hungry and on the verge of getting cranky, she still managed a quick scan of the main floor, the grounds and the garage before she had to slow down. Nothing. That left the upper floors and the attic.

Sonya was taking a look around the second floor when she heard a shout. Arlen?

She looked up. He wasn't on the main floor. Where—?

This time she didn't debate her options. A bolt of power crackled from her fingers and shot unerringly in a straight line, curving around the corner. She followed it in a dead run.

She found him sitting at the bottom of the basement stairs.

His antigrav unit. Had his intruder taken it? She took one step down—and then decided on a short-cut, jumping down.

She landed in front of him. "What happened?"

He jerked back. "What did you do? I only heard you take one stair!"

"I only needed one. What happened? I heard you call out." She looked around. "Where's your antigrav unit?"

"It's there," he said, pointing. "Son of a bitch." He got up, leaning on the banister.

She looked where he was gesturing. The unit was still covered with the blanket. "Have you taken a look at it?" she asked. Something struck her as being off-kilter. She could have sworn that the unit had previously been—

"No."

"Why not?" she asked, losing her train of thought.

"Because whoever was here decided to move Gloria to the other corner of my lab, just to rub my nose in the fact he was here. Son of a bitch."

Arlen pointed at the corner where the unit had been. "Just to make sure I didn't miss the point, whoever it was chose not to vacuum that area of the floor." There was a nice, clear ring of cleanliness where there was no dust. If Arlen hadn't pointed to exactly where he had left the device, she could have sworn the corner where it sat currently was where she had first seen it.

"That's why it seemed odd," she muttered. Then, "Gloria?"

He gripped his crutches and didn't answer. "I'm going to take her apart to make sure she hasn't been tampered with," he said grimly. "Did you check the attic? The garage?"

"I checked the garage, but I heard you before I got a chance to go up to the attic." She looked around the space, then at the window where she had first entered the house. Someone else could have done what she had done—but she didn't think that was likely.

He frowned. "I thought you went up to the second floor."

"I did." She couldn't have done a clean sweep in the time she had been gone, she realized. "You were pretty loud. I came down to check."

What the hell—he had something tucked into his belt. What was it? Oh no. "What is that, an Enfield?"

He flushed. The antique revolver looked precarious. "I'm going with you up to the attic. And how do you know it's an Enfield?"

"You're not going up with me." Her voice got sharper. "You can't climb comfortably with those crutches. And Enfields aren't safe, for God's sake, Arlen!"

"I'll manage. I'm not going to let you walk into a dangerous situation alone."

"John, I can take care of myself." She rubbed her temples. Still hungry, but at least the nausea was gone. "I'm safer without that thing in your pants."

It took her a moment to realize what she had said. She felt her cheeks flush. "You know what I meant."

Way to go, Sone. It's not easy to sound authoritative if you don't even listen to what you're saying.

Fortunately, he wasn't paying attention. Or maybe he was just ignoring her. "You're sick!" he exclaimed.

Sonya groaned. "I'm fine. Now stay here or you can find another physical therapist. I mean it, John."

"Why, because I want to make sure you're okay?"

"I can deal with anything I find. Stay here."

She started to turn before she remembered. "Get rid of that thing before it goes off and hurts you." She pointed at his weapon. The World War II vintage revolver was firmly tucked in his pants. Fortunately, the gun was old enough that she had her doubts whether it still worked. "Rule Two-hundred forty-seven, never trust an Enfield."

"I needed something to defend myself." His tone was defensive.

"Do you even know how to use it? Get rid of it. I'm not going to be happy if you accidentally shoot me. And you'd be really unhappy if you shoot you." She shook her head, disgusted.

Brushing past him, Sonya was up and out—and this time she made a point of letting him see her take the first step on the stairs and then jump to the top.

"Who are you, Wonder Woman?" she heard him yell.

"Not quite," Sonya muttered. Wonder Woman would have whupped his ass, not placated him.

She was starving by now. But she took a quick tour of the second and third floors, not to mention the attic, this time letting her sensitive hearing do the work. There wasn't anyone on those floors. The only heartbeats she could detect were her own and Arlen's. Nothing ticking, either.

That was enough. She decided to get back to the basement, just in case the idiot decided to try out the revolver.

One, two, three, four seconds—by the time her burst of speed had spent itself, she was back at the head of the stairs. One more step—the stair squeaked, giving him plenty of time to react. And she was in front of him again. "Nothing," she reported, not even breathless. She was getting used to this again. "Whoever it was is not in the house or the garage. Or in the gardens."

"Figures." He was standing in front of the antigrav unit, but it was still covered with the blanket.

"Why haven't you taken a look at—uh, Gloria?"

He looked grim. "It occurred to me it might be booby-trapped." He walked around it, peered under it.

Something occurred to her. "Do you want to dust for fingerprints? I have a kit in the car."

He stared at her. "Why do you have a fingerprinting kit?"

Sonya snorted. "It's too bulky to carry in my purse, of course. Just in case you were considering calling in the police."

"The same police who told me they couldn't do much to help me? They'd put a warrant out for the arrest of the Engineer, but that was all they could do? I don't think so." He hesitated. "Why do you have a fingerprint kit again?"

She shrugged. "Another parents thing. I'll go get it."

Sonya came back with a small plastic case and opened it. After a few minutes, she stood up.

"Unless you polish the surface of this thing every day, whoever moved it also took the opportunity to wipe it clean."

He set his jaw. "Son of a bitch."

"Is that why you've avoided leaving the house?" She paused. "My notes about you mentioned you refused to go out. And you looked around the house yesterday when we came back and then again today. And with the cameras around the property smashed..."

"After I got home from the hospital, I found my office trashed."

Oh, that was interesting. "Why would someone do that?"

He shrugged and looked away. She knew what that was about. The less he said, the less likely he would be caught in a lie. "Looking for the formula my father perfected, maybe."

"Which you don't have. You were afraid whoever trashed your office would come back. Why didn't you tell me?"

"Why do you imagine? You probably think I'm crazy to start with. Why should I tell you something that's going to make you think I'm paranoid, too?"

She smiled and leaned in. "It's not a secret, Arlen. You're not paranoid if they really *are* after you."

She looked him in the eye. He smelled good. "I never sense anyone is in the house when I'm here," he confessed. "It's only when I leave and come back that I find something moved, or something wrong. It's as though—"

"They're waiting for you to leave." She leaned against the staircase. "I can't believe it. I spend years trying to avoid—"

He stared at her. "Avoid what?"

She glanced at him before she focused on the antigrav unit again. "Life can be weird, have you noticed?"

"My life was just fine until you knocked at the window."

Sonya almost laughed. "Your life was down the toilet until I got you to open that window, Mr. Arlen."

"What's that say about you? Did your life change when I opened that window and acknowledged you were there?"

This time she did laugh. It felt good. "Yeah, it did, John." She packed up her fingerprint kit and stood up. "Are we through here? It's time for your physical therapy session."

He waved her off. "Not now. I need to take a look at this." Kneeling stiffly, he turned back to his unit.

She knew it wouldn't be easy. She placed her hand on his shoulder. "John. Let's go on up."

"Give me a couple minutes."

She didn't move. "You know you've got to do it."

Sighing, he reached out to steady himself on her, holding onto her arm. She reached out and helped him up, feeling his shoulder shift under the faded workshirt. "Ready?"

"Yeah." Shaking his head, he touched the antigrav unit. The unit shifted a little.

That was odd. Why was it off-balance?

He frowned. "It's not supposed to be—"

EEEEEEEEEEE

What the—?

Bomb?

"John!"

Startled, he staggered back. Sonya ran over from the staircase. "You okay?"

"Yeah," he gasped after a second. "What the—"

"I'll find out," she said, reaching out.

"No, don't!"

"It's okay, I know what I'm doing," she lied as she examined the unit. Noticing something that didn't belong, she detached it. "Here it is."

It was a small buzzer, the kind found in joke shops. "Whoever moved the unit over here decided to play a practical joke and set this to go off if you bumped the unit."

His eyes narrowed. "Why didn't you find it when you were dusting for prints?"

"I didn't dust underneath the bottom lip. I only saw it this time because I was looking right there."

He gritted his teeth. "This is starting to piss me off."

"If this were aimed at me, I would be trying to figure out how to tear this guy's head off."

Arlen glowered. "I'll do that once we find him. Now come on. I need my physical therapy session."

He was determined, Sonya had to admit. His jaw set, he didn't make a single comment, about pain or otherwise, throughout the session. Then she finished up with a massage and she could feel the tension melt from his shoulders.

When she finished, he grabbed her hand. "Thank you."

"You're welcome." She didn't step away this time.

They sat for a few minutes before she got up. "I'll make sure you get your car back tonight, so don't shoot me if you hear the gates opening." She grabbed the edge of the cot, intending to fold it to get it back into her SUV.

He looked alarmed. "You're coming back tomorrow, aren't you?"

"Yeah, of course. Why?"

"Then leave the cot here. There isn't any reason for you to put it back into the car again, is there?"

Sonya stood still. "It won't be in your way?"

He curled his lip. "There are forty rooms in this house. I don't use thirty-seven of them. You haven't noticed?" He reached out and ran his hand across a side table. Sure enough, a fine layer of dust came off on his fingertips. "My housekeeper can't keep up."

She smiled. "Just making sure. Are you going to be okay here alone? Do you have another pair?" She gestured to his glasses.

By the expression on his face, she knew he had forgotten about his cracked lens. "I'll be fine."

"Good." She paused. "Are you sure you're going to be okay?"

A flash of something flitted across his face but she couldn't identify it. Then he said, "I've been alone. I'll be fine."

* * * * *

He watched her go.

The house had been quiet before, but it was even quieter after she left, with only the clock in the great hall chiming the hour. As night settled in, even the clock seemed to hush. The drizzle deepened into a gentle rain, dulling residual noise off the street.

Before he turned in, he made sure every lock was locked, every window closed, every door wired and live. He made sure the alarm system was working—he set it off twice to double-check—and even slowly, carefully, descended to the basement and back up to make sure everything there was okay. That in itself was a workout for him. Once he was on the main floor again, he stopped for a minute to get his breath. "Damn it, I've got to get stronger," he whispered, though there wasn't anyone who could have overheard.

He even put the Enfield away in a wardrobe in his bedroom, deep in the back. Ordinarily, he kept it close to him, but right now he felt safe enough to put it away for the first time in weeks.

Then he couldn't sleep. Perhaps it was the excitement of the day. It wasn't fear—this had been his house since he was born, and his family's house for two generations before that. No, he had too much on his mind.

It was the first time he had admitted someone might have been breaking into his house.

Was he ever going to walk again? How had he gotten across the street with only a scratched hand and a cracked lens, when he could have sworn he was going to be mincemeat?

Was Sonya sick? Was that why she had looked so ill?

Who was taunting him and why?

Groaning, he sat up. The deep, satisfying sleep he had enjoyed the previous night would not be repeated, not for a while. He turned on his reading lamp and grabbed his other spectacles. Maybe the latest issue of *Science* would help.

Then he remembered. "Damn it," he exclaimed, snapping his fingers. The triangle. He forgot to give her the triangle. He knew exactly where he had left it, slid between the couch and one of the side tables in the library. He had to put it somewhere so he would remember to give it to her tomorrow.

If she came back. She'd knocked on his window looking for a client and instead she'd found — what? A mystery? A future patient at a mental asylum? He couldn't blame her if she begged off.

Was there anything in the house to help him sleep? No sleeping pills, no pain pills, he knew that. He had dumped them all down the toilet after coming home from the hospital.

Milk. Sonya had forgotten her groceries. She had put a gallon of milk in his refrigerator.

Maybe warm milk would help him sleep. She wouldn't mind, he was sure.

He didn't bother with the lights as he limped through the corridors, but for once, he felt uneasy. Nothing had changed as far as he could tell, but he was seeing everything through a new filter, making him aware of every shadow. The back staircase never seemed so lengthy — or unlit.

This was the first time he'd decided to venture downstairs in darkness since he had come home from the hospital, and certainly since he knew beyond a doubt someone had been in his home.

There wasn't much he could do if he did run into his intruder. He was on crutches, alone.

Screw it. This was his home.

The stairs felt good under his feet, worn in familiar patterns. He considered jumping over the one squeaky step, but decided that falling down the stairs and being unable to crawl to the phone would not help him any. So he stepped on it square and listened as the squeak echoed through the house.

He really had to get that fixed one of these days.

He reached the bottom of the stairs. He held his breath and listened.

Nothing. John had let his imagination go overboard.

With that, he turned toward the refrigerator.
He didn't see the shadow move until it was too late.

Chapter Four

The phone jarred Sonya awake. Groaning, she fumbled for it and pressed it against her ear, her eyes still wielded shut. "'Lo," she muttered.

"Is this Sonya Penn?"

Her eyes popped open. "Yes."

The last time she heard those words in the middle of the night, she had been informed her parents had been in an accident.

"This is the Morrissey police. Do you know a John Arlen?"

The conversation was short and to the point. She was rolling out of bed by the time she hung up. She yanked on her jeans, stumbling in her haste.

Damn it, I should have known!

Someone was out to get John Arlen, whether he knew it or not.

The blue Mustang that nearly hit him had been weaving slightly. An out-of-control driver on rain-slick streets, or had he been aiming? And Arlen? An easy target on crutches, crossing against traffic, helpless to jump out of the way?

She could have killed him. But someone else was trying to.

Only a couple of hours before, when she had dropped off his car, aided by Addy, the house had stood quiet, the gates closed. Now the gates to Arlen Manor stood agape, having been forced open by the police. The paramedics were there as well, lights flashing. All the excitement must have caught the attention of the neighborhood because the lights were on at the tony estates and around the cul-de-sac.

Damn it. Shouldn't these people be in bed, getting ready to take over companies or something?

Sonya pulled behind the squad car closest to the house and ran up to the uniformed cop who was looking around outside the front entrance. "Where is he?" she demanded.

The cop—a young one, by the looks of him—looked at her, surprised. "Are you a friend of Johnny's? You're not his ex-wife, are you?"

Despite her hurry, she did a double-take. Johnny? The cop had to know John Arlen well. John had a cop friend?

John had an ex-wife?

First things first. "Where is he?" she demanded. "Is he hurt? I'm Sonya Penn. I got a call—"

"Oh yeah. No, he's okay, but he asked us to call you. He's in the kitchen," he called after her as she pushed past. "That's—"

"I know where it is," she said over her shoulder as she hurried.

Until yesterday she had a nice, thriving little PT practice, making sure people got the most out of their lives by being able to move easily again. It might not have been what her parents had had in mind for her, but she'd managed to make her own way. But all of a sudden her practice wasn't so simple anymore.

She rubbed her eyes. She hadn't turned her back on them, she told herself as she sprinted down the connecting corridors. She had simply found another way to "protect and serve".

But damn it, John Arlen was wrecking her reasoning. As his protector and guardian, she was doing one lousy job.

She burst into the kitchen, her senses alert. The previous day, when she had organized the groceries in Arlen's refrigerator, the room had looked spacious and cheery. Now, it looked crowded and confining—and menacing.

He was huddled on a stool, gingerly trying to stroke a butterfly bandage being attached to his temple and the paramedic attending to him gently moving his hand away. John had a blanket around his bare shoulders. Only then did she realize he was wearing a pair of sweatpants, and that was it.

He was okay.

She took a step, then another. On closer inspection, he was pale and the circles around his eyes were more pronounced than the previous day. But he was alive. "John?" she said, glancing at those around him. Besides the paramedic, a uniformed policeman and a firefighter stood in the kitchen, checking out wiring in a half-hidden panel in the backdoor entryway.

John saw her and mustered a smile that looked like an afterthought—but it didn't matter. *He's all right, he's okay,* she said to herself. He started to slide off the stool, but the paramedic stopped him. John shrugged. "I'm fine," he said to Sonya, waving her over. "I'm sorry to disturb you in the middle of the night, but I figured you should know."

"I went over this place top to bottom and it was clean," she burst out, equal parts uneasy their conversation was public and angry her first duty as protector had already gone bust. "Was there any sign of a break-in? Are you hurt?"

She glanced at the paramedic, who took that moment to dab at John's temple. "Not too bad," the medic commented for him. "He should get checked out tomorrow, but otherwise, nah."

Tap-tap-tap.

Her breath caught.

"You Sonya Penn?" a new voice rasped.

She turned, her heart pounding. Another man stood at the entrance to the kitchen, but this one she recognized as a plainclothes cop, tapping the counter with the edge of his notepad. This cop she knew. Unfortunately.

Her lip curled. It had been a long time. "Yes. And you are?" she asked, though she knew perfectly well.

"I'm Detective Malone," he said, flipping open his ID and just as quickly flipping it closed. "Where were you between ten pm and midnight?"

"Hey!" Arlen snapped, but Sonya wasn't listening. She was staring at the detective.

"I'm sorry? Are you accusing me of something? Are you insinuating I hurt him?"

"It wasn't her," John interrupted. "I can assure you of that."

"But according to the statement you gave, Dr. Arlen, you didn't see your assailant," Malone said.

"I just know," John insisted. "Whoever it was, was taller." He gestured at his temple. "Angle's wrong. Right?"

Sonya closed her eyes and counted to five. Then she opened them and spoke as tranquilly as she could. "I was working out at my gym. I spoke to a couple of the attendants. Do you want their names, or do you not need any facts?"

"Maybe you wanted to check this place out. Just in case something caught your eye," the rumpled detective suggested to Sonya. "It's not unheard of. And it's happened before."

He remembered her, she knew it. She narrowed her eyes, but kept her voice steady. "You've been on the force a long time, haven't you, Detective? You were on the force when my father was alive," she said. She turned back to Arlen and smoothed a strand of hair out of his eyes. He was bristling. Their eyes met. *I'm sorry,* she wanted to say. *This guy's a jerk.*

The detective, meanwhile, leaned against the counter and grinned as he scribbled. "As in Sam Penn. Well, what do you know," Malone said, and the amusement in his voice infuriated her even more. "Small world."

"So it is," she said, her lip curling. Her father hadn't liked him and she knew the feeling had been mutual. Sam Penn's suspicion had been that Malone was on Gentleman Geoffrey's payroll, but her father had died before he could prove it. "What are you accusing me of?"

Malone shrugged. "You got bills to pay, maybe you thought you could pawn something here. You know—rich guy, lives alone."

She started forward, but felt Arlen's grasp on her shoulder. She could feel his fingers digging into her skin. She eased back, but she could still feel his hand on her. "Detective, are we through here?" she heard him say. "She wasn't the one."

The look on the detective's face was palpable disappointment. "You sure? You said it was dark—"

"Thank you," Arlen said, cutting the other man short.

The detective shrugged. "If you remember any details, give us a call." He ambled out. Sonya watched him leave, wondering if Arlen would be missing a silver candlestick or two. She wouldn't be surprised.

One by one, the reports came in from the others. The paramedic gave Arlen a clean bill of health, save the contusion on his temple. The firefighters concluded there was nothing to indicate the security system had malfunctioned and there was no wiring problem.

Eventually, they all left.

Finally, the kitchen fell silent. Inside the house, Sonya could hear the boiler and the rhythmic beat of the grandfather clock. Outside, she could hear the voices of the cops, the firefighters and the short whoop of the paramedics' truck as it left the premises. Then those noises faded into the night.

They were alone again. "What happened?" she asked. She touched his cheek. The bruise wasn't bad and the paramedic had dealt with the cut. His pulse was regular. "I double-checked, and I'll bet you did. No one could have been in the house."

Arlen pushed up his glasses—another pair, Sonya was glad to see, with lenses intact—and shook his head. "There wasn't anyone in the house then," he argued. "They had to have come in later. Let's look at the system." Grabbing a crutch, he hopped off the stool and went over to the security panel. He opened it.

He stared at the panel, glowing with red and yellow lights. "You have a full security system," she noted. She even recognized the system. "The firefighter just checked it. You've checked it. There has to be something—"

"I checked it again after you left, and I set the alarm off a couple times to make sure it was in working order."

She frowned. "There's got to be something. You just got mugged in your own home."

John didn't answer. He hit a few buttons—and stopped. "Huh. Look at this."

Sonya came and stood next to him, looking at the lit panel. "Wait," he said. They watched as the lights indicating the system's alert status flickered once then died.

"It's not working?" she exclaimed. "What good is a security system if it doesn't work?"

"Now wait again." Again, the lights flickered back on.

She frowned. "Bad wiring? I don't see how—"

He shook his head. "Someone programmed it to turn off and then turn back on. Someone just waltzed in here and knocked me out because I was in the wrong place at the wrong time."

Sonya stared at him. "What were they after?" She looked at the butler's pantry that led to the dining room. "I thought you said there was nothing much in here. Besides the antiques and the paintings."

He waved those off. "Everything else that could possibly be useful to anyone got trashed over a year ago. So what was all that with that detective? You knew him."

"I'll tell you later," she said, troubled. She didn't like this. Not at all. "Are you sure you're okay?" He was pale, but otherwise he seemed to be fine. Tired, of course. It was three a.m. "Tell me exactly what were you doing."

Arlen shrugged. "I couldn't sleep, so I decided to warm up some of your milk. I came down the backstairs—and then boom."

This wasn't good at all. She didn't have a choice. "I'm going home to pack a bag," she told him. She started for the back door. "You can't be alone right now. It's not safe."

"Sonya, I'll be fine," he protested. "I can reprogram the system. And I'll fire the security firm tomorrow. This morning. Later."

She looked back. He had made his way back to the table and sat down. His shoulders were slumped and he looked so tired. She didn't blame him. "I'll be back in twenty minutes. Don't move."

She was back in fifteen, breaking a few speeding laws along the way. That was one thoroughly practical thing her parents had taught her—how to pack in a hurry. Another was how to dress and undress in a flash, but somehow she didn't think that would be appropriate under the circumstances. He was cute…but he was also under her protection. Such as it was.

Fewer lights were ablaze in the neighborhood by the time she got back, and only two cars she recognized as police issue. But Malone was still lingering outside the house, and him she had had more than enough of.

She walked up the steps and stopped in front of him. "You can go now," she said. "He'll be safe with me."

Malone sneered. "I'm sure. Just in case, I've given Dr. Arlen my direct number."

Sonya glared at him, but John came out then. "Thanks for coming so promptly, Detective. I should be fine with Sonya here."

You're lucky this time, Malone, she thought. But she smiled. "Nice to see you again, Detective," she said sweetly. "I'll walk you to your car."

She escorted him to the end of the driveway. "Thank you, Detective Malone, and good night."

But he wasn't going that easily. She heard his heart rate skyrocket. "Don't think I don't remember what happened when you were a kid," he said, teeth gritted. "You and your father—"

She cut in. At least the jerk had waited a while before he brought it up. "Charges were never pressed, and if I remember, you had problems of your own."

Malone's heart rate spiked, but he snarled and left. She watched as the last of the police cars left and waved at the neighbors watching from the safety of their own properties. Then she closed the gates and hurried back to the house.

Sonya closed the front door behind her and took a deep breath. "They're gone," she called out.

"I'm in here," she heard. She made her way to the kitchen again, where she found Arlen balancing the gallon of milk and trying to pour, hampered by his crutches.

Now that the circus had left town, he looked more tired than he had just minutes ago. "Relax," she advised. She came round and touched his shoulder. "I can do that."

"So can I." But his hands shook as he tilted the heavy container.

She covered his hand with hers. His hands were cool. Shock? Or just tired. His pulse was steady. "Sit."

He did, resting his head on his arms.

"So you're sure there's nothing in the house someone would break in for?" she asked a few minutes later. The microwave pinged. She popped it open and retrieved the steaming mug, which proclaimed "World's Greatest Son!" on its side. Watching the steam rise from the warm milk, she slid the mug across the table. "What about the formula you and your father worked on? You're sure you haven't worked on it since you came home from the hospital?"

At that, his head came up, his eyes flashing. He slapped his hand on the table, startling her. "I told you. There is nothing else."

"What about that antigrav unit you're working on?"

"What about it?" He sounded testy. He was tired, he probably hurt and he might even be frightened, though he'd never admit it. "It's old tech. There isn't a freshman at MIT who hasn't taken one apart." He looked at her with a clear-eyed intensity that made her uncomfortably aware he was half nude.

"Then tell me why someone would want to waltz in here after reconfiguring your security system."

Arlen looked away. "I don't know."

He was lying and he wasn't very good at it. But all she said was, "We'll figure it out. Drink the milk before it cools down."

"What are you, my mother?"

"Are you always this grumpy?"

"In the middle of the night? Yes."

"And if you're interrupted during the day, too, if I recall."

The adrenaline high was wearing off. His eyelids drooped. She could hear his pulse slowing. "There were extenuating circumstances," he said.

"There always is. Want any cookies to go with that milk?"

"My cupboard is bare. That's why I went for your milk."

"Actually, the milk was for you. And there should have been some oatmeal cookies in the groceries I left." She got to her feet. "Want some?"

"You don't need to take care of me. I couldn't sleep before," he said abruptly. "That's why I thought of the milk."

"Well, you look tired enough now. Give it a try."

By the time she helped him back upstairs, his head was nodding. Sonya slipped her arm around him. Her hands slid over his cool bare skin—the blanket had been abandoned downstairs on the kitchen floor—and she could feel the faint impression of his ribs under her touch.

The house had been updated in recent years, but not the back stairs, with no lighting added. That became clear when they got to the second floor and the corridor flared with blinding light. "Motion detectors, but they're rigged so they only come on if it's not me," he mumbled. "Something new I've been working on."

"Interesting idea, but dangerous," she told him. "Tomorrow, you're going to adjust it if you can so you have light all the time."

The only answer she got was a mumble. He was going to be out cold as soon as his head hit the pillow. That reminded her. "Are you allowed to sleep?"

"I don't have a concussion," John said wearily. He shuffled into what she assumed was his bedroom. He staggered over to the bed and fell on it.

"Are you sure you don't have a concussion?" she tried again.

"I'm sure. Good night. Take the bedroom at the end of the hall," he muttered, subsiding into a soft sigh.

She watched him for a second before she slipped out. "Good night, Arlen," she whispered. She closed the door.

Only one of the other bedrooms didn't have sheets covering the furniture, so she took that one. Whether he was expecting a guest or simply kept one handy, she didn't know. But before she got a few hours of shut-eye, she decided to go through the house one more time, top to bottom, just in case.

Dusty and dim, the attic looked untouched from when she had been there before. It also seemed to go on forever, filled with random pieces of furniture and miscellaneous cardboard boxes, taped shut and only some of them marked and identified. If Arlen's assailant had been searching up here, there certainly was no sign of it. The dust was intact except for a single set of footprints—hers.

What had the assailant been looking for? It had to be the formula. Even unfinished, perhaps it had value to someone. But Arlen insisted the formula no longer existed.

Would anything up here give her a clue? She started to prowl, her senses alert, until she stopped in front of a small wooden chest. She gingerly lifted the lid and began to look through its contents wonderingly.

A yo-yo. A slingshot, a comic book—*Adventure* #247, well thumbed and worn—an English essay marked with a B+ and in a brittle, yellowed envelope—jackpot—old family photos of a very young John Arlen and what had to be his parents.

A glance at the one sitting on top told her immediately why it had been hidden away. She recognized Jonathan and Lorraine Arlen from the photograph on the mantel. In this one—a snapshot—they were sitting on a sterile-looking bed—a hospital?—a newborn in her arms. John, she guessed.

The next one was of a little kid John Arlen and his father, John's teeth obscured by braces. The glasses perched on his nose were big and thick, and his father looked at him proudly as they stood in front of a messy blackboard. Sonya smiled wistfully. Like father, like son.

Speaking of which...she listened, searching through the stillness of the house. She smiled, satisfied, when she heard Arlen stir, murmur in his sleep, then subside.

Why had she agreed to help him? There was no good reason to go back into the family business now, conscience aside. In fact, she was doing all sorts of things she had sworn off.

"It's been too long, Dad," she whispered into the darkness. "I don't know if I remember what to do."

She knew what her parents would have said. As long as someone was in need, she had to be there to help. But that philosophy had gotten them killed.

She studied the next photo. She smirked when she recognized the scene as a birthday party. John Arlen, circa age five, dressed as a cowboy, wore a party hat, cake smeared around his mouth.

When was the last time her parents threw her a birthday party? It had to have been her ninth birthday. She had invited her fourth-grade class and her kung-fu class. Her parents had hosted with her aunt and been called away halfway through — but she didn't realize it until her classmates and friends went home and only her aunt was left. Sonya's aunt, who didn't know about her sister and her brother-in-law's other life, told her there had been an emergency.

They didn't come home for hours, but she knew the routine by then and listened to the late-night news on the radio. She nodded, satisfied, when the news told her why they weren't home.

And so it went, until the day of her sixteenth birthday. The plan to introduce her to the world as Sonika fell through when her parents found out that Gentleman Geoffrey was back in town. She had intended to join them on her first mission, but they told her to enjoy her birthday and she could become Sonika the next day.

But that day never came, not for Sounder and Velocity. Sonya spent the evening out with her friends. Coming home afterward, she had turned on the TV — and found out the bad news.

To this day, she didn't want to think about the arrangements she had made to retrieve her father's body and her unconscious mother. And then she had had to wait for the call from the police, informing her of her father's death and her mother's serious accident, so it was official, and she could start to grieve and deal with it all.

No. She couldn't do all that again. Granted, agreeing to help John Arlen wouldn't leave behind an orphaned child, the way her parents had. Her aunt, who had raised her after that, had died of cancer during Sonya's college years, so Sonya wouldn't have her to worry about either, just the lingering hospital bills. If she was also killed in the line of duty, there would be no one left to worry about, no one to endanger for fear of exposure.

Funny, she mused. She was in the perfect position to get back into the family business but she had little desire to do so.

So why was she agreeing to do it?

She looked at the photo again. John Arlen was a geeky kid, but he had grown out of it. The glasses added to the quirky charm.

Was that what attracted the ex-wife?

Don't get too close, she could hear her parents warning her. *Don't get too involved. Protect and serve, but always protect your identity.*

The way they had. The three of them had had plans to protect their identities in case of emergency. To set plan B into motion had been Sonya's responsibility. The night her father died, she had had to slip out of the house without her aunt knowing, her eyes full of tears, after she watched the news and found out the most disastrous thing in her world had occurred—and it was up to her to protect and serve her parents, this one last time.

What was that?

Sonya listened. It was Arlen, and he was restless.

There was a good reason she didn't like to think about the past. Sonya wiped her eyes as she shot down the stairs, once more skipping all but one in her need to move as quickly as she could. The lights in the corridor switched on, blinding her temporarily, when she hit the floor sprinting. One, two, three steps—and she was at his bedroom door.

Sonya slipped in. He was tossing and turning, his murmuring growing louder and louder.

She winced. He'd had a big day. He had decided to take a chance and actually gone out for breakfast, nearly got run over, been mugged in his own home, found out his security system had been tampered with, and now he had a virtual stranger living with him. His having nightmares didn't surprise her.

"Arlen," she whispered. She touched his shoulder. "John. Wake up. You're having a bad dream."

"No," she heard him say. "It can't be. I can't have. No!"

His heart was racing and he was sweating. Whatever he was dreaming about, it wasn't good. "John. Wake up."

His eyelids fluttered. His eyes rolled before he finally focused on her. "Sonya? What are you doing here?"

His pulse was slowing. She wiped the sweat from his forehead—his skin was clammy. "You were having a nightmare. Can't take what away from you?"

She could see him swallow, his Adam's apple trembling. "The formula," he murmured, his voice fading into the dark. "I was dreaming about the formula. I dreamed I forgot it." It was a secret, she guessed, and he had to make sure no one would hear.

She frowned. "You don't have the formula," she whispered to him. She knelt next to him.

He kept twitching as though something or someone was still following him from his dream state. But he was awake. His heart had slowed to almost normal and his eyes finally focused on her. "I recreated it," he answered, his voice getting softer, and only Sonya's sensitive hearing caught it.

"You mean you dreamed you recreated it."

"No. Dad memorized half and I memorized the other half. After the Engineer killed him, I said Dad was the only one who had the formula so he wouldn't suspect, and that's when—"

She winced. "That's when he hurt you. You told me you don't have the formula."

"I lied. I had to." There was a trace of apology in his voice. "I was dreaming I forgot it and Dad died for nothing."

Irritation shot through her—she was tired too—but she tamped it down. She couldn't blame him. Some secrets had to be kept. She knew that. "Why tell me now?"

"I think the Engineer's after me again," he whispered. "I think that's why—" he hesitated.

His tumultuous day had affected him more than she had realized. She touched his arm. "Why didn't you tell me before?"

"I didn't know if I could trust you. You could be working for the Engineer and I didn't have any proof otherwise." He struggled into a sitting position and rubbed his head. The Band-Aid on his hand shone white in the dark, like the bandage on his temple.

Sonya touched his arm again. "You still don't." At least she knew she couldn't trust anyone—he didn't have that luxury. She rocked back on her heels, letting him have his space.

"I had to tell someone." He exhaled. "If I didn't, I would go crazy."

She rubbed her eyes—she was tired too. "You haven't had anybody to talk to about this since your dad died, have you? You holed up in your house, trying to figure out what to do next, because you didn't know if the next person you put your trust in was going to try to kill you."

His jaw set. He glanced at her, but he didn't say anything.

"So," she had to ask, "was that bit about getting me to help you a ruse, or did you decide a half-truth was safest?"

He looked at her. "That was the truth," he said, his voice stronger. "I figured if you were working for the Engineer, at least I could steer you in the wrong direction."

"Why tell me now? For all you know Malone was right, and maybe I *am* involved. Maybe I really did sneak back in here—maybe I was the one who reprogrammed your security system. Maybe I didn't expect you to come downstairs and that's why I had to jump you. You don't know squat about me," she said, warming to the subject. "I know about antigrav units. Where did I learn about that? I'm obviously athletic. I know martial arts. I have gymnastic skills. I—"

He shook his head. "No, I think you're pretty much what you say you are." She watched as he turned to look at her, his head a shadow in motion. "There's one thing I can't figure out. How did your father really die?"

Chapter Five

Sonya stopped. She hadn't expected that one.

Damn it! This was what happened when she let someone get too close. They asked questions she wasn't going to answer.

She stood up, looking John Arlen in the eye. "I'm glad you're feeling all right," she said, making sure her voice was steady. She wasn't going to let him get the better of her. She wasn't. "I think you can deal with things on your own now. I'll send you my bill tomorrow. Good night."

One, two, three steps and she could be out of there.

But he wouldn't let her go. He grabbed her hand. "It's a simple question."

For someone who needed physical therapy, he had a pretty good grip. But then, she had a pretty good grip herself. She shook him off. "And I don't want to answer. Let me go, Dr. Arlen."

Even in the dim light of his bedroom, she could see his puzzled expression. "I opened my veins for you, the first time I've done that in years, but you can't answer a simple question for me? What does Detective Malone know that I should?"

She stiffened. *Go to hell,* she wanted to tell him. But she couldn't. "You can ask him anything you want, but if I were you, I wouldn't trust anything he says."

"Why not?"

She shook her head. She didn't want to talk about this, but she didn't want to talk about what he wanted to talk about, either. "My father thought he was on the take. He never got a chance to prove it." That, at least, was the truth.

John Arlen's eyes narrowed. "That was what, ten, twelve years ago? You glared at him as though that happened yesterday. Meanwhile, he's still on the force. And Malone looked as though he was going to pin this on you."

"Some things die hard." And took a long time.

"Sonya, what's going on?"

She sighed in exasperation. "Nothing is going on. And if you don't believe that, I'll find you another physical therapist."

She didn't want to go. She wanted to help him get better—she wanted to help him get his revenge. She knew how it felt. She knew it hurt. But—

"I can't tell you. I made a promise, and I can't break it now. I wish I could, John. But I can't."

For a moment, she thought he would let it go. But then he shook his head, and she knew she had lost. "I'm sorry, Sonya. I've got to be able to trust you."

"And you can't unless I tell you something that's none of your business?"

"I don't want another therapist. Damn it, I want *you*. I have to know if this secret of yours is going to kill me."

The room went still, charged with tension. She was aware of his breathing, shallow and rapid, his bare chest rising and falling.

She hadn't even known him a week and she wanted to tell him everything. This was not good.

"Not a chance," she said, meeting his eyes. "This much I can promise you—I will die before I let anything happen to you."

All of a sudden, that electricity between them seemed to scatter, leaving her almost dizzy in its wake. She stared at him, her head swimming. She watched him swallow.

"Very melodramatic," he croaked after a moment, and she knew the current between them had not been her imagination.

Sonya smiled a little. "But it's true." She took a deep breath—then regretted it, because all around her was his scent, male and distinctive. "You'll be safe."

She had to get out of there. Right then, right away. She turned, headed for the safety of the world outside that room, but then she felt his hand on her arm again. "Don't go, Sonya."

Don't do this to me! Don't touch me. Don't—" And I don't want to go. I wish I could tell you, but—"

"You don't have to," she heard him say. "Just—stay."

She squeezed her eyes shut. "Thank you." Her voice quavered and she had to clear her throat. Then, ever so gently, he turned her to face him again. She felt him press his forehead against hers.

She drew back after a while. "I'm not used to having a conversation like this after two days' acquaintance." Sonya opened her eyes and looked at him. "Maybe you are."

He smiled briefly, his eyes uncertain. "No. But it's been a very strange two days." He looked toward the windows and her gaze followed. Slivers of light were coming through the drawn curtains. "Three days."

"Maybe this day's going to be a little calmer."

"You believe that?"

"No. Think you can get back to sleep?"

"No. It's time to get up anyway."

She glanced at her watch. "You get up at four-thirty?"

"I didn't before," he said with a sigh. "But I've done it a helluva lot since I've been back."

The tension was gone, thank God. She took a deep breath and stretched her arms above her head, willing herself a second wind. Food. Food would help. "In that case, can I interest you in an early breakfast?"

"I don't think Addy opens this early."

"Live dangerously. No, forget that. You already live dangerously. I can cook for you at my place. You don't have any equipment in that big kitchen of yours."

"I want a banana split for breakfast," he informed her. She was relieved to see what looked like a glint in his eye. He was being playful. "Not unless I can get a split for breakfast."

She laughed, though she didn't feel much like it. "You can have whatever you want. But I'm going to fix you a real breakfast, and then you can make your own split."

"Addy wouldn't let me have one yesterday."

She rolled her eyes. Being protector of the meek she could deal with. Food monitor, no. "I'm not condoning it, but you're buying your own supplies," she warned.

There wasn't anyone in the vicinity when Sonya and John left in the early hours before dawn, with only a light here and there to break the darkness. Sonya saw nothing, but more important, she heard nothing out of the ordinary.

He was quiet during the drive over to her place. He spent most of his time looking out the window, she noticed. "Anything wrong?"

He shook his head. "No, I was just thinking how long it's been since I've seen any of this."

Since before the hospital. Before and after. "The new ballpark's the big thing," she said, striving for a light touch. "The traffic's hell around there on game days. But the new thing next to it, the Pavilion of Peace, is pretty. It-it's built over the old Wasserman mines."

"I guess I should see it one of these days," he said absently.

The darkness in Sonya's working-class neighborhood, unlike the posh area in which John lived, was punctuated with flickering street lamps that were the main source of illumination, leaving the sidewalks looking bleak and deserted. But they weren't—Sonya knew that. It was already time for her neighbors to start their day. She felt safer there than she did in John's part of town. No one had tried to run anyone over on these streets.

"They could be back there right now."

Sonya knew what he was referring to. She shrugged. "If they are, at least you aren't there this time," she pointed out. "If they're watching you, they might also have noticed you went to Addy's twice. So make them wonder where you are now and when you might be back."

She sensed him bristle. "Are you implying Addy's in on it?"

"You don't know she isn't. And until we find out—"

"I'm supposed to suspect everyone?"

Sonya slid into her parking space in front of her brownstone. She glanced up at the first-floor front windows, dark and shuttered. Her landlady was still asleep. "Let's go pick up some supplies," she said, her voice traveling in the quiet.

She walked slowly so he could keep up. The all-night grocery was just down the street—not far, even with Arlen on crutches. She waited for him, as though she had done so before.

It felt comfortable, and that was a problem. She was getting too comfortable and she couldn't afford that. But how would she extricate herself? She couldn't, not yet. And she had to admit, she didn't want to.

"Good morning," she said pleasantly as they passed by the big, burly man who squatted outside the brightly lit Greek diner, glowering at them. He had a cigarette between his fingers.

"What's so good about it?" the man growled, taking a drag.

Sonya stifled a grin. "No one's complained about your cooking yet today."

The man nodded. "True. Here for breakfast?" He started to get up, dusting off his apron and stubbing out his cigarette.

"Oh, not this morning. I'm treating my friend to a home-cooked meal. And a banana split."

"No split for breakfast," the man growled. "Not until lunch. Good morning."

Sonya nodded and they walked on. "Should you be talking to vagrants?" John asked.

"He's the owner and chef of the diner."

John glanced back. "I wouldn't eat if that guy was cooking."

"You would if you tasted his cooking. No sudden moves in here," she cautioned John as they approached the grocery.

He snorted. "Why, does somebody have a gun on me?"

"Yes. Good morning, Mr. Polokoff," she greeted the storekeeper as they stepped over the threshold. "How are you today?"

The wizened old man looked up from his *Time* magazine. "Very well, Miss Penn," he said with a nod. "The tomatoes are exceptional this week, if you so choose. I would recommend against the zucchini, however." He shifted the machine gun over his skinny shoulder as he resumed his reading, with a careful glance at John before he did.

Sonya tugged on John's sleeve, gesturing for him to follow her. She grabbed a basket and began to walk down the aisles. The store—run by the same elderly couple as long as Sonya could remember—was garishly lit and amply supplied. And efficiently protected.

John trailed behind her. "That was an AK-47," he whispered, with a glance over his shoulder. He tossed a can of chocolate syrup into the basket. "The old guy, he was carrying an AK-47."

"His wife usually carries a .357 Magnum," Sonya told him. "She used to use a bear-hunting rifle, but it got too heavy for her. She gave it to her daughter." She paused in front of a display of cans. "Do you like mushrooms in your omelet?"

His voice rose. "The whole fam—?"

"Shh!" Sonya glanced up at the ceiling, making sure John did as well. Sure enough, the tiny camera blinked red, recording their shopping expedition. "Do you like mushrooms?"

"Sure," John said after a moment. He looked up again.

He was quiet until they stepped out of the store, all of the shopping done. He took a deep breath. "I can see why you said no sudden moves."

"Everyone in the neighborhood knows them. Nobody bothers them," she added. "And you can pay me later."

He slapped his hip. "I don't have my wallet again. It didn't occur to me—"

She waved him off. "That's all right." She looked around, enjoying the predawn cool. The morning rush would start up soon, she knew, and the tranquility of the dawn would be replaced by the bustle of the day. She walked slowly, making sure he could keep up. The last few feet, however, she sped up, so she was fishing out her keys by the time he arrived. He leaned against the stoop to get his breath.

"It's only down the block. How can you be out of breath?"

"You were running. Nice place," he gasped.

"I was walking. Home is one flight up. Let me go first."

She opened the door and hurried up the stairs, allowing John to come up at a slower pace. From what she could hear, her landlady was awake, watching the local news. Sonya unlocked the door and slipped into her apartment noiselessly, but Rover knew. The calico cat on the couch stretched a mighty stretch and jumped down to greet her.

"Hi, sweetie," Sonya said. The little cat rubbed against her leg with a vengeance. "Miss me? Was Mrs. Mensch nice to you?"

She shifted the bag of groceries and reached down to pet the cat. When she did, however, she saw the folded slip of paper tucked into the doorjamb. She picked it up and unfolded it—and her blood ran cold.

I know who you are.

"A note from your landlord?" Arlen asked, coming up behind her. Rover, never used to strangers, took the opportunity to vanish, but Sonya didn't notice. She was staring at the note.

I know who you are.

Nothing else was on the paper except those words, laser-printed, anonymous on a plain white sheet.

I know…

Sonya held her breath, barely hearing Arlen as he tried to converse with the cat that was hiding under the sofa. She looked around. It was quiet—no radio, no TV bled through the walls. No one else was breathing in the apartment. The only other things she could hear were the swish of her cat's agitated tail and John's soft wheedling.

Whoever had planted the note wasn't in the apartment anymore.

The note crackled in her hand, posing questions she couldn't answer. How? There was no way anyone could know. She'd kept her end of the bargain—she'd sacrificed her life to make sure of that, much in the same way her parents had sacrificed theirs, for the greater good. She had never told anyone, and there was no one else who could know.

She crumpled the paper, then changed her mind and refolded it, tucking it in her back pocket.

Arlen noticed. "Something important?" he asked. The little cat glared at him, but didn't shrink away—a promising sign.

Sonya shook her head. "Some work on the apartment."

She hated lying. Whenever possible, she tried to avoid it, so she would have fewer things to remember. Her mother had told her that. Rule Five. She shouldn't have let him come up here.

Sonya felt something at her ankle. Sure enough, Rover had come on out, and now the cat's furry little head was butting against her. Wordlessly she picked the cat up and stroked her head as she did so. "Give me a minute, John," she called out. Still holding the purring cat, she dumped her groceries on the kitchen counter. And then she searched the apartment.

That didn't take long. Sonya always kept her closet doors open, so she searched the bedroom in a visual sweep. The shower curtain was always tied back when not in use. Her bed was a captain's style, with drawers underneath instead of empty space where someone could have hidden. Hidden storage space was at a minimum, since she always opted for open shelving instead of cabinets with doors.

Whoever it was probably hadn't searched the place. If he or she had, the place had been put back together neatly.

Whoever it was wouldn't have found a thing.

Her parents had taught her a lot about paranoia, but they had referred to it as "being cautious".

Just to make sure, she opened her refrigerator. Just food. She let Rover down, then opened a can of cat food. She could hear Arlen flipping through the magazines in the living room.

Her apartment was clean. But she still didn't know who had left the note.

She started for the living room—and stopped. Breakfast. She'd promised breakfast. She started to put away the groceries, her mind awhirl.

Who? Why? How?

"Hey, I forgot to get something," she heard. Too close.

Introducing Sonika

Sonya jumped a little. John was leaning against the doorway, one of her magazines in hand. "I need some pepperoni for my omelet. I'm going back to the store. Could I borrow a few bucks?"

"No," she said abruptly, shoving the can of mushrooms back into the bag. She didn't want him to go alone. And she wasn't so sure she wanted him here. "I'll go with you."

She didn't bother to listen to his agreement. She repacked the groceries, then went into her bedroom and pulled out a duffel bag, courtesy of her college days. The cat joined her in the room, watching her pack from the vantage point of the bed pillows.

Sonya looked around the room. Nothing was out of place—it was as neat as she had left it and would leave it.

But someone had been here. Someone who thought he or she knew her secret.

Standing up, she petted the cat again and whispered, "Keep an eye out. I'll be back soon."

She hoped.

She swung the duffel bag onto her shoulder and forced a smile as she picked up the groceries from the kitchen and went into the living room. "Ready? Let's go back to your house," she suggested. "I want to try out that fancy range of yours. My landlady's doing some repairs, it turns out."

He nodded, sliding his crutches into position and pushing himself up. "Do you want to take your cat? I don't mind. Won't she get lonely? What's her name, anyway?"

I don't want my cat in danger immediately came into Sonya's mind. But the cat was in as much danger here as she would be there. Aloud, Sonya said, "She'll be fine here. Her name's Rover," she added. "She spends more time with my landlady than me, anyway. And she likes her own territory." Patiently, she waited at the door for Arlen to join her.

"Like you."

"I'm sorry?"

"She likes her territory. Like you," he explained. "You seem to be a little antsy with my being here."

"I'm not used to having people over," Sonya murmured as she opened the door. And that was the truth.

She was keenly aware of the slip of paper in her back pocket.

It was the beginning of a pretty morning, but she didn't see it. The note burned in her back pocket, reminding her of a secret that wasn't a secret anymore.

She hadn't done anything out of the ordinary, not since her parents died. She had grown up, gone to college and then to graduate school, watched her aunt die of cancer and had gone to work. It hadn't been easy. For a long time, she looked over her shoulder, terrified someone would find out. Her dreams had been punctuated by that odd, disturbing *tap-tap-tap* that never ceased to wake her. It was all connected, but she had never known how.

To make sure her parents' secret was safe, she cut off contact with her parents' old friends. That was hard. Several had offered to take her in and train her, which would have lessened the burden on her aunt, but the temptation would have been too great. Her parents' way of living had killed them—her father outright, her mother later. She wasn't going that route.

"Sonya?" Arlen nudged her. "Are you all right?"

She snapped back to the here and now. "I'm fine. Why?"

"Because we've been standing here for the past few minutes, and I was wondering what we were doing."

She looked up. They were at the corner of Siegel and Shuster, across from the diner and the store. "The delicatessen," she said, deciding abruptly. She looked around, glanced at her watch. "They have great pepperoni. They should be open by now."

The doors of the deli were being unlocked as they approached, and the neon sign flickered on. The deli owner, a sweet-natured bearded man, asked, opening his arms wide, "My first customers of the day! What would you like? We've got it all—roast beef, turkey, pastrami, ham and more."

"Pepperoni. And pastrami," she informed him.

The deli owner slid open the glass door. "Pepperoni and pastrami you will have. How much?"

The door opened behind Sonya and Arlen, the bell chiming. The deli owner froze as he reached for the meats. Sonya knew without looking that trouble was afoot.

Arlen turned. "Oh, hell," she heard him mutter.

"Don't move!" a voice rasped. "Don't move and nobody gets hurt!"

She rolled her eyes. First thing in the morning and she had to be caught in a stickup. She turned around.

Two men, stockings pulled over their heads, dressed in worn denim and wearing cracked brown gardening gloves, stood near the front door. The digital clock above the door read 6:05.

And judging by the hammering of their hearts, she guessed they were very, very nervous. "Didn't I tell you not to move?" one of them barked. "Do you want to die?" He cocked his weapon at her—a .38 special, she noted.

"No, and I'm guessing neither do you," she said pleasantly. Their hearts were hammering. Not their first job, but they weren't seasoned pros at this, either.

Well, neither was she. But she knew what to do.

"Up against the counter," one of them ordered.

She put down her duffel and her bag of groceries and crossed her arms. "No. Turn around and go before we all regret it."

The talker looked in her direction. "Are you crazy? You stupid bitch, I have a gun!" Just to make sure his point was made—Sonya assumed—he unlatched the safety, the click echoing in the deli, and aimed the pistol at her head.

"No," she said. "If you shoot me and kill me, you'll not only have armed robbery on your record, you'll also have murder one. Small-time hood or murderer? It's so hard to choose."

Maybe a little too sarcastic, she mused. "And you," she said, addressing the one who hadn't said a word, "accessory to murder sounds better to you? Will that make you feel better?"

"Shut up!" the talker screamed.

"Missy, don't say any more," the deli owner said in alarm. "This guy means it."

"Sonya, what are you doing?" Arlen exclaimed. "They're armed!"

"I'm making sure nobody gets hurt." She tensed, watching the talker, keeping track of the silent one out of the corner of her eye. The talker had his weapon pointed at her, but his hands were noticeably shaking, while the other one... The other one was inching away from him. "You," she said, switching her attention now. "You're still going to be an accessory to murder. Trying to disassociate yourself now isn't going to do you any good."

"Sonya, they're two-bit punks. Don't get them riled!"

"Shut up!" the talker screamed, and pulled the trigger.

The blast of the gun exploded in the confines of the shop. *Oh, you idiot!* Sonya thought fleetingly. A glance confirmed the weapon had been pointed at Arlen when it was fired. She lunged in the direction of the bullet in the way she had been trained, all those years ago. She could see the bullet exit the barrel, she could gauge — pun intended — its trajectory, and she knew it would, if unstopped, hit Arlen square in the chest.

She knew what to do.

She reached out toward the bullet and let her nature take its course. She opened her mind. All of a sudden, the world was a clearer place, full of color and texture, and the world was much slower than it had been just seconds before.

Sheer, unadulterated joy. Her heart filled with it and it made her body tingle, saturating her soul. She remembered what her mother had told her once—to use her abilities should be no obligation, it should come from her heart and pour from her soul.

A clear and shiny film, touched with green, crystallized around the bullet. In a nanosecond it solidified, settling around the projectile. Sonya grabbed an edge of the substance with each hand. She swaddled the bullet in the stuff and pulled it away from John.

Eight seconds.

But she didn't throw it to the floor. First, she had to cover her tracks—and there were big tracks to cover. She swung the substance, with the bullet still swaddled in it, toward the shooter and his partner—but not to hit. Years of practice, years of work—years other teenagers had spent giggling on the phone and shopping in the malls—she had spent on exercises like this.

Five seconds.

The sack-like substance swung close but didn't hit them. She watched as the shooter and his sidekick stumbled and fell, their eyes glazing. They hit the door behind them, rattling the glass, before they slid to the floor like ragdolls.

Three seconds.

Without pausing, she swung the sack in the direction of the deli owner. Again she didn't swing to hit. She swung to get the sack, which was changing consistency even as it was swinging, as close as possible to the man without touching him. He, too, slid to the floor.

One second left.

She threw the sack to the floor, where it dissipated. The bullet bounced out, harmless.

Her feet felt leaden. The exultation that had suffused her body had disappeared as quickly as the substance around the bullet had, leaving her tired and hungry and queasy again.

The sack hadn't gone anywhere near slack-jawed Arlen, who was against the deli counter, but not for the lack of her wanting—there hadn't been time.

She was so tired. And it wasn't even seven o'clock in the morning yet. Looking at Arlen made her remember too many things she couldn't afford to think about right now, so she didn't. Instead, she secured the two would-be robbers with the string the deli guy kept on the counter with which to wrap purchases. Then she called the police.

Next, she turned to the deli owner, who was showing signs of waking up. Once he was, she knew she had to get out of there. He wouldn't remember anything—but it was still best not to be around for a while.

"Are you all right?" she asked the deli owner once his eyes opened. "Will you be all right until the police get here?"

He was still shaking his head. "I'll be here. What happened?"

Sonya smiled and picked up her things, slipping her business card toward him on the counter. "I don't know. I think they tripped. I tied them up. We've got to get going now. Here's my card in case you need me to make a statement. Good luck. I'll be back later."

The deli owner waved as Sonya pulled Arlen out the door.

She noticed John's lips were moving, but nothing was coming out of them. Her stomach twisted.

"We're going back to your place," she told him. She pulled his hand, stopping only to grab his crutch when it clattered to the ground. "We've had enough excitement for today."

"R-right," he stuttered. Out of the corner of her eye, she saw him take a deep breath.

Here it comes. "Let's wait until we're in the car, okay? We don't need to have this conversation in public."

He nodded and climbed into the SUV. Sonya looked at him out of the corner of her eye—he was still in shock.

They were both in the car when he finally managed to get his lips to do what his mind was telling them. Sonya knew she was in for it. "What was that?" he said as she started the car. "What happened? What did I see?"

"I don't know," she answered. "What do you remember seeing? I can tell you right now the deli owner doesn't remember anything. All he knows is one minute he was held up and the next minute the guys were down on the ground."

"We left the scene of a crime. We have to go back!"

"No, we don't. Not right now. We'll go back later and make sure those guys are in custody, but as far as the deli owners concerned, we were bystanders and he has my cell phone number if the cops need a statement. We don't need to be there right now."

She steeled herself for what was coming. She could hear his pulse rate dropping a little—that was good.

What really bothered her was how easy it had all been. Even after all those years.

"What was that?" he finally sputtered. She was pleased to notice he was probably ready for an intelligent conversation. But he wasn't looking at her. That was not good.

"That was a solidification of the sound of the bullet being discharged from the barrel of the gun."

She drove down the street that, at last, was showing signs of life as her neighbors began their workdays. The deli owner should be fine. She saw a police car, lights flashing, stop in front of the delicatessen. That had been quick. Good.

Arlen finally spoke. "What was that?"

"It's a sonifer. It's a materialization of sound."

The car was quiet again. "Are you all right?" she asked.

"I'm fine. What did you call it? A son—"

"Sonifer. My mother coined the word."

"Your mother," Arlen repeated. "Your mother was a forensic scientist for the police force."

"Yes." Then, when he said nothing else, she added, out of the blue, "I was around three when my father dropped a dish." She stopped for a light, glanced at him.

He still looked dazed and turned to stare at her. "What does that have to do with anything?"

"He made a noise," Sonya explained. "The dish was from my mother's favorite china. Her grandparents gave the set to her the day she and my father got married." She paused. Now he was staring at her as though her marbles had vanished.

"It was instinctive," she went on. She bit her lip. "He made a noise, and I reached out to try to catch the dish even though I wasn't anywhere near it and a thin layer of—I don't know how to describe it, even after all these years—"

"Goo. I'd call it goo," Arlen said. He was still staring at her. His heart rate was speeding up again. On top of everything else, she didn't want to deal with a heart attack.

"I reached out and scooped up the dish in this stuff—and saved it. After I had it in my arms, the goo dissipated."

"And you were three?"

"I was three," she confirmed. "Before that, my life was a little girl's, but after that, I started to train as a superhero, with my mother and father."

Now, she could feel his eyes on her. She stopped at a light.

"Your parents were Sounder and Velocity," he finally said. His voice was hoarse from shock. "The superheroes."

Chapter Six

ஐ

Say something. Anything, Sonya urged silently on the drive back to Arlen Manor. *Say something so I can say something back!*

A glance at her passenger didn't do anything to quell her anxiety. He sat, not even blinking. This was the first time she had told anyone her parents' secret. It had been the secret that had prevented her from getting too seriously involved. She had always come to the conclusion that no, it wasn't safe — and eventually, she had decided it never would be.

But now the cat was out of the bag.

When they arrived at the gates, Sonya turned to him. "I can use any noise, any voice, except my own. Mom never figured out why I was exempt from it — she thought maybe it was because I'm attuned to my own voice. The sonifer exists for ten seconds, tops, depending on how complex the sound was. Then it dissipates, with nothing to show for it."

Say something, she urged silently. *Anything.*

"Can't you wave your hands and make the gates open up?"

She drew a deep breath. She was tired, a little nauseated and hungry — it always happened after she used her abilities, that had never changed — and now, she was more than a little pissed. "No. Go to hell, Arlen," she snapped as she reached out the car window. "Now what's the code to open the gates?"

Before her fingers could reach the keypad, the gates swung open, startling her. She glanced over her shoulder and caught Arlen's eye as he finished tapping his watchband.

"Thanks," she muttered as she slipped back in behind the wheel. He nodded, but didn't meet her gaze. She couldn't blame him.

Sonya parked close to the house, but not too close. She put her hand on his shoulder before he could open the passenger door. "Follow me," she said, taking her hand back quickly, just in case he brushed it off. "We have to have a little chat."

She felt uncomfortable around him now, and that wasn't fair to him. She'd lived with her abilities most of her life, and it continued to startle even her. She found a path in the gardens, half-hidden in the tall laurel bushes, and took it, guessing it led to the house sooner or later.

To her relief, John followed her. "Do you know where this goes?" he said, panting. She really had to make sure he got more exercise.

Physical therapist by the hour, superhero twenty-four-seven. Her days were full. She got tired just thinking about it. "No."

"Well, I do. Slow down."

At least he was talking to her. She paused, letting him catch up. Not wasting the opportunity, she dove in. "Whoever's after you isn't going to be jumping you in daylight, in case—"

"What happened yesterday?" he interrupted. He was starting to breathe hard. She slowed down but didn't stop. His glasses slid down and he shoved them back up.

She gritted her teeth. This was what happened when she stuck her nose where it didn't belong. "I'm just trying to figure out if there's anything dangerous around here before we go in—"

"You did something yesterday when I nearly got hit by that car, didn't you?"

"When the car nearly ran you over? Yes." Her body was beginning to recover—the nausea was drifting away and the headache was almost gone. She was still hungry, though. Junk food would hit the spot, but was there any in the house? She had to remember to keep some chocolate bars around. "But I didn't figure the driver was aiming for you until last night."

"No, what did you do?" he persisted. "I would have been a goner if you hadn't—done whatever you did, right?"

She sighed. "Yes."

Sonya pressed her hand against her stomach. The family secret wasn't so secret anymore. The note crackled in her pocket, reminding her. "Sorry, Dad," she whispered. "I tried."

"Pardon?"

"Nothing," she said quickly. "When the car skidded—when it was aiming for you—I used the sound of the brakes to make a net around you and yank you out of the way. But it was close. I didn't pull you fast enough, and you scraped your knuckles before I got you on the sidewalk on the other side, and your glasses broke before I could grab them. I'm sorry."

If she hadn't been conflicted over revealing her secret, the expression on John Arlen's face, one of outraged disbelief, would have amused her. "And there wasn't anyone on the street who saw all this happen?" He rubbed his bandaged hand.

For a moment, she resented his reaction. She saved his life—she patched him up—now he was questioning her? Why did she bother to do anything, anyway?

Because it was her job, that's why. "It happened pretty fast," she reminded him. "And most people don't realize what happened if it happens that fast. And I move fast when I need to. Not long, just long enough."

She started to walk again, but then he spoke. She stopped. "I couldn't figure out what happened," he said rapidly, running a hand through his hair. He hadn't said a word in the car and it was all pouring out now. She couldn't blame him for that, either. "It was weird. Was that part of it? Did you do something else? How do you do it? Were your parents from another planet?"

This was probably why she had been told never, ever to tell anyone—too many questions. She fiddled with her ring for a moment, trying to find the right words. She looked around.

Only an expanse of verdant lawn and garden, that was all she saw—and it was a good thing he knew where they were, because she realized she couldn't see the house anymore. It was time.

Sonya didn't know where to start. Did he want to hear about her parents, about how they became Sounder and Velocity, how they died—but she decided to take his questions one at a time.

She took a deep breath. "There's a property of the sonifer that seems to suck the oxygen around it before it disappears," she began. "Mom never could figure out why. If I get it really close to people, they black out for a few seconds—"

John frowned. She halted, and despite her misgivings, she watched his face change as he struggled to understand. "And they forget what they saw," he whispered. "Oxygen deprivation. None of them remember, do they? Why didn't you swing it near me?"

She shook her head. "It was more important to make sure those thugs didn't remember what they'd seen."

"But if you had had more time?"

"I would have made sure you didn't, either. Don't take it personally, John. I had to."

"Was this the thing you couldn't talk about? Why you were willing to walk away when I asked about your father?"

She stopped walking. Sighing, she sat on a stone bench and gestured for him to do the same. The bench, cool beneath her fingers, was sheltered under a trellis clustered with tight buds of roses, pink and yellow, courtesy of impending spring. No cameras, no listening devices, nothing with feedback she could detect. They were safe. "Pretty place," she said.

He sat. "It was one of my father's favorite spots. Shouldn't you be on the lookout?"

She shrugged. "The chances of something trying to attack you in your garden aren't that high. I wanted to get this over with before we went back inside."

There was so much to say. "It was my sixteenth birthday," she began. "If they weren't home by the time I went to bed, I watched or listened to the news to find out what they were doing. That last time, though," and she made sure her voice didn't tremble, not after all these years, "instead of hearing Sounder and Velocity had brought another criminal to justice, I heard they were in a showdown with Gentleman Geoffrey in the old Wasserman mines. Geoffrey was trying to blow up the entire mine system, which would have caused an earthquake."

"He was trying to find something, wasn't he? Uranium?"

She nodded. "My mother and father managed to corner him, but in a geologically fragile area. If Dad used his voice to get him, the mine would collapse. If he didn't, hundreds of thousands would die when the system of explosives Geoffrey rigged went off. My mother was caught in the mine, too—her legs were trapped, and she couldn't use her speed to vibrate the rocks off her, because that again would have set off the explosives."

She bit her thumbnail. It had been twelve years since that day and she could barely talk about it.

"'Care for a wager?'" she quoted, a bitter taste in her mouth. "Do you remember? That was Gentleman Geoffrey's trademark, what he always said. That time, surviving was the bet, and none of them, not him, not my folks, won that one."

"They didn't have a choice," Arlen said softly.

"No. My mother and father did what they had to do." She shook her head. "I had to retrieve Dad's body. And Mom. She got caught when the mine collapsed, and she was alive but paralyzed from the waist down. She never walked again."

"Velocity, the Mistress of Speed," John whispered. Sonya remembered those dark days. The city of Morrissey had mourned, so her own, intense mourning had not been out of place.

"She didn't live long after that."

"How did you get her away? I remember the news stories—"

Sonya shook her head. "She managed to change to street clothing before the authorities got there. As far as they knew, Victoria Penn had been held hostage. And Velocity's body was never found, buried under all that rock, like Gentleman Geoffrey's."

She was silent for a minute, remembering. "Some girls have debutante balls. I was supposed to come out as a superhero on my sixteenth birthday. That day." She faltered. "Instead, I retrieved my father's body."

He murmured, and she knew she had said too much. Once she got started, it was hard to stop. She just wasn't going to cry. "So what did you tell people? About what happened to him?"

"I said car accident—but Malone. That Malone," she nearly snarled, "found out there hadn't been a car accident. Or at least what he said was he 'couldn't find evidence' there had been one. He spread the word Dad was killed in a drug bust, and not as the arresting officer, either. No details on that, either."

John's head reared up. "That's why you and he didn't seem chummy."

"There's more, but that was the worst of it. He's been on the force for years, so I can only guess he's gotten smarter."

"Are you—" He paused, and she didn't know why. "Are you sorry you had to tell me?"

She laughed. It felt like her first in years, rusty and stiff. "I'm only sorry I had to tell you this way."

"I'm sorry I had to press."

Sonya shook her head. "If you hadn't, your questions would have become accusations, and that would have destroyed us." Reaching into her back pocket, she drew out the folded note. "I found this in my apartment when we were up there. I have bigger problems than you knowing my secret."

She watched as John read the words. He frowned. "This doesn't have to mean what you think it does. Could someone believe you lead a double life?"

"I haven't had a double life. I've barely had one."

"So you haven't done anything to attract attention all this time?" he asked incredulously. "How can that be? Maybe you slipped and used your powers. Maybe someone caught you."

"I'm not my parents. I'm not a superhero. I don't have a double life. I haven't even tried on my uniform since they died. Haven't you noticed? This city hasn't had resident superheroes since Sounder and Velocity. It nearly killed me when they died. I wasn't going to have anything like that happen to anyone around me. My only secret is their secret—and I got this note right after I agreed to help you. So we're back to my original question," she said. "Who did you tick off?"

* * * * *

Not surprisingly, John decided against breakfast, so the groceries they bought went straight into the refrigerator. Surveying what was in it, she realized that the switch was complete—currently, her own fridge only had Diet Pepsi in it.

"I'm staying here for a while. I don't know if I mentioned that," she added as she closed the refrigerator door. She rummaged for the cookies, coming up with oatmeal and chocolate chip in triumph. "Ah. A fine breakfast."

"That explains the duffel bag you dumped in the foyer," John said, biting into a chocolate chip cookie. Though he had decided against an omelet, the cookies apparently were an acceptable substitute. "So what exactly can you do?"

"At the moment, not much. I can protect you, but until we figure out what we're up against—"

"No, your abilities. What exactly can you do?"

Sonya glanced around the kitchen. She should have known this would happen. "I can keep you safe," she said carefully, shaking her head in warning. She hadn't had a chance to determine if the place was bugged. Probably not right here—she would know. But it was a very big house, and she hadn't had time. "You know I grew up taking martial arts classes. You're less likely to be a target if I stay here."

He shook his head, misunderstanding. "No, I meant—"

"The cat food," she interrupted, laying a finger across her lips. "I have to make sure Mrs. Mensch gets the cat food for Rover. Let me give her a call."

He looked confused. "I'll be fine. You know, if you don't want to, you don't have to stay here. I can protect myself."

She checked her first reaction, which was to snort. "You weren't touched in your own house until you met me," she pointed out. "You weren't nearly run over until after I took you on as a client. Have you swept your house?"

He shrugged, looking more and more confused. "I have a housekeeper, and I assume she does. Why?"

"No. Have you," she paused, then decided there was no longer any point in not saying it, "searched your house for listening devices?"

He gaped at her, and for the first time, she saw him comprehend. He looked around and, she knew beyond a doubt, it was no longer simply home and shelter anymore. "Search for bugs?"

Sonya closed her eyes. "Rule Three, always assume you're being listened to."

"So—"

She opened her eyes and looked at him. "We're going to start assuming." She looked around. "You got that?" she raised her voice. "We had a conversation and you couldn't hear it!"

The expression on his face said it all. "Maybe you're overly suspicious," he said finally.

Sonya glanced at him again before she started to walk around the spacious kitchen, listening for any evidence of electronic feedback. Nothing. The kitchen, at least, might be clean. "Maybe. And maybe by talking out there we cut our chances of being listened in on. I hope you like long walks in your garden."

"My dad and I talked about—" John stopped. "We walked a lot in the gardens. We're not safe anywhere."

That was the sad reality. "No, we're not." She placed a finger across her lips again, this time more of a warning to think before he spoke. "You know, I should keep my cell phone close. It's out in my car. I'll be right back."

Sonya could feel his wondering gaze as she slipped out. He may not know what she was doing, but then, she wasn't so sure herself. It didn't take her long to get her phone. On the way back to the house, she called Mrs. Mensch, but got no answer. She'd have to go home herself to take care of Rover.

He was waiting for her when she came back, his face full of questions. "Got it," she said aloud, gesturing for paper and pen. Rummaging, he found a ballpoint from the bank in the shopping center and a notepad from a Marriott hotel. She nodded and said, "My cell phone's too big to carry most places, but I haven't had a chance to do much research on what would be better. Do you like yours?"

"My— Yes, I do," he said, recovering quickly. She liked that. He wrote, in a quick, spiky hand, barely legible—*Arlen Labs has had a recurring problem with corporate espionage. Maybe bugs there too?*

John Arlen was brighter than he looked.

But then he started to cough. He coughed so hard his eyes teared. "Are you all right?" Sonya asked, concerned.

He nodded, but he kept coughing. Not asking again, she came around and began to give him the Heimlich maneuver—but then he stopped choking, turned around, and placed a finger across her lips.

What the— Sonya froze.

John turned his face and coughed one more time, placing his lips next to her ear. "I know where there might be a bug," he whispered, his lips barely moving, not much more than puffs of air. And he coughed again, clearly for good measure—she caught on. "My office upstairs and the lab downstairs."

He breathed deeply and so did she, aware of every inch of her body against his. She had to concentrate, she couldn't pay attention to the spicy scent of his aftershave, the tang of perspiration on his skin—

He turned around so they were face to face. Her breathing picked up speed. She was acutely aware they would have been lip to lip if she'd turned her head an inch. They couldn't have been closer if they'd been in an old-fashioned phone booth.

Sonya felt a little lightheaded, but that wasn't going to stop her. She shifted and placed her lips next to his ear. She felt him tense. "What makes you think that?" she breathed.

To reply, she felt him dip his head—not much, just a little—and felt warm air envelop her ear. Her mouth went dry, but she ignored that too. "It's logical," he answered, barely audible. His voice, low and gravelly, caressed her earlobe and sent her entire body on alert. "I keep finding evidence someone's been in both places."

She resisted the urge to close her eyes and enjoy the sensation. First things first. "I've got to pop on home for Rover. I'll come back and take a look after I make sure my cat's okay," she whispered.

"Good," he murmured.

It took her a moment to process his reply. The curve of her ear was almost at the tip of his nose, she could tell. One shift, one breath, and—

She could feel him run his hands over her back, down to the flare of her hips— "Be careful," he said. Or so she thought, but she wasn't paying much attention by then. She said something too, barely uttering into his ear, though she couldn't say exactly what, because by then her hands were on his butt and she lost track.

It was a very nice butt. She appreciated every muscle of it, every way it shifted. But she had work to do. She squeezed, causing him to startle. "I'll be back as soon as I can," she whispered. She gave him one more squeeze—and then tried to step away.

His arms stayed put. "Is there anything I should look out for?" he murmured, clearly determined to stretch out the moment.

It wasn't as though she could claim he was harassing her. Her hands were still on his cheeks. But there was work to do.

"Yeah," she breathed into his ear. "Remember this."

Abruptly, she pulled back and slapped him. Not hard, but firmly. "We'll have to set up some rules about personal space, Mr. Arlen." Then she placed her lips on his temple, light, cool, almost impersonal. "I'll be right back. Be careful."

And then she was gone.

* * * * *

He rubbed his cheek—the one she had slapped. What had he been thinking?

All he knew was once he had her in his arms, he hadn't wanted to let go. He could have written more notes, but his handwriting was execrable, and his notes would have been unreadable. He had had good intentions. *She's trying to save your life and you've got to cop a feel.*

But it was a hell of a feel.

The house was usually quiet but he hadn't realized how much. It was the first time he had been truly alone in the house since the night before.

Funny. He had lived in this huge house all his life, save his college years. He knew every noise, every sigh, every rumble. But it had taken him this long to realize he was lonely there.

Belatedly, he remembered the other reason he had gotten up last night—the triangle. The gift for Sonya.

John wasn't sure how she would react to it now.

He retrieved it, then started up the stairs to his office, holding onto the banister. The wide staircase was comfortable, the steps broad and shallow, and ordinarily, he would have had no problem—but the crutches slowed him down.

The step beneath his foot squeaked, disrupting his musing.

In fact, the step was very, very squeaky. It was a problem not just for the back staircase, but for the main one too. How could anyone go up and down these stairs and not be heard? There were squeaks all over the house. He had never noticed them because they had always been there, as long as he could remember. But now, he heard them.

Were the intruders still in the house? Was that it?

Helluva time for his own private superheroine to take care of her cat.

A superheroine. He had made a pass at a superheroine.

He got to the top of the stairs. He refused to admit he was breathing a little harder. He hadn't been going up and down the stairs regularly, let alone getting exercise any more strenuous than that. He was woefully out of shape.

And he had just made a pass at a superheroine.

It had been a helluva day already and it wasn't even noon.

He veered off the main hallway, past suites unused for decades. This house had too many rooms, too many secrets.

He slowed as he approached his study. The last two times he had been in there, the place was in a shambles. If the place was a wreck, he wasn't going to bother cleaning it. Not again.

Why did they keep searching through it? Why weren't they searching through the rest of the house?

Maybe it wasn't the formula they were after. Then what?

He cracked open the door, dreading what he would see. This was his study, his respite. It was where he had retreated to when the rest of his life was too hectic.

Be a man, Arlen. Open the damn door.

He shoved it open. The door banged against the wall. For a moment, he stood in the doorway, gaping.

It was clean.

In fact, it was cleaner than it was the last time he was there. Which pissed him off more. Whoever was breaking into his home was also cleaning it up.

He stepped in. It didn't feel like his anymore. The only thing he felt when he walked in was a sense of unease, as though he were a stranger in his own home.

The room was a large one. That was one of its strengths—the other was the view of the swamp, genteelly referred to as the family lake. Its walls were lined with overstuffed bookcases, the rickety steel-cased desk was the same one he'd had since college—he had hauled it out of the dorm garbage his first week—and the rug, while ruefully stained and torn, kept his feet off the scuffed, cold wooden floor. His ex-wife had gone through most of the other suites on the floor, redecorating up a storm, but not his office. His office was sacrosanct.

He shivered. There had to be a bug around here. Something out of the ordinary. Something that would explain what was going on.

Damn it, he'd made a pass at a superheroine. If he were eighteen, he would have been proud of that.

He approached his desk in the same way he approached anything he didn't want to deal with—by making a mess of things. He yanked out the first drawer, flipping its contents onto the floor. He ran his fingers around the edges of the drawer and peered at the corners. Using his foot, he pushed around the papers that had fallen out, and carefully and deliberately stepped on everything.

There was a distinctive *crack!* under his foot and a distinctive scent. He liked the smell because it cleared his sinuses. Those peppermints were going to be messy getting out of the rug, he mused. Maybe it was time to replace the carpet.

Next was a key ring with an emblem of a college. "So that's where it went," he said aloud. He remembered buying one when he was a freshman—and promptly losing track of it. He tried to pick it up but nearly lost his balance, thanks to the crutches.

He was *really* getting tired of the crutches.

He improvised. He picked up a pencil from the top of the desk and deftly looped the key ring with it, finally bringing it up to eye level. He stared at it for a second, squinting.

It wasn't his college emblem. In fact, he didn't recognize the college.

That was odd. He set it aside. Sonya would need to see it.

The next thing he stepped on was a pencil, and it snapped. It seemed to reverberate in the very quiet house. He tensed.

That might have been why he felt the pressure around him change, and heard the slight *snick!* behind him.

Chapter Seven

୨୦

Rover didn't want to leave home, even if it was to just go downstairs to the landlady's. She mewed indignantly when Sonya tried to pick her up, then wriggled out of her arms and scampered under the sofa, where she stayed.

Sonya sighed, her teeth set. "What's the matter with you, kit-cat?" she muttered. "You spend more time down with Mrs. Mensch than you do with me, anyway. She spoils you rotten." She reached out and tried to grab the cat, finding dust bunnies instead. She finally cornered the calico and, apologizing, slipped her into her carrier.

A helluva few days for Rover too, Sonya mused. She had to have had at least two strangers in her cozy domain, Sonya's apartment, one of whom had actually tried to pet her. "It's just for a few days, Rove," Sonya told the cat. "Just downstairs—you like Mrs. Mensch, don't you? John was trying to be friendly. He didn't mean any harm," she cooed, her stomach turning over in embarrassment. If her apartment was bugged, she'd pay extortion money just to make sure her conversations with her cat were never revealed. "I'll be back soon."

The indignant expression on the cat's face didn't look as though she believed any of it. Sonya gave up. "Think of it as a vacation, Rover." She picked up the carrier.

And then put it down. Since she was here she might as well look around, see if any other notes were tucked away somewhere.

Whatever she found wouldn't be much of a revelation. After all those years of absolute secrecy, she had spilled her guts to the first guy who hadn't made a pass at her as a client.

No, he waited until she told him she came from superhero stock to make a pass at her. Helluva few days.

The paranoia was ingrained in her. It came part and parcel with being raised to be a superhero. There were guidelines—not written, of course. That went with the paranoia, because writing anything down was unwise. She hadn't dated much when she was a teenager because before her parents died, she had been in training. She didn't date much after the death of her parents because she was distrustful of almost everyone by then. And she hadn't dated recently because she didn't have the time. Sounder and Velocity had reared her, trained her, taught her so many things, but in the social graces they had left her sadly bereft.

Arlen had made a pass at her.

She would have been interested before she revealed her secret. But after? The last thing she needed was a groupie. Her parents' friends had run into problems like that. Groupies tended to drift away after the glory was gone—and she had no interest in the glory in the first place.

Sonya straightened, looking around. The place was squeaky clean. No messages tucked into a doorjamb, not even a hairball. Maybe the message was a joke. Maybe it was just something to throw her off-balance. If so, it had done its job.

"Let's go, kit-cat," she said to Rover. "I've got to get back to someone who really is in danger."

Then she noticed the cat was huddled on something in the pet carrier, a piece of paper that looked just like—

Rover jumped out and disappeared into the bedroom when Sonya opened the carrier door.

He's dead and so are you.

She didn't have any more time.

Sonya wadded this one into a ball and threw it back into the carrier. "You win, Rover. I'll see you later," she called out as she ran out the door. She locked the door but didn't bother to deadlock it—clearly it didn't make a difference. She'd leave a note for Mrs. Mensch.

Who was it?

She ran a couple of red lights in her haste to get back, surprisingly not gathering cops on her tail by the time she got there. She shinnied up the gates because it was faster than punching in the code and waiting for the gates to open. She was through the front door inside a minute.

"John!" she shouted. At first, she heard nothing—then she heard her name, choked off, then a crash.

Where was it coming from? Where?

"Arlen! Where are you? John!" she screamed.

He had to be upstairs. Sonya raised her hand and tried to concentrate, trying to pinpoint where the sounds were coming from. She felt the telltale warmth envelop her, but she started to run up the stairs before the thin stream of light could identify John's precise whereabouts. *Control, control.* Desperately she tried to maintain control, trying to remember those lessons her mother and father had taught her.

Where is he?

A part of her had never been trained, never gone through the process of hardening to the possibility of losing someone again, the part that kept screaming, *Please, no!*

The corridor lights were on. Somebody had to be here.

Sonya heard the second shout just as she was about to turn the corner. She focused on a closed door. *There!*

She threw herself at the door, kicking it open. Once she was inside, she somersaulted away, gave herself a running bounce against a handy metal file cabinet and landed in a struggle between Arlen and a big, burly man dressed in a gray jumpsuit. She pushed John out of the way with her left hand and lashed out, hitting the thug with a right uppercut, then a left hook, then a sharp jab at a strategic spot—

The scream was fortuitous, because it gave Sonya the opportunity to reach forward—and the scream materialized into a large, hulking hammer. *Ten seconds,* she chanted to herself. She grabbed the hammer and swung the business end.

Jumpsuit guy dropped like a log.

She stood, panting, staring down at her opponent. The hammer crumbled into nothingness, right on schedule.

She rubbed her hip. That was going to hurt later. Kicking open a door isn't as easy as it looks, she mused. She looked up at Arlen, who was panting too. He gripped a crutch in one hand and had a stapler in the other—a big, old-fashioned metal one.

"You can put the stapler down now," Sonya said. She looked around. The place was, predictably, a mess, his other crutch on the floor.

"It pisses me off, you make it look so damn easy."

She stared at him in disbelief. "I arrive in the nick of time to rescue you and that's all you've got to say? Not even a 'thank you'? And incidentally, it's not easy at all. It hurts to crash through a door! You try it sometime."

"Thank you," he said, still sounding surly. He hopped over and lowered himself onto the floor to pick up his other crutch.

Sonya rubbed her hip. That was going to leave a big bruise, she could tell. "This isn't a macho thing, is it? Because it looked as though you were holding the guy off pretty well with the stapler and all."

"Shouldn't we tie the guy up?"

She shrugged. "He's out cold. He's not going anywhere for a while. But now that you mention it, got any rope?"

"I might," he grumbled.

He looked around and so did she. Everything she assumed had been in drawers was now on the floor and all the scattered paper made walking around slippery. "Did he do this or you?"

"I did some of it before."

Meaning he had made a mess and then it had gotten messier. The male ego—a delicate thing at best. "What happened, anyway?"

"I came up here after you left. I turned and there he was."

"And you managed to keep him busy until I got back," she said lightly. "That was nice of you."

John, however, wasn't having any of it. He started to shove the detritus around, his jaw set. "The only reason I heard him behind me is because the papers crackled on the floor when he stepped on them and the air—I don't know—felt funny. I swung at him with my crutch. I nearly fell on him. I grabbed the stapler when I got the chance. Hey, here's something we can use!"

She grabbed the roll of duct tape he tossed at her—she wasn't going to ask why he had some in his office. She ran the tape around the wrists of the unconscious man. "How did he get in? This place is supposed to be secure—"

"He materialized out of nowhere," he insisted.

"Was he in the shadows?" She looked around. Daylight was pouring in. No closet, Venetian blinds took the place of drapes. "Under the desk? No, you were there," she muttered.

"No. I told you, something crackled, I turned around, and one minute he wasn't there and the next he was."

Sonya frowned. She could have dealt with a simple breaking and entering. She could have dealt with a casual robber. But this didn't sound like either.

She turned to the man in the jumpsuit and grabbed him by the collar. His head rolled a little. He looked out of it still—bald but for a pigtail and the size of a football player, he probably alarmed and intimidated his victims—but not her. She slapped him. "Wake up," she ordered. She slapped him again and then flexed her fingers, because it hurt to do that too. She had to toughen up again. "Wake up or I'm going to kick you in the balls again."

That did the trick. "No!" His eyes popped open and he wriggled, trying to get away from her. He nearly bucked her off as he began to struggle.

Sighing, she grabbed his knee and held it. "Stop moving now," she ordered. He froze. She leaned in, squeezing slowly as she did. "Who are you working for?"

"I-I'm not at liberty to say," the man stuttered.

"For God's sake, let me beat it out of him," John snarled.

"And you think he's going to be more willing to talk that way? When has that ever worked?"

"Oh, yeah? How many times have you tried it?"

"You think you can make me talk by pulverizing me with your crutch, Arlen?" the man burst out. "Screw you."

Arlen and Sonya turned to stare at the tape-bound man. "Don't make him mad," she advised the thug. "I don't have any control over him and he's feeling touchy. That crutch is a deadly weapon. Now why are you here?"

"What makes you think I'm going to tell you?"

She leaned in and tapped the guy on his battered and bleeding nose. "Because I just kicked your butt and I can do it again." Her voice was soft, but it was menacing—without saying much. Rule Forty-three, speak softly but say nothing during interrogation.

Unbelievably, the guy sneered. "It was a fluke, girlie. You hit me from behind."

She smiled. "Is that what you're going to tell your boss? If he bothers to bail you out." She got even closer until they were nose to nose. She could hear his heartbeat quicken, the blood start to race through his veins. He was trying to keep his breathing even, but he was having a hard time. He swallowed and the sound was like thunder in her ears.

Sonya smiled a toothy smile. "Or is that the last time he's going to tolerate failure? You failed when you came into the house before, didn't you? You failed to run Arlen over—that was you, wasn't it? And you got interrupted last night when he decided to come downstairs." She smirked. It was a very broad smirk, maybe too broad. But then, she hadn't had much practice since she'd learned this lesson from her father. "So how much longer do you have to live?" she whispered. "Maybe I should just let you go and see what happens. Maybe next time your boss will send someone competent. What's going to happen to you then?"

She deliberately closed her fingers around the collar of his shirt and twisted, staring him in the eye. Her mother's variation on the brute force bit was softer than her father's, designed specifically for the superheroine's interrogation.

"Tell me now and you might have an easier time at the precinct house," she suggested, her voice pitched low. "Tell me now and I'm not going to beat the crap out of you. Or let him." She nodded toward John.

Unbelievably, the guy snorted again. "Girlie, *you* don't scare me. *The boss* scares me. I tell you, I'm toast."

That did it. Time to use Rule Forty-four. She yanked him to his feet and shoved him against the desk. "Hey! That hurt!" he whined.

"What do you think is going to happen to you, you idiot?" she exclaimed. "Either I'm going to lose my temper and beat the crap out of you, Arlen's going to beat the crap out of you or your boss is. Your choice." She lowered her voice. This was Rule Forty-four, part b—her own variation. And considering her lack of experience, a tricky maneuver. She leaned in. "At least if you talk to me, it might be kind of fun," she breathed. "So how about it? Tell me now and at least enjoy it."

Huh. It wasn't just a saying—he stopped breathing.

Come to think of it, so had John.

Sonya decided to put a flourish on her request. "I'm going to kick you again and this time I'm not going to be gentle."

This time, both men groaned. The bound man whimpered and she almost felt sorry for him. "It's the Engineer. He's sure Arlen's hiding the formula," he rasped. "He's going to find it, even if it means tearing the place apart."

John pushed himself to his feet. "Killing me isn't an efficient way of doing that."

"No, but you have a will."

Sonya looked at the thug. "What about his will?" She turned to John. "What about your will?"

John glanced at her in confusion. "I have one."

"If you die, your nearest relative inherits your share."

Sonya glanced at Arlen, then back at the thug, then back again. Arlen was even paler than when she had met him.

"My share goes to my sister," he whispered. "And if not her, my cousin Jasper gets a small bequest."

She stared at him, loosening her grip on the thug. "You have a sister? And what's that about your cousin?"

"He's the Engineer."

* * * * *

It had been in front of him all this time and he hadn't seen it. "Hell of a family," he whispered. "What's left of it."

"John? Are you telling me you're related to a major crime figure? When were you going to tell me?" Sonya's eyes bored into him—and he was grateful laser eyebeams were not included on her list of abilities. As far as he knew.

"I would have gotten around to it," he said weakly.

"We have a lot to talk about, don't we?" Her tone was as cold as his basement lab on a winter's day.

He took a deep breath. "I'm sorry. I should have— *Hey!*"

Sonya turned. The thug was dematerializing in front of their eyes. She lunged for him, but too late. By the time she had placed her hands where the thug had been, he wasn't there.

"Damn it! We were so close! How?" she exclaimed.

He sat. He felt sick. "I'm sorry," he said again.

She turned back to him. He braced himself. "You couldn't have told me the Engineer was your cousin? All that talk about wreaking revenge, and he's your *cousin*? Just a little detail," she raged, and he wasn't inclined to interrupt.

"Until he showed up wanting the formula, we hadn't seen each other since we were kids. As for—" He paused, not quite sure how to say it. "His father, Gentleman Geoffrey—my grandfather disowned him and Geoffrey never forgave him for it." He closed his eyes.

John opened them when he heard her laugh. It wasn't a warm laugh, but considering the events, he was happy enough to hear it. "So the late Gentleman Geoffrey and the Engineer are actually Arlens, and they're ticked they were cut out of the will?"

"By the time Grandfather died, my dad hadn't seen or heard from my cousin in years," John muttered. But that sounded weak. That *was* weak.

"This is starting to sound like a soap opera," she muttered. Sonya leaned against his desk, rubbing her neck. She hadn't had much sleep either, John knew. "So your grandfather disowned your uncle. Your uncle became Gentleman Geoffrey, the mastermind behind some of the most bizarre crimes in the world, who left a legacy of crime in this city the police haven't been able to control since the death of Sounder and Velocity. His son, your cousin, is trying to kill you for the formula you and your father devised. Am I up to date here?"

He scratched his head. This wasn't going to be fun. "More or less. I have something else to tell you."

"*More?* I'm not going to like this, am I?"

"You know the disappearing act that guy just pulled? That's something Arlen Labs was working on. There was a case of industrial espionage while I was on sabbatical a couple years ago and the blueprints disappeared. I'm guessing it was Jasper."

The look Sonya gave him was downright murderous. "So that's how your house got broken into all this time, and you only see fit to tell me that now?" She stood up and dusted off her hands. "Every time I turn around, there's always something else I didn't know about. I don't know how to protect you because you don't want to be helped. To hell with this."

"Sonya," he protested. What John did next was nothing planned. One minute he had his hand on her shoulder and the next, he pressed his lips against hers.

If he had any sense at all, what little rational mind he had left would have pointed out this woman could tear him apart without thinking twice about it. If he had had any sense, he never would have done this. If he had any sense…

Vaguely he felt her shoulders stiffen, sensed her breathing hitch…

Felt her mouth soften, her lips part, her hands—

Where were her hands?

That was his only warning before she slapped him. He slid to the floor. His face exploded in pain. "I guess I shouldn't have done that," he mumbled, cradling his cheek. "Ow."

"Have a nice life, Arlen," she snarled. "What's left of it."

She turned to leave. "Wait," John said, scrambling for the small packet on the desk. "Sonya, wait. I— This is for you."

He grabbed the packet as she turned in the doorway. He froze when he saw her expression.

"What?"

Maybe this wasn't such a good idea. "I-I got you a present when I was out yesterday," he said. He held out the packet.

Her nostrils flaring, she grabbed it and tore it open. She lifted out the triangle. "What the hell is this supposed to be?"

Oh hell, this was not promising. "It's a triangle. You majored in music theory, right? I figured you might like a triangle."

The look on her face got worse, making him fear for his life. "You checked up on me? To hell with you, Arlen!"

Then she was gone.

The room was still after her footsteps died away. Nothing. Not even a creaking, not even the clock.

He pounded his fist in sudden rage against the floor. He had screwed this up royally.

Then he heard something. He was braced for the sound of a closing door, but instead he heard voices. One was Sonya's. The other…

He raised his head. Clumsily, he brought himself back up to standing. He opened the door as he rubbed his aching jaw.

"Johnny? Are you up there?" a familiar voice floated up the staircase. "Johnny? I'm back!"

What the—? He relaxed when he identified it. Then he tensed again. He heard a murmur, then what might have been a heated exchange—at least on the part of Sonya—before he heard, "Johnny? There's someone here who's claiming you're here. If I don't hear from you in the next five seconds, I'm going to call the cops on her. I know kung-fu, you stay right there!"

John groaned. With his luck, Malone would end up back here and he'd arrest Sonya. And Sonya would *really* be ticked at him. And he'd get his butt kicked five ways from Sunday.

"I'm up here," John shouted. He made his way down the hallway, holding onto the wall. He belatedly realized that he wasn't using his crutches. He was unsteady and he wasn't going to last long without them, but at least he was on his feet for the moment. Something he could thank Sonya for, if he could get her to not walk out of his life.

He turned the corner and slowed down when he realized the voices he had heard before were conversing, and the exchange was a heated one.

"Honey, I don't care who you say you are. If my brother doesn't say he knows you, straight into the hoosegow you go!"

Oh, hell, he was toast now. Either one of them could whip his ass. And one of them had, on a regular basis.

John paused at the top of the staircase, gripping onto the railing for dear life. "Hey, Janie. Welcome home."

His sister—his older sister by more than a decade—was, as usual, dressed like a vagrant. Or at least that had been their father's description of her sartorial sense. Janie Arlen was wearing the same glasses he had always associated with her. In contrast to his own tortoise-shells, the ones she wore were harlequin-shaped, with rhinestones around them. Her dark brown hair, shot with silver, was—

Well, that was new. "Why is your hair in cornrows?"

She shrugged, and in the way those with doctorates in applied physics did—at least in his experience—she said, "We got bored in McMurdo. Why not?"

His father's description would have been right. The sweatshirt tied around her shoulders was faded and torn, and the T-shirt she was wearing was emblazoned with the Sorbonne logo. "So how was Paris? And Antarctica?"

"*Bon, bon.* And cold." She glanced at Sonya. "So who's the cookie, Johnny?"

His sister had a firm grip on Sonya's arm. And she didn't look as though she was going to let go anytime soon.

Sonya, the superheroine, wasn't wrenching herself away from Jane H. Arlen, Ph.D., M.D. Instead, she was allowing herself to be dragged around by his sister, who was even shorter than she was. Sonya looked as though she were going to kill him and dump his body somewhere once she got a chance. If she were a practicing superheroine, he wouldn't be worried. As it was...

He gripped the railing as his legs weakened. If he wasn't careful, he was going to break a bone or two, possibly before one or either of the women did it for him. "The cookie is my physical therapist, Janie. And she'd probably appreciate it if you not grip her arm."

As soon as those words were out of his mouth, Sonya yanked her arm away. "Whoops. Sorry about that," Janie said, and she truly sounded contrite. Undaunted, she stuck her hand out and beamed at Sonya. "Hi, I'm Janie Arlen. And you are?"

Sonya glared. "Leaving." She turned to Arlen. "I'll ask around for a new therapist for you. Although since you're walking again, I guess I don't have to look for one who specializes in severe cases. Goodbye," she said. She headed for the foyer.

No. "Sonya, wait," he called out desperately. "Please. Janie's been out of the country for a while. Paris and McMurdo Base in Antarctica," he added, as though the detail would make a difference.

"And a fine welcome home I get too," his sister added.

John ignored her. "Sonya, please. Don't go."

Sonya turned to look up at him. "Then I suggest you tell her what's going on. She's going to be in the same danger you are, unless your cousin has something against you personally."

Janie looked from Sonya to him, alarm on her face. "Cousin? Jasper? What's Jasper done now?"

"He just tried to kill me again and Sonya stopped him. He's also wanted for questioning in the death of Geoffrey's old bookkeeper."

Janie looked at him for a second. "What do you mean, 'again'? I'm sorry I couldn't get back before, little brother, but the weather down there—"

"He tried to run me over, and he hired someone to break in here to look for the formula. A couple times."

"And she *stopped* him? Who is she, Sounder junior?"

He choked back a laugh and tried not to look at Sonya, who looked as though she was going to explode. "Not exactly."

Janie turned to the younger woman. "You may be too young to remember, but Sounder was—"

Sonya, thank God, cut that short. "I remember Sounder. It was nice to have met you, but I've got to go."

"Sonya, please. Give me another chance." It was humiliating to beg in front of his sister, but he had no choice. If Sonya left now, he might never see her again.

"What part of adios don't you understand? Go to hell, Arlen."

The door shook when she slammed it. The house was very, very quiet after that.

Janie finally put down her duffel bag. "What the hell have you been doing, little brother?"

Chapter Eight

ஐ

If Sonya had been Supergirl, she would have slammed her fist into a concrete wall and had the satisfaction of watching it crumble. Instead, she stubbed her toe when she kicked a rock in the rock garden on the way to her car. She yelped and stifled a curse.

Stupid, stupid, stupid! How stupid *was* she? All this had started because she needed one more gig to pay off her aunt's hospital bill. Otherwise, would she have bothered to climb the gates? Would she have bothered to pound at the door?

Would she have bothered to tell the jerk the one secret she had sworn never to tell anyone?

She broke a promise to her parents. *The* promise. And look where it had gotten her.

Sonya swore again. Helluva few days.

Limping, she opened the door next to the gates and left that way. She had been in such a hurry to get in that she had never bothered to open the gates to put her car inside the property. She started up the SUV and started to turn around. He could save his own hide. Or his sister could. For all Sonya knew, the Arlens were teeming with relatives she didn't know about.

"Get out of the way!" Sonya shouted as she stopped behind a Mercedes that was waiting for a Boy Scout to help an elderly lady cross the street. Sonya hit the horn and got a dirty look from the Boy Scout, the little old lady and the driver of the Mercedes, who turned out to be a steely-eyed matron in a St. John suit who really shouldn't know gestures like that.

By the time Sonya got home safely—she was in a bad mood, but her driving skills were intact—she managed to talk herself out of her anger. She was also tired.

Helluva few days.

Rover came trotting over when Sonya walked in. The cat rubbed against her ankles, purring. Sonya reached down and stroked the cat's nose. "At least I know what you're about, Rove," she said. On impulse, she picked up the cat, and surprise of surprises, the cat didn't squirm. Rover was not one to enjoy being picked up. Instead, the cat purred and butted against Sonya's shoulder.

Sonya scratched the cat between the ears. "I'm home for a while, kit-cat," she whispered.

She could pick up another client without much trouble. She would be a little delayed in paying off her aunt's final bills, but she could deal with that. And she could get on with her life with a clear conscience. Arlen—well, John Arlen could clearly take care of himself.

But he knew her secret.

Sonya stroked Rover. "I told someone something I shouldn't have, and it's going to drive me crazy, cat," she whispered. "I don't know what to do with that."

She was pretty sure he wouldn't do anything with it. She was fairly sure her secret would remain a secret. Fairly sure.

Not sure at all.

Worse, she had to think of the Engineer—John's cousin—who clearly had no scruples when it came to what he wanted. If he decided to hurt Arlen somehow—hurt him, torture him, if he decided to find out if Arlen knew anything else about that fuel formula—her secret would be lost.

Of course, her secret was already lost. And for all she knew, the Engineer knew it. Somebody certainly did.

Rover butted her head against Sonya's chin, demanding more attention. Sonya obligingly scratched the cat's head.

Her secret wasn't much of a secret anymore. She'd already broken her promise and she couldn't even figure out how anyone had known.

The phone rang but she chose to ignore it. She could guess who it was without looking at the caller ID. She let the answering machine pick it up.

"Hi, Sonya, this is Janie Arlen," came a chirpy voice with which she had just become acquainted. "My brother said you would hang up if he called, so I called instead. I guess he didn't realize you'd just let the answering machine pick up."

Sonya rolled her eyes. "You wanna eat?" she asked her cat. "I think I have something for you. What about some tuna?"

Janie Arlen's voice floated through the apartment as Sonya walked to the kitchen and opened a can. "Anyway, I just wanted to say you did something great — I couldn't believe he was back in his study, because I know he hadn't been there in months. I couldn't talk to him very often when I was down at McMurdo, and he didn't answer my e-mails that often before that. I — well, thank you. And I guess he's been eating, which is great. I couldn't get out of McMurdo when Dad died and he got hurt—"

Good God, the woman could talk. Sonya tuned her out — or tried to. "Here's some tuna, kit-cat," she cooed as she spooned the contents of the entire can into the cat's bowl. "I haven't spent enough time with you, have I?" Rover paused in her eating for a moment and looked up at her — almost with suspicion, Sonya could have sworn — before resuming.

"Maybe a vacation. I haven't taken a vacation in years," Sonya mused aloud.

Janie, meanwhile, hadn't paused. "Johnny told me you saved him from the crazy car and you came when he got mugged—"

Sonya could hear the fumbling of the phone as John's voice came through from the background. "I did not get mugged. I came down for—"

Then she heard Janie's reply. "What do you call it when someone whacks you over the head? You got mugged." There was a muffled discourse Sonya wouldn't have been able to make out if she weren't used to hearing things that were ordinarily muffled. "'Breaking and entering' is when they come in and take something, but it's different if they actually lay a hand on you. How do you think I know? You should try it sometime."

"Anyway, Sonya," Janie Arlen's voice became clear again. "You came when he got mugged— Stop that," she said, her voice muffled again. "I'm still not sure what's going on, but it sounds like our cousin's come out of the woodwork and I'd appreciate it if you could talk to me about it, since Johnny's babbling—" Then there was the muffled "Yes, you're babbling."

Then, back into the phone, "Johnny says you know what's going on. Our cousin's been confused ever since he was a kid—but then, his father wasn't exactly well. Anyway, could you tell me what's been going on? You know the number."

Finally, the apartment was quiet again. Rover finished and decided to groom herself. Sonya petted her. "Maybe I'll have something to eat now," she said aloud. "I think I'll relax. Would you mind if I go out?"

As if in response, the cat mewed, a short, decisive sound, and Sonya could have sworn the cat was glaring. "Fine, I'll order in."

Sonya snagged the kitchen phone. The Greek diner delivered, fortunately. The order took all of two minutes. Once she was done, she hung up and looked around.

This was the first time in years in which she had absolutely nothing to do. After her father died, she had started on a roller-coaster of activity. After his funeral, most of her time had been taken up with her hospitalized mother, and then she had moved in with her aunt.

After Sonya graduated from high school, she went to college, and eventually, cared for her ailing aunt. In between were jobs, studying, friends who came and went, boyfriends—and always in the background, the secret that could never be told.

School, school, school. Then paying off school. When would she have had the time to suit up and take after her parents? Being a superhero took time. She had spent most of her youth studying and working out. She deserved a little time off. She did. To hell with John Arlen anyway.

The doorbell rang. She got up, checking her pocket for her wallet—and encountered, instead, the first note. The second one was still crumpled on her bedroom floor.

Whatever else she did, she had to find whoever was leaving her those notes. She grabbed her wallet and unlocked the door.

John Arlen stood there on one crutch, with Janie behind him. Janie was holding a brown paper bag. "We intercepted the delivery kid," he said with no preamble.

Sonya rolled her eyes. No peace and quiet, not for her. "Give me the bill and I'll pay you back."

"I'll just take it out of your payment for therapy services."

"Like hell you will," she snapped. "One has nothing to do with the other. How much?"

"My treat," Janie said, thrusting the bag at Sonya. "Can we come in?"

Sonya stepped aside. "I take it you called on the way?"

The Arlens walked in—actually, Sonya observed, John was leaning on his crutch. She closed the door. "Are you back on the crutch because you think I'm going to feel sorry for you?"

"Would it work?"

"No."

"Would doubling your physical therapy fee?"

"Money is not the point! I told you I'd help you, but you won't let me."

"I guess you don't really need me here to talk," Janie said.

"I'm sorry I didn't tell you!" John yelled. "I didn't think it was relevant!"

"You didn't think it was relevant the guy who killed your father and maimed you is your cousin? You didn't think it was relevant that all this time I thought you were an only child and it was just the two of you, your dad and you?"

"Mom died when Johnny was just a baby," Janie supplied helpfully. "He was a late-life kid. Spoiled rotten."

"Why couldn't you have said that? Why was it so hard?"

"I'm not going to say I was spoiled rotten!"

"Of course you were spoiled rotten. You didn't have to say that, I already knew that."

"Then what was I supposed to say?"

"You know, he's never been any good at stuff like this," Janie cut in. She peeked into the bag. "Hmm. Greek?"

"You ordered from that guy at the diner? Aren't you taking chances with your life?"

"No more than hanging around with you," Sonya said.

"I love spanakopita," Janie said enthusiastically.

Sonya sighed. "I'll set out some plates," she said, heading into the kitchen. "Seeing as I have guests for lunch."

Plates. Plural. As a rule, she didn't have people over. Her home was her fortress of solitude, so to speak. She dragged out three plates that most resembled each other, a pure accident from regular trips to the Salvation Army. Her parents' china was long gone, broken in a frenzy of grief around her eighteenth birthday. She still regretted that.

Well, she had a few plates, at least. She fished out some flatware. They were a little twisted—on occasion they doubled as tools—but they would do. If not, she had chopsticks left over from the last time she had ordered Chinese.

Janie stuck her head in. "Need any help?"

Sonya shrugged. "No. I can deal with it."

"Let me help. We're intruding on your lunch," Janie persisted, coming right in.

You got that right, lady, Sonya thought. "Here." She thrust the plates at Janie. "Let me look for spoons. I ordered some avgolemono while I was at it."

"I wouldn't have rushed down here if I'd realized you would be eating."

Sonya looked at her. "Am I supposed to believe that?"

"I'm just being polite, but I really didn't realize you'd be in the middle of lunch."

Sonya had to grin, though reluctantly. "Why can't your brother be more like you?"

"Because he was the baby. Seriously," Janie said, lowering her voice. "I don't know what's going on, but he was ready to spit nails after you walked out. I figured if nothing else, taking a drive might calm him down."

"Did it work?"

They paused and listened. In the living room, John was pacing—or the equivalent, with the awkward gait of the crutches probably driving Mrs. Mensch crazy downstairs. "I guess not," Sonya said. "And coming here's not going to help him any."

"But he needs you."

"He doesn't need me specifically. He needs a physical therapist who'll force him to do his exercises. If he never regains full mobility, it'll be his own fault."

Janie clattered the forks against the plates. "He hasn't been doing them? He promised me he would!"

Sonya snorted. "And you believed him?"

Janie glanced at her. "Why haven't you thrown us out yet?"

"Because despite what you or he may believe, I was actually raised with some manners," Sonya said grimly. "Here are some soup spoons. Let me find some bowls and some napkins."

By the time she was ready to go back out, she had calmed down. She was going to be polite if it killed her. Or him.

Janie was portioning out slabs of spanakopita by the time Sonya came back out. "Did you know we were coming? There's so much of it," the older woman marveled.

"The guy at the diner doesn't believe I eat enough, so he always puts in extra. I end up eating Greek food for days after I order from him."

"Well, I'm sorry we're cutting into your food for the week. The avgolemono smells heavenly. Johnny, sit down," Janie ordered. "Eat something instead of annoying me."

Cantankerous, obstreperous John Arlen obediently sat down at the dining table without arguing. "You were walking back at the house," she observed. "Why the crutch now?"

"I feel unbalanced without at least one. And I got tired."

"You're going to feel tired and unbalanced unless you exercise. Of course, this could be your ploy. I'm on to you."

"It's not a trick, okay? Good God, woman, is this how you treat all your clients?"

"I quit your case, remember? Now you're just another guy and I can treat you however I want."

"Yes, but I'm a guest in your home and I should be accorded some respect."

"You're eating my food. If I want to harangue you while you do it, that's my prerogative. Now eat."

He stared at her. "I'd walk out of here, but that would make you happy."

"It would, but since you drove here with your sister, you'd be stuck, unless you find a cab, but that's not likely in this neighborhood."

"Johnny, have some soup," Janie urged. "You'll like it."

"That's right, Johnny, have some soup."

"Lay off me, will you? What have I done to you?"

Sonya could hear her own heartbeat speed up, and not coincidentally, she could hear his do the same. They glared at each other across the little melamine-covered table. "You've wasted my time and that's the worst thing you could do to me."

His expression eased up and he looked at her now as though he had a secret. And she realized he did—hers.

"Is that the very worst?" he said, his voice lowered.

She could smell the hot, fragrant soup filling the air, drifting around them, touching their senses.

She swallowed. "You know it's not."

"Then give me a chance."

"You've had it."

"Then give me another one."

"Why should I?"

"Because you need me as much as I need you," he said, and it was true. She could have cursed him for it.

Sonya put her spoon down. "Janie, please excuse your brother and me. I need to say some harsh words to him and I don't want to disturb your dining."

Arlen protested. "What about me? You'll be—"

"Shut up, John," Sonya said. She grabbed him by the arm. "We're going—" What was the farthest spot from the dining table? "To the bedroom and having a little talk."

"The bedroom? I'm too young to hear about this," Janie said. She cut into her spanakopita.

Sonya noticed the older woman had a look of satisfaction on her face. "She'd better be happy," she muttered as she dragged Arlen away. "Bob's spanakopita is great."

"If it's that good, why don't we go back and eat?"

"Because we have a few things to talk about." She slammed the bedroom door behind them and turned to face him.

The bedroom was in shadows with only one lamp lit. She couldn't see his face, nor his expression, making him suddenly unreadable. "Why didn't you tell me about your sister?"

Arlen shrugged. "I didn't think it was relevant."

"I got the impression it was just you and your father as you were growing up."

He shrugged again. "It mostly was. Janie's a bit older than I am. She went to college out of town, so I didn't see her frequently until after she finished her undergraduate studies and she came home to work at Arlen."

"Why couldn't I find anything about her in my research?"

"Did you find *anything* about us? We pay through the nose so there isn't anything," he said. "I'm sorry —"

"I thought the Engineer was out to get you and you were all alone in this house!"

"I never said that," he said defensively. He shifted his grip on his crutches, wavering a little. Sonya pushed him down gently onto her bed. "And if you'd asked, I would have told you our housekeeper's retiring and we haven't found a replacement and Janie was out of the country."

"If I had known you had a sister and she lived at Arlen Manor, the situation wouldn't have seemed so dire."

"I guess not," he answered, his voice rising a little. "Wouldn't you have thought it was strange if I'd just volunteered all that out of the blue? She hasn't lived here steadily for years. So you would have said no if I'd told you all that?"

Introducing Sonika

Sonya's nostrils flared. She couldn't deny it. She had a weakness for the weak and downtrodden — even if it happened to be a six-foot-two guy on crutches. "You're right," she said after a moment. "I didn't do my homework. Or at least enough."

"You thought I was all alone?"

She dropped heavily onto her bed. "This is why I'm not a superhero. There's a lot to remember and I just flunked the simplest test. You could have wormed your way into my confidence and killed me without much trouble." She buried her face in her hands, too embarrassed to look at him.

His voice softened. "It wasn't fair of me to drag you into a situation you weren't comfortable with. And considering you had a secret of your own to protect, it really wasn't fair."

"Well, it's not much of a secret anymore," she said, picking up the crumpled note from the floor and sitting back on the bed. "This is why I came running back to the house. I got a second note. I never got a chance to tell you."

He unfolded the note and read it. "Bad to worse," he said, staring at it. "And with Janie back, she's involved too."

His heartbeat picked up again as he turned to her. Her gaze met his. "Thank you for not telling her," she said. She squeezed his hand.

He gave her a half-smile. "How do you know I didn't?"

She matched his smile. "Because you wouldn't."

"Then how are we going to explain this little chat?"

The sharp rap on the door startled them both. "I'm coming in," they heard Janie announce. The door swung open. "I'm sorry, it took me a while to realize what was going on. I'm clueless sometimes," she said. "But if I'd been paying attention, it would have been obvious."

Sonya stared at her. "What?"

"About you and Johnny. That was quick work, brother dear," the woman said. "Didn't you say you met her three days ago? I never would have thought he would have the charm to sweep you off your feet, Sonya—"

Arlen groaned. "That was not a nice joke."

"Not intentional. Anyway, when I look at him, I see a grubby five-year-old who's buried my brand-new purse in mud because he thought it looked like a treasure chest."

"Oh, thanks a lot, Janie!"

"Wait," Sonya said, looking from Arlen to his sister and back again. "Hold on here. You think John and I—"

"I told you we couldn't keep it a secret," he told her, bringing her closer to him.

She sat for a moment, confused, until he kissed her on her forehead. "What's going on between us is too obvious, babe."

Babe? Sonya pulled away. "Janie, I don't know what you think is going on, but—"

"It's okay, sweetheart, she guessed," he interjected. He gave her a little squeeze. "We don't have to keep it a secret."

She coughed in disbelief. He rubbed her arm. "I'm sorry, did I squeeze too hard? Come back to the house and we can talk about it later, Sonya," he said, this time kissing the back of her ear.

"Janie," Sonya gasped, ignoring the molten lava coursing through her by now—if she hadn't been enjoying it, she would have slapped him silly. "I don't know what John's told you—"

"Honey." This time, he guided her face to meet his. He put both his hands on her face, forcing her to look at him. "It's okay. She knows we're together."

Chapter Nine

೫

Sonya gaped at Arlen. "What?" She looked at Janie.

"Sweetheart." Arlen turned her head. This time he kissed her.

For an audience. Infuriated, Sonya shoved him away. "Do that again and you're going to be sorry."

"I'll be at the table. Is that Greek restaurant around here? I'll have to check it out," Sonya heard Janie muse. The older woman closed the door behind her.

"How dare you," Sonya said to Arlen. She tried to control her own breathing. She was so angry a red haze dulled her vision.

To her surprise, he backed away. "This way if there's anything we have to talk about, it's not going to look peculiar if we excuse ourselves to be alone," he said quickly. His breathing was still rapid, but his heartbeat was slowing. That was the truth then. "Two's company."

"Three's a crowd." She took a deep breath. Her stomach was doing a dive she wasn't used to. "Next time, warn me."

"I tried. But you weren't listening."

"What are you going to tell her?"

He shrugged. "That our dear cuz tried to kill me, he's been threatening you, you're trying to protect me—"

"What are we going to tell her that's not true?"

He paused. After three days, Sonya was starting to recognize his expressions. This one meant he was editing his response. So much for being honest.

"I'm going to tell her we're involved, and you're protecting me, but nothing else. Can I tell her you're a master of kung-fu, for real, if she asks how you're protecting me? Otherwise, she'll want to hire someone."

She grimaced. "I haven't practiced in years, but I can brush up. As for hiring a bodyguard, tell her we can't trust anyone right now, so it's best not to."

"How are we going to protect *her*?"

Sonya paused. "I don't know. Especially since I don't know her and you can't control her—"

He rolled his eyes. "She isn't easy to persuade."

"You're sure she can be trusted."

Sonya watched his face as he struggled to reply. "I've trusted her all my life. She's always been there for me."

"But can she be trusted?"

"I'd trust her with my life."

"But can I trust her with mine?"

She watched again as he struggled to answer. Finally she said, "I can't share my secret. Please."

He nodded, unhappy. "We'll figure out a way. I don't know how we're going to make sure she doesn't see what you can do—"

Sonya fingered her ring. "There's a way. We'll see." Getting up, she put out her hand to him. "Let's see if Janie's left any food."

Arlen took her hand. She steadied him as he got up—he was stronger than he had been. Good. "I don't know if I want to eat," he grumbled. But his face was relaxed as he said it.

"Why, because you think Bob looks like a vagrant?" By this time, they were almost back to the dining table.

"I'd worry about ptomaine poisoning— Janie, have you left us anything?"

Arlen's sister was still at the table, her cheeks bulging as she chewed. She smiled beatifically. "It wasn't easy, but I didn't touch anything on your plates. But I polished off the soup, and I took the extra dolmeh."

Sonya slipped back into her chair as Arlen eased into his own. The slightly pinched look around his mouth told her it still wasn't easy for him to walk. "John, you have to eat something," she said. The sound of her own voice surprised her. Even she could have sworn she was involved with him.

He started to wave her off before he too seemed to remember. "Thanks—sweetheart," he said, "but this is fine. Even though I'm not fond of the guy, he does good food."

Janie sat back and beamed. "He does *great* food. Why don't you like him?"

"He told John he couldn't have a banana split for breakfast."

"Johnny, I tell you what to eat. I don't recall you paying one bit of attention to me."

"He owns the diner!"

"Then don't go there!"

Sonya made quick work of her lunch and watched Arlen eat. He wasn't an enthusiastic eater because he let everything bother him. She guessed he usually had too much on his mind to eat much.

"Have a dolmeh—honey," she said suddenly. She speared one of the leaf-wrapped delicacies on his plate and thrust it at him.

Predictably, he recoiled. "I'll try one, Sonya. Later."

"Oh, come on," she wheedled. She moved her chair a little closer and waved the dolmeh in front of him. "You'll like it."

He glared at her. "I can eat on my own."

"You wouldn't like to try some? For me?"

She tried to communicate... *Eat something. Eat something so you're strong enough for what's ahead.*

He didn't get it—typical male. She smiled again and nudged the entrance of his lips with the dolmeh. "Trust me."

Their eyes met. Their gazes held. All their breaths were held—hers, his, even Janie's. The dolmeh wavered—and he parted his lips.

His eyes still holding her gaze, he bit into the dolmeh and started to chew. "You're right, it is good," he said.

Sonya could feel her own heart speed, like his. His respiration was up and the room felt warm, as though she had turned up the thermometer.

"Have some more," she invited. "You've got to eat."

She watched his Adam's apple shiver. "In that case, you've got to eat too," he said, his voice hoarse. He swallowed hard.

He speared her own dolmeh and brought it to her mouth, brushing the grape-leafed delicacy across her lips. "Tit for tat," he whispered. "Just a taste. You like dolmeh, don't you?"

She laughed a little. She should have been embarrassed at this exchange. "You know I do."

"Then taste."

She parted her lips and she kissed the leaf—just a little—before flicking it with her tongue. She opened her mouth just a little more and he paused the morsel, waiting for an invitation.

Janie coughed. Loudly. "I'm going to see if you have any coffee I can brew, Sonya." She stood up.

Sonya blinked, the spell broken. She sat back. "Second shelf over on the left from the sink."

Janie pushed through the door to the kitchen. They could hear her rummaging.

Sonya exhaled. Arlen was chewing, but slowly—his gaze was averted. "Think she bought it?" she asked.

He laughed. "I think she did. I nearly did."

She felt her cheeks flush. "John—"

"Mmm?" She watched as he cut his own spanakopita into smaller and smaller pieces, pushing random chunks around his plate.

Keep on track, she told herself. "Right now, our only goal is to keep you safe. We don't know it's your cousin who's after you," she pointed out. "It seems likely, but we can't be certain. So we need a plan. We need to know who our friends are, who we have to beware of, and why."

He didn't answer. She grasped his hand. "Trust me."

He squeezed hers and swallowed. "I do."

* * * * *

He was such a lousy liar. That was going to be a problem. But it wasn't going to be much of a problem, because if he wasn't careful, it wasn't going to be much of a lie.

She was short and curvy. He preferred tall willowy brunettes, not little strawberry blondes. He preferred bookish types, not athletic types who could beat up a couple of thugs, or him, without blinking an eye.

Who was he kidding? There wasn't a man alive who wouldn't find a petite superheroine a turn-on. He didn't know what was more alluring, the abilities she didn't seem to want, or the almost kittenish persona the steely personality hid.

Not only that, she smelled really, really good.

"I'm going to help your sister make coffee," Sonya said, standing up. "I've got to persuade her to let us protect her, and if you can't do it, I've got to try."

"I'll help you," he offered, starting to push himself up.

"Making coffee's not a three-person operation, Arlen."

"I'm not going to sit here while you two are in the kitchen."

"You haven't finished eating."

He speared one last piece of spanakopita and swallowed. "Yes, I have."

He liked following her. But he would never have connected her to the neat little kitchen he followed her into, which Janie was attempting to make a mess out of as they entered.

"The coffee will be ready in just a minute," his sister said cheerily. He watched as his sister, seemingly comfortable in the kitchen, bustled around, making herself at home.

"Here, let me do that, Janie," Sonya said, disarming the other woman of the can opener and opening the can of coffee without losing a finger. "That opener's a little tricky."

"Thank you. I like her, Johnny," Janie said, beaming. "I approve of your taste."

He smiled back, cringing internally. "Good. Then please don't embarrass me."

"Oh, I'm not embarrassing you, Johnny. I'm not digging out the photographs of you as a baby, am I?"

"That's only because we're not at home!"

"Just use the coffee measuring spoon and put the amount you want into the— Oh, you don't have the setup quite ready," Sonya said, unperturbed. Arlen had to hand it to her, she could have been alone for all the emotion she was displaying. "You have to find the filters—"

"She usually drinks tea," he informed Sonya.

Sonya stopped as she placed the filter into the basket. "Then why are you making coffee?" she asked the older woman.

"I didn't think you had any tea. You look like a coffee person."

Sonya looked at the open coffee can and the filtered basket. "Canister near the sink. I don't make a pot of coffee for just me very often."

"Oh." Janie looked at him. "Johnny, do you drink coffee?"

John stifled a smile. "Yeah, I do. I'll drink it."

Janie was his sister. He had the utmost respect for her professionally, and he trusted her implicitly, but personally, he didn't know her that well. He knew what—or who—had driven her away and why. At least he thought he did.

Janie chattered what seemed nonstop, but at least she didn't allude to his relationship with Sonya. Thank God.

"Janie, what can you tell me about your cousin?" Sonya asked after the coffee had brewed and she had poured it for him. The tea, nicely made in a fat white teapot, was steeping.

Arlen coughed, a feeble warning it wasn't the right time. Sonya ignored him. "The cops must love you guys. Well-respected old family cooperating with the police on the matter of master criminal relative."

Janie and John both snorted. He had to admire the attempt—Sonya was forthright and direct. But in this she was misguided. "We have a battery of lawyers on retainer," he commented, not sure what to say in front of Janie and Sonya both. "*They* love us. We've called the police only when absolutely necessary."

"The police are polite to us, but that's about it," Janie volunteered. "If nothing's changed since I've been gone, they keep as close an eye on us as they do the hookers over on Wolfman and Wein."

"They called out a crowd when I got mugged," John said. "Including—" he stopped. He took a gulp of his coffee instead, yelping when the hot liquid burned his mouth.

Sonya sipped at her tea. Whether she noticed his hesitation, he couldn't tell. "So you have no idea where he might be?"

Janie shook her head. "The time before last I saw Jasper, he was trying to beat up my brother over a plagiarized paper. Johnny was eleven, Jasper was ten, I think. Then I didn't see him until he showed up at Arlen Labs a couple years ago, and I felt sorry for him, so I gave him an intern's job. He didn't have any natural inclination but he learned fast. And then he disappeared the same time some blueprints did, so I have to assume he took them. And that was the last I saw him. The next thing I knew, I got a message from the hospital about John—and my father."

When Jasper murdered Janie's and his father, John filled in. He and his sister were going to talk about it, but not now.

"Sonya knows about the project, Janie."

His older sister made a face. "Did he tell you all the plans for it disappeared? I was beyond angry."

John grimaced. "We got to see it in action. You'll be happy to know it works."

"Dad would have been pleased. It was one of his pet projects."

"It's probably how they got into and out of the house," Sonya added. "Any known allies?"

"Just the hood trying to knock me out when you came home."

Sonya ran her finger around the rim of her cup. He watched. Her hands were so small. "Any known hobbies?" she asked.

Janie shrugged. "Mayhem and murder. No, that's not fair," she amended. "Maybe it was manslaughter. But like father, like son."

John watched Sonya's face, but she didn't blink. "And Gentleman Geoffrey died a long time ago," she commented. "Was that before or after Jasper was convicted for grand theft auto?"

"After. I think he escaped and vanished during a prison riot."

"And how long ago was that?"

When had Sonya had time to look up Jasper's record? John glanced at his sister. "That would have been, what—ten years ago? Then about five years later he showed up at Arlen

Labs and told me he was on a work-release program. Like an idiot, I believed him. He asked to borrow some money, and like an idiot, I gave him some. Then I found out the police wanted him."

"And you didn't see him again for a few more years. Janie encountered him next when he wanted a job at Arlen Labs, and then he disappeared. And then you saw him last year, when he showed up at Arlen Manor. Right? Johnny?" Sonya asked.

"You can call me John, sweetheart," he said drily.

Sonya gave him a look that could kickstart a dying man. "Why don't I just call you 'Arlen'?"

"That'll do just fine, honey," he answered, hoping she wouldn't decide to do to him what she had done to the intruder at the house. "And yeah, that's when it happened."

"You're sure it was your cousin, right?"

"Yes. He called me by name and I called him by name."

Sonya gave him a long appraising look. Then she glanced at her watch.

"Got a date?" he asked.

She looked at him again and her lips almost curled. "I wouldn't run around on you, sweetie. But I want to make sure you're both safe, so I want you to go home, pick up some clothes and stay here with me. Let me find another key. I've got a spare around here somewhere." She disappeared.

Janie turned to him. "You didn't have a key before?"

Unbidden, he felt his face flushing. "We haven't known each other that long."

"I guess not," his sister mused. "Does she have any family?"

"No." He kept an eye on the kitchen door, hoping against hope Sonya would find the key quickly and come back out before his sister continued her impromptu interrogation.

"So have you discussed any…arrangements?"

He stared at her. "What arrangements?"

"When is she moving in?"

He snorted. "At the moment, we're moving in with her, Janie."

She waved that off. "We have such a huge place, I think she should move in with us after this is over. We have room."

"Janie, we can talk about that later," he said hurriedly. He watched the door—the crashing sounds of items being sorted through a drawer finally ceased.

Sonya came back out holding a brass-colored key. "Found it!" She handed it to him. "I'll make another copy when I get a chance. It unlocks the door downstairs and my front door. Jiggle it in the lock downstairs, because it sticks." She glanced out the window.

Arlen's gaze followed hers. Although it was only midafternoon, the light was fading quickly, thanks to the gathering clouds. "I want you both back here before sundown," Sonya said. "I want you here for the night. That place of yours," she glanced at him, and then Janie, "seems to be open to anyone who wants to break in, so I think it's easier to keep you—us—safe here."

Damn her and her hearing. She must have heard Janie's comments. "That's fine," he said. He narrowed his eyes. "You're going with us, right? I don't want you alone either."

"No. I've got some errands to run, so just let yourself in. Order pizza, whatever, for dinner. Order from Bob, the number's next to the phone in the kitchen, tell him it's for me, he'll deliver it himself. I'll be late."

"You can't go alone," he protested, not knowing exactly what she would be doing, but knowing that errands would not be involved. "I'll go with you."

"No, you're not," Sonya said calmly. She glanced at Janie. "If you do, who's going to protect your sister?"

"I can protect myself, thank you," his sister piped in. "Where are you going, Sonya?"

"I have to go alone," she said again, as though Janie hadn't spoken. "I can't make sure you're safe and keep myself safe."

She looked as though she would have broken in half in a windstorm. She looked as though she could have used all the food that Bob sent over. But there was more to her than that.

"Who's going to watch your back?" he whispered.

She met his gaze. "Don't worry, John. I know what to do."

"I can help you."

She sighed. "That's why you have to do those exercises, Arlen," she reminded him. "Without them, I'm sorry, you'd put yourself in danger. Stay here, protect your sister. I've got to see if I can find some answers."

John couldn't let her go. Not without—

He found her lips with his. They felt warm and soft and right. "Be careful," he whispered.

* * * * *

Sonya huddled into her jacket. She should have worn gloves. It was chilly, but more than that, she didn't want to touch anything. She could have sworn there was slime on the surfaces.

She hadn't done this since she was a kid. True, it probably hadn't been the most responsible thing in the world for her father and mother to have done, bringing their twelve-year-old daughter to the Mission Mercy district, the seedy part of town, but they insisted it was the only way for her to learn how the criminal element lived.

She remembered thinking the criminal element lived in very rundown housing.

What had fascinated her as a kid were the smells and the sounds. With her abilities, the sounds fascinated her. When her ability began to define itself, she had become interested in all noises and how they wrapped around her ears, shaping themselves to her. But the smells—they had lived in a quiet, middle-class neighborhood, not far from where she still lived—the smells were so different from home. There was the putrid scent of rotting fish and the rank odor of urine and the acrid smell of other things she hadn't been able to identify in her youth. She did later and she shuddered to think of them.

Until then, she never realized despair had a scent and a sound of its own.

Right now, Mission Mercy was quiet, with only an occasional squeal of tires. All she could hear were the echoes of her own footsteps, ringing through the cramped alleyways, the occasional gloop of water spilling from a split gutter, the skittering of a rat and the yeow of a cat in heat, the heated murmurs behind closed doors. Somewhere, a window slammed.

Tapping. Somewhere behind her, someone followed her.

Someone quiet. Someone who knew she would be ready for someone to be close behind her.

But someone bold enough to get closer and closer. Someone who was obviously looking for a defenseless target.

Deliberately, she turned into a blind alley. There were three trash cans, metal, and nobody in any of them. Whoever might have been hiding in them would have been too small for her to worry about. Shallow puddles on the ground—probably water. No dripping.

No way out except the way she came in. Just what she was looking for. A little hubris—she was confident enough to know she could get out of the alley unharmed.

But not too much, her mother would have warned. Pride goeth before a fall. That wasn't one of the superhero rules, but it should have been.

Sonya waited, listening for a footstep. Whoever it was had a distinctive step, with a slight shuffle on the left foot. Either a shoe problem or a weak ankle. Big and smoked too much—she could hear the rasp. Whoever it was hesitated a little.

And that was all she needed. Unerringly, she turned, reached up and grabbed his throat, shoving him against the damp wall of the building. A couple of rats squeaked and skittered out of the way, the echo of the rodents trembling in the close space of the alley as Sonya pinned her stalker.

A familiar face. It was the big intruder she had caught at Arlen Manor, the one who had disappeared in her presence. Mr. Baldy with the pigtail. "What, the Engineer send you out for all his errands?" she snarled, shoving him again for emphasis. "Can't you just materialize in front of me instead of stalking me?"

His face was less alarmed than it had been the last time she had seen him. That puzzled her for a second, until she realized she was in his element now. "What is it about you?" he snarled back. "I wasn't aiming for you. I was just walking down the street and you jumped me. I should call the cops on you."

She snorted. "Fine. I can testify I found you trying to rob Arlen in his home. Or were you trying to kidnap him? Why don't we add attempted kidnapping to the list? Then you can make your complaint about my roughing you up. That reminds me, did you mention to your boss that I beat you up? Me, a defenseless little female?"

The thug's eyes widened. "I'm not crazy."

She tightened her grip and leaned in. She heard his heart rate skyrocket. "Where can I find him?"

He started to struggle. "I'm not going to tell you that. I'm not suicidal!"

She shoved him back again. "Then you're going to rot in jail. And you're going to stay there. How's that?"

She knew, from the way his heart rate actually slowed, that something was going on. Then she looked into his eyes and realized it was behind her. Without taking her hand away from her stalker, she turned—

And nearly decked John Arlen.

"Oh, for—go home!" she ordered. The thug under her hand squirmed and she tightened her grip. "Go home now. I mean it!"

"It's not safe out here!" John exclaimed.

He looked like a lamb ready for the slaughter. He was using a utilitarian cane instead of his crutches, which she would have commended him for under different circumstances, and he had to be tired, because he was leaning on it. His eyes had bags under them. Her heart would have twisted in empathy because she was tired too—except she was pissed.

"It's not safe for you," Sonya said. She turned back to the thug. "Stop moving," she commanded. "Or the bruises are going to have bruises."

"This is brutality!" the thug squeaked, his voice climbing. She could feel his pulse running amok under her fist, and she loosened her grip a little—but not by much.

She turned back. "John, go home. This isn't something that you should be involved in. I can deal with it on my own."

"You need someone to watch your back—look out!"

She started to turn but sensed, more than she saw.

She twisted and struck out to her side, but felt a blow glance off her shoulder. Hissing with pain, she still wouldn't let go of the thug under her hand. In desperation, she kicked blindly, hoping to find her target.

She connected with something solid, hard enough to rattle her teeth. She heard a strangled shout. In frustration, she shoved the man in her grip down to the ground so she could deal with what was behind her.

The thug on the ground took that opportunity to yank at her leg and that threw her off-balance. She slugged him as hard as she could. She connected and again she heard him slide to the ground, out for the count, bouncing his bald head against the wall. That was going to hurt.

The scene she saw was almost a replay of the scene from Arlen Manor, but with a new, added player. This one was bigger, even stronger—which explained why her shoulder hurt—and he was making mincemeat out of John with a massive, tattooed fist.

She grabbed Arlen's cane from the ground and whacked his attacker over the head, breaking the solid piece of wood in the process. When that didn't work—the thug didn't even notice—she grabbed a sliver of fabric at the back of his jeans and gave him a wedgie.

The guy squealed—*What a sissy!* she thought—and turned around. She slugged him in the jaw before he finished moving.

Ow! Unlike his partner in crime, he didn't have a glass jaw. Her hand throbbed as she tried to hit him in the stomach, but he blocked her. She tried to knee him in the groin and that did have an effect—but again, he managed to protect himself.

This wasn't good.

He backhanded her, the blow glancing off her face. She wavered, seeing stars.

Think about the next move! Momentarily blinded, she backed up a step and put up her fists, cursing herself for having been goaded into an argument when she should have been paying attention to her surroundings. Meanwhile, John was on the ground, wiping blood off his lip.

"John, keep an eye on the guy who's out," she ordered without taking her eyes off the mammoth thug in front of her and without lessening her auditory surveillance of the area. "Just do it."

This time he didn't argue, she was glad to note.

"Do you like picking on girls and crippled guys? Pick on someone your own size," she taunted. She reeled, still dazed, and estimated she could only have one or two more shots before he knocked her out. She had to get into position to take him out and unless she bought herself some time, the outcome would not be in her favor.

Speak, damn it, say something, she thought in desperation. *Give me the time I need!* She lashed out with a kick but the burly thug grabbed her leg. She kicked him away and he reached out to grab her throat. She did a backflip that got her away from him, but she miscalculated and tripped over a trash can, taking her deeper into the alley. She ended up sprawling.

In the background, she could see Arlen keeping a grip on the thug on the ground, who was starting to wake up. The overgrown linebacker, though, was advancing on her.

Her ankle hurt but that didn't matter. She just needed more time.

Come a little closer, you big ape. Just a little closer.

He did. And he finally spoke, "You got anything to say, you little bitch?"

She grinned.

Chapter Ten

ಸಿ

Sonya reached out without thought, on pure instinct, and crystallized the echo of those words. In a split second, an oversized croquet mallet formed. She seized the handle and swung.

The burly thug didn't see it coming. But then, why would he? He thought he had her where he wanted her. It would never occur to him she had *him* where she wanted him.

Pow!

The impact echoed in the close confines of the alley. *Imagine that,* Sonya thought. The sound *makes* sounds.

The thug stood there, blinking. Slowly, he toppled, like a bowling pin after a well-placed bowling ball hit its target. *Strike!*

He hit the ground with a solid *thunk*. Sonya sat there on the ground, breathing hard for a minute.

What do you know, she mused. *Words can hurt you.*

"Sonya, are you okay?"

She closed her eyes for a second. John. He was safe. "I'm fine," she said, opening her eyes and willing her voice to have a semblance of normalcy. "But you and I are going to have a nice long talk after we get these guys to the police station."

She wiped her hands off on her jeans — she preferred not to think about what was on the ground in the alley — and tipped the bigger thug, the tattooed one, over, examining him as John Arlen made use of his cell phone. She grinned. "The best part about what I can do," she muttered.

"What?" John asked as he spoke into his phone to his ear. "Yes, I'll hold."

"There isn't a mark on either of them. The noise I solidified was just that—noise. And the guy won't remember anything."

She stood up, twisting her face in distaste. She couldn't get the sensation of slime off her. She would have to scrub when they got home. "Are they coming?" she asked as John closed his phone.

He nodded. "How's your guy?"

"Out like a light. How's the other one?"

"He stirred once, but other than that, he's still out. Is this what it's like?"

For a moment, she was confused, but then she understood. The superhero gig. She shrugged. "I don't have that much practical experience. I just knew what to do."

"So," he paused, looking around. "How did it feel?"

Sonya looked at him. John was crouched next to the man who had assaulted him in his own home, but he looked curious, not angry.

She would have been angry. Angry and satisfied that finally, the man would be behind bars. "Aren't you mad?"

John Arlen looked up at her, startled. "Yeah. But that's not going to help me here."

Sonya stared at him. "Don't you want to kick him?"

"That's not fair. He's unconscious," he pointed out.

"He would probably do it to you if he had the chance."

John glanced at her. "I'm better than he is. Would you?"

She looked at the man sprawled on the ground. "I'd be tempted," she said finally. "But probably not."

The sound of sirens cut through the miasma of the alley. He looked around. "The cops are finally coming. Are you okay?"

Sonya laughed shortly. "I'm going to be sore and bruised, but that's about all."

She hesitated. "John. We have to get our stories straight. Remember, we were on our way to—the Armenian restaurant over on Kane. You had to run an errand…"

His eyes widened for a moment. Then he suggested, "I was trying to find a flower shop that was open along the way."

She had to smile. He was a natural—she didn't know if that boded well or not. "Good."

"It came to mind because I passed one that was closed."

"Even better. You caught up to me and realized I was being mugged and tried to help."

He winced. "I could have had a shot with this one, but—"

She shook her head. She didn't have the heart to tell him even one of the thugs would have been too much for him. "We were both overpowered by the bigger one," she went on rapidly. "But he slipped in the alley and knocked himself out."

"Is this what's known as establishing an alibi?"

"What do you think?" she asked with a faint grin. "Think that restaurant's open? The Armenian one?"

"We can find out," he said, and she liked his smile.

She had to remember to yell at him for following her.

* * * * *

Arlen was happy about one thing—it wasn't Malone who responded to the call.

Of the two who showed up, he knew one of them, the younger one, still in his twenties. John knew his age for a fact. "Thanks for coming, Henry," John said when he saw who it was, and feeling only slightly uncomfortable. "I didn't think this was your beat. Come to think of it, you showed up at the house, too."

Henry Keats shook his head. "This isn't my beat and your neighborhood isn't either. Sarge was short a few guys, so I said I'd fill in. What are you doing here, Johnny?"

Arlen took a deep breath. Here it started. "Sonya and I wanted to try out the Armenian restaurant down on Kane."

Henry shook his head. "They moved last month—nobody wanted to come to this area after dark. Sorry, man."

John exhaled. "I didn't know. Helluva way to find out."

"Not to be too paranoid, but do you have any ID on you?" Sonya asked, turning away from the other, older policeman.

"Sonya, it's okay," John interrupted. "I know this guy."

"I'm a friend of Janie's," Henry added earnestly. "Have you heard from—" he paused.

Of course the kid wanted to know. He looked as though he were steeling himself for the answer. "As a matter of fact, she just arrived home today," John said.

"So—" said the kid—because he wasn't much more than that, in John's estimation—taking a deep breath. "How's she doing?"

She hasn't mentioned you, John thought, but didn't say it.

At the station house, the sergeant on duty needed his own questions answered. "Hell of an area for you to be walking," the grizzled cop drawled. "Mercy's not safe in broad daylight, let alone in the evening."

"We were going to the Armenian place," Sonya explained. John marveled at her earnest look. "Down the street, on Kane?"

"I got lost," John chimed in, confident of his story now. "I'd never been there—" He almost started when she linked her arm with his, but managed to stay still. He started to sweat.

The sergeant was as suspicious as Sonya was. He glared at the two of them. "Wasn't your father a cop?" he said finally, shifting his attention to Sonya. "Sam Penn?"

She nodded, getting doe-eyed. It was hard for John to take his eyes off her. She was a natural.

"Pretty convenient, the guy knocking himself out," the sergeant observed.

"Hey! What do you mean, 'convenient'?" Arlen demanded. "Would you have preferred she got mugged or raped?"

Almost immediately he felt the pressure of her hand, squeezing. "It's okay, he's just doing his job," she said soothingly.

Then he felt her foot step hard on his. He shut up.

"I thought I was in real trouble," she explained. "Maybe you should have someone go over to the alley and check it out. I guess it's slick because it's been so wet lately."

Arlen stifled a sigh of relief when, finally, the sergeant waved it off. "I know those alleys. Don't wander around in areas you don't know after dark, okay? It's not like we got Sounder and Velocity around anymore."

By the time they left the police station, the stars had come out. Together they looked up at the sky. Did she come from up there somewhere? John wanted to ask, but decided this wasn't the time. "It's a nice night," he ventured.

She didn't answer directly, choosing to link her arm with his. He liked it. "Let's take a walk along the riverfront," she said. He ignored his need to lean on her, considering his cane had met its demise in battle.

The riverfront wasn't far. It was also decidedly more populated with shoppers and tourists than the area they had just been in. They paused along the lookout over the water, away from a gaggle of tourists watching a street performer and his dancing cats. The lights of the bridge reflected on the waves of the water. She let go of his arm and leaned against the railing.

"It's a beautiful night," he ventured, watching the river.

"Something you wouldn't have been around to see if we hadn't been lucky," she shot back. She was looking around, at anything and anyone but him. She smiled. John realized it wasn't for him—or anyone, for that matter. It wasn't a warm smile.

"I thought you might need some protection."

"Then next time hand me a condom or a shield, but don't follow me." Her voice was still soft, her lips curving, but the tension under her words overwhelmed her tone. "I could have gotten myself killed, not to mention you. I need to train, and until I do it's not safe for you to come with me."

He set his jaw. "Then it was lucky I decided to follow you, isn't it? I'm sorry I was worried about you. I came prepared—look." He swiftly unbuttoned his jacket and flipped it open and closed, glancing around as he did so. The Enfield was heavy.

Her eyes widened. She looked around, then hissed, "Are you *insane*? Do you know how to use that thing?"

He gritted his teeth. "I know enough. And I'm licensed."

"John—" she shook her head, looking around again. "When you get home, put it away. Leave stuff like this to people like me. It may not have looked like it, but I have trained for it."

"But you were great!" he exclaimed, then lowered his voice. "You did exactly what you had to do."

"John," she said, her voice softening. "Let me take care of this."

"You said you wanted to help me get the Engineer. You didn't say anything about doing it yourself."

"My priority is to make sure you don't get hurt. And you will if you're not careful."

"I'm not going to sit at home and let you endanger yourself!"

She looked away. He noticed she hadn't stopped looking around, keeping an eye on her surroundings. And she managed to do it effortlessly, without rousing suspicion. The waterfront was filled with people, all enjoying the clear night, none of them paying any attention to them. As far as he could tell.

"What do you think you did back there, John?" she asked. She smiled. He realized anyone watching would assume they were having a pleasant conversation. "You distracted me. I shouldn't have let you, and it could have turned out a lot less positively."

He turned to face her. "Who's going to watch your back?"

She sighed. "I can watch my own back."

He shook his head. "I can't accept that."

"You'll have to," she said with a lilting laugh. "And put away that revolver before you hurt someone with it."

"No." He could feel his heart race and he knew she could hear it. "I'm going to help you, whether you want it or not."

All he could see in the dim light was her silhouette, but he thought he could see the weight of responsibility slip onto her shoulders. She seemed to slump. Maybe it wasn't his imagination.

She straightened and linked her arm with his. "Ready to go home?" she said, her voice light and carrying. The conversation was tabled for now, he guessed. "How did you get here, anyway?"

"I hailed a cab after you left."

They strolled down the boardwalk, taking care not to get too close to any of the other late-evening wanderers. "In my neighborhood? Amazing. How did I not see you?"

"The cabbie dropped me off two blocks from where you parked. He took off so fast he was on two wheels."

"I heard tires squealing," she murmured. "It never occurred to me it might be you."

"I'm sorry you didn't get what you were looking for."

She didn't answer. Instead, she squeezed his arm, surprising him. "I didn't find the information I came for, but the first guy said he hadn't been following me. I'm betting he wasn't out on a casual mugging expedition, either."

"If he wasn't following you, what was he there for?"

"Even if he'd been lying, his partner showed up out of nowhere," she went on, squeezing his arm again. "I'm betting another visit to that neighborhood might be in order later."

"Like—my cousin?" he said, lowering his voice. "You think my cousin might be there?"

"Maybe." He could hear the excitement in her voice.

They were walking a little faster. "The chase is afoot?"

"Tomorrow," she whispered, leaning into him. "After Tweedledee and Tweedledum make bail, we're going to be right behind them."

* * * * *

They made it home without incident. Considering their lives in the past few days, that in itself was a miracle, Sonya mused. Also considering what they'd been through, she was leery that Arlen had left his sister alone in her apartment.

"Janie?" John called out when they walked in, the lights in the living room were low. "Are you here?"

"In the kitchen," they heard. Sonya noticed the light beneath the door to the kitchen. He pushed the door open.

The kitchen never looked cozier to Sonya—or messier. Janie sat at the table, the newspapers that had been set aside for recycling spread out. The smell of coffee filled the room, and in the background, the radio played jazz.

"Are you all right?" he asked, adding, with Sonya's jab to his ribs, "Sonya had some errands and I went along."

"Oh, I'm fine. I found these newspapers after I got back and I realized I haven't read a real newspaper since I got to McMurdo. I was getting caught up. It's not the same reading everything online," John's older sister added as she neatly refolded a section. "But I'm going to sleep, so don't worry about me. Let me just get ready."

"I'm sorry I don't have much room," Sonya apologized. "I don't get many overnight visitors."

"The couch is fine, dear," Janie answered, beaming. "And I was thinking. The translocator—"

Sonya had just spent the evening fighting a pair of thugs, but she managed to get back to business. "The Engineer swiped the plans for from Arlen Labs?"

Janie nodded. "And most likely how they got in and out of the house. It needs space to work. We could never get around that. And Arlen Manor has plenty of space. There isn't enough here for them to be able to pop in and out safely. Otherwise, they could pop in and get stuck in the walls or between the floors. So we're safe here."

"So it's not that precise. That's good to know."

"We hadn't been able to adjust for the Earth's rotation when Jasper stole the plans," Janie explained. "Among other factors. As it is, I wouldn't want to risk it, but he is obviously willing."

"Maybe he perfected it."

Janie shook her head. "I don't think so."

Sonya sat at the table, wincing. She was starting to stiffen.

Janie noticed. "Are you all right?"

"I'm fine. I tripped over a crack in the sidewalk," Sonya said, flinching. "So there's an advantage to small spaces."

"That's right. And he wouldn't have a battalion of scientists to iron out the problems," the older woman said with a sigh. "Anyway, let me just skedaddle to the bathroom."

After she was gone, Sonya and Arlen stared at each other. "I only have the one bed," she said.

"I gathered."

"You can share it with me."

"Thank you."

"But first, I need a shower," she added, standing up slowly as the aches started to pound at her body. "And I want to burn these clothes after touching that ground."

By the time she showered, she was even stiffer, muscles shrieking. She just dumped the shirt and jeans into the garbage because she wasn't going to even try to clean them. This was the part of crime-fighting she had mercifully forgotten — the bruises and aches.

She also had to consider sleepwear. *We're both adults,* Sonya reminded herself as she got ready for bed and John was in the bathroom. She usually slept in the nude, but for this occasion, she chose a T-shirt and sweatpants, for modesty's sake.

And there was the bed. She took a deep breath.

"At least it's big enough for both of us," she heard behind her. She turned.

Arlen was at the doorway, dripping wet. He also wore a T-shirt with his boxers.

She sank onto the bed. "We almost look like twins," she said. He sat on the other side. She stripped her hand of her ring, and he stripped his face of his glasses and his wrist of his watch.

"No one would think we're twins," he said as he lay down, facing her. "They'd think we were an old married couple."

She got under the covers. After a moment, so did he.

His heart was pounding and so was hers. She smiled and so did he. She could hear the blood coursing through their veins. She switched off the lamp, plunging them into darkness.

"I haven't done this in a while," he said. He touched her face, trailing his fingers down her cheek. "Who would have thought I'd end up in bed with someone like you?"

She moved, suddenly uncomfortable. "What does that mean?"

"I've spent most of my life in the realm of theory. You're as far from theoretical as I can get." He tucked a strand of her hair around her ear.

She wished she could see his face. "For a lot of people, I'm as theoretical as you can get," she offered in a whisper. "How many people out there think superheroes are a figment of someone's imagination?"

"That's because they don't know you. They don't know how vital and real you are."

"Are you turning into a superhero groupie? Because if you are, I'm not the superhero to start with." Her eyes burned. She could feel the hot tears trickling down her face. She tried to stifle a cry, but she couldn't do it.

"It's okay. Shhh," she heard him say. He stroked her hair, and no matter how hard she tried to control her trembling, she couldn't. Some superhero she was. She nearly got beat in a simple fight and now she couldn't stop crying. "Calm down," she heard him say soothingly. "Come on, Sonya."

She felt his arms close around her. "It's okay," he said again, and she tipped her face into his chest.

All those years of studying and practicing, and she nearly bought the farm, courtesy one big, stupid, burly guy. Who didn't even have a gun. What if he had had one?

She turned over, unable to face John. She was losing it. All these years of holding herself in—and she was losing it now. She turned her face into her pillow, letting the cloth absorb the tears.

"Chill out, Sonya. It's okay."

She clenched her fists, burrowing her fists into the soft cotton of her bed linens. All the while, he held her, stroking her back. Presently she stopped trembling. He turned her over and settled her against him, letting her breathe.

John stroked her hair. "What was that all about?"

She hesitated, then shook her head. "I'll be okay."

"In my experience—limited though it is—when someone starts to cry, there's something wrong." She felt a whisper against her hair. "Especially when it's you."

"I nearly got us killed," she burst out, tears flowing down her cheeks. She gulped deep breaths, because all of a sudden she couldn't get enough air. *I'm hyperventilating*, she realized. She tried to calm down. "I nearly got us killed."

She started to sob and she was so embarrassed. "I'm an embarrassment to my parents, to my heritage, to every superhero out there who's overcome Kryptonite and overambitious mad scientists and alien conquerors. I nearly got you killed with a couple of thugs."

"Is that all?"

"Is that all? Isn't death enough?" she cried, pushing away from him and glaring at him.

He smiled broadly. She stifled an urge to hit him. "What?"

He leaned in. "It's called dress rehearsal. It wasn't the real show. So there were problems. We'll iron them out."

We? "What if we can't?"

He came closer still. "What if we can?"

John filled her vision. His eyes, almost iridescent in the dim light, seemed to dance.

For someone who had been on the wrong end of a fight, he didn't seem to have his spirits dampened at all.

"You could have died because of me."

He shook his head. "I could have died because of *me*. You didn't expect me. I was overly optimistic, I admit it. If I'd gotten hurt again it would have been my own fault. Not yours."

"Why *not* mine?" she whispered.

He reached out and smoothed a moist tendril of hair off her cheek. "The only fight I've ever been in was for the last textbook available for my introductory quantum mechanics class, and the nebbish I was arguing with stepped on my foot, grabbed the book and ran."

She smiled a little. "How embarrassing for you."

"Especially since he grew up to be Bill Gates. Imagine what I could have done for the world if I'd hit back." His eyes softened. "Feeling better?"

She buried her face a little deeper into her pillow. "I guess. I don't know if I'm horrified, or—horrified."

Sonya felt a whisper of something on her forehead—a kiss? She couldn't tell. She heard him say, "You've been so hot on making sure I do my exercises. Well, tomorrow we're going to make sure you do yours. Now get some sleep."

He stroked her hair. And as far as she could remember, he was still doing it when she finally drifted to sleep.

By the time she woke up the next morning, he was gone. His pillow had been smoothed and his side of the bed looked as though it had never been touched.

Dressing quickly, she staggered out into the living room, her muscles screaming in protest. The couch did have some sign of life. The linens and blankets were neatly folded, pillows on top.

Her nose twitched. There, at least, was one sign of life. Even two. She knew that smell—and that heartbeat. She tracked the scent, and the sound, into her kitchen.

John was at the kitchen table, a newspaper open in front of him—not the one she subscribed to—a red Sharpie in his hand, the coffee perking behind him. It was a scene of domesticity she hadn't expected.

"Good morning," she said, her voice rusty. "I didn't think you knew how to use the coffeemaker."

John Arlen looked up and smiled. She faltered. It was a friendly smile, but it was not the smile of a man who had held her as she cried.

Unaccountably, she felt her heart crumble around the edges.

"Good morning," he said. "I don't. Janie made it."

"I didn't realize she was domestic." Curious, she craned her neck, trying to read what was on the newspaper in front of him. "What are you marking up the newspaper for?"

"The police blotter. Your newspaper doesn't run one, so I went out and picked up the other daily, which does."

She sat down opposite him, pouring herself a cup. There was a reason she subscribed to the paper that didn't run a police blotter. She hadn't wanted to look at police reports. But now she did. "Looking for anything in particular?"

John had a yellow legal pad next to the newspaper. By the looks of it, he had been at it for a while, since the pad was covered with scribbles. "The crime rate," he said. He sipped his coffee. "I think it's escalating."

From the number of circles in bright red, she would have gauged that crime was indeed afoot. "Something's going on," she said, guessing what was on his mind. "Something connected with the Engineer."

"They're not afraid of the police anymore."

She thought of Malone and grimaced. "Depending on how many of them are on the take."

Surprisingly, he shook his head. "Not many, I'll bet. Not unless things have been going downhill a lot longer than I think. Essential services still seem to be intact. That includes police protection."

Sonya snapped her fingers. "That reminds me. Let's check on the guys from last night." She snagged the phone. "Thank you," she said, seemingly out of nowhere.

He looked up, and she knew he understood. "My pleasure," he said. "How often do I get a chance to hold a superhero?"

Sonya smiled a little. "I don't know. How often?"

A few taps on the phone pad, and she was connected to the precinct house. A minute later, she hung up. She was numb.

"What is it?" he said in alarm.

She put the phone down as gently as she could. Otherwise, she would have thrown it across the room. "They vanished. Literally. Five officers saw them do it," she told John.

Chapter Eleven

No, his mind rebelled. "How—" He stopped. His fist clenched. He *knew* how. "Damn it!"

Infuriated, he stood up. "I should have known, damn it!" He banged his fist on the kitchen counter, rattling the dishes and splashing the coffee. "They used the translocator!"

"Well, I guess it works."

"Of course it works..." His voice trailed off as he looked at her. "Are you all right?"

Her hands were shaking, wrapped around her mug in a way that made him fear for its fate. "Their attorney—" Her voice thickened with fury. "Shook their hands and walked out. Then they stepped outside the station and popped into nothingness."

"The cops must have loved that."

She laughed, short and bitter. "From the sounds of it."

He grunted as he thought about it. "The translocator uses a homing device. The lawyer must have slipped them one, because neither of them had one when they were arrested. That's the only reason I can think of why they didn't disappear before the cops showed up."

Sonya twisted her ring. He'd never seen her lose her temper—and he wasn't sure he wanted to. What would she do if she did?

"They can't materialize into a small space, right? And that's why my apartment's safe? Do you know its range?"

He shook his head. "We can find out. Janie's the best one to ask. She went into the office." He shook his head. "Not back two days and she's already got to go back to work. Let's go for a visit."

The Arlen Industries complex loomed as they approached, as large and impenetrable as ever. It wasn't particularly attractive—it never had been, with its rows of broad concrete buildings, some of which were labs and some of which held offices—but that didn't matter. "It hasn't changed at all," John murmured as Sonya stopped her SUV at the gates. He glanced at the closest building, remembering happier days. "Right down to those lawns over there," he said, pointing. "And the name of the company written out in pansies. Janie did that one year."

"Why would it change?" Sonya asked practically. "Hi, he's going to do the talking here," she greeted the guard at the gate, gesturing to her side. "We're here to visit Janie Arlen."

The guard, however, wasn't listening to her, having caught sight of John. "Dr. Arlen!" he said, his craggy face lighting up. "Welcome back! Comin' back to work?"

John beamed. "Not yet. Kenny, this is Sonya Penn. She's a friend of the family. Does she need a visitors' badge?"

"Naw, if she's with you. Hope to have you back soon," the white-haired guard said, waving the car through.

It felt good to be back. This was home, as much as Arlen Manor was. "Kenny's been with Arlen since I was a kid," he said as they moved through the compound. "He helped me play a practical joke on my father when I was ten. Park there."

She parked in a space that had "ARLEN" written out on the cement. "What did you do? For the joke?"

"Kenny helped me nail the furniture in my dad's office to the ceiling. Took us all night," he added, the memory still warming him, more than two decades later. He got out of the car and leaned against the SUV. "But it was worth it. Dad was doing some antigravity experiments. The look on his face…"

That was the one time he had actually surprised his father. He grinned at the memory. "I'm still amazed he let me get away with it. Dad made Kenny and me take all the furniture off the ceiling and repair the ceiling. He laughed, though."

Sonya came over to give him a hand. "I'm surprised Kenny went along with it."

"Dad knew I put him up to it. Thanks," he said when she put her arm around him. They started to walk. "I wasn't looking forward to having to request a wheelchair."

"Since you didn't bring along your crutches and the cane you were using is now kindling, I figured I'd better help you until we get you a new walking stick."

"Thanks," he said again. She kept her arm around him. He would have liked it, but it felt too much like support.

"I need to try this on my own," he told her as they approached the doors of the building. Bullshit, he said to himself. He just didn't want to walk into his home away from home unless it was on his own two feet.

He felt Sonya's glance on him. "Can you do it?"

"For a while." He grimaced. "Just a while longer."

Unlike Kenny, the security desk attendants for the building were relatively new. John had to produce ID. He curtly turned down the offer of a wheelchair. "We're going to my dad's office before we go see Janie," he told Sonya. He looked grim.

"Okay," she said, but she looked worried. *It'll be all right,* he wanted to tell her. But he couldn't.

The elevator ride was uneventful and they ran into no one John recognized. "When was the last time you were here?" Sonya asked once they got out and they walked down the corridor.

"The day Dad was killed. It happened in his office," he said abruptly, fishing out his keys. He fingered the one he knew was the right one. "There should be something in here I could use."

Introducing Sonika

Entering wasn't as traumatic as he thought it would be. He held his breath as he pushed the door open. The light was dim, the curtains drawn, probably had been since the day of the incident. He looked away from the area of the carpet where the chalked outline had been drawn—cleaned since then, but he would remember forever where it had been.

"What are you looking for?"

John looked around. "Something my dad always kept here." He eyed the credenza near the far corner of the room.

He had to try three keys before he found the right one. "You could have picked this lock by now," he commented as he pulled open the cabinet door. He pulled out something he had never thought twice about before that day. He held it in his hands. "I think I can use this."

They both admired the object he held. He hefted it, rolled it with his fingers. It felt good. It had been his father's and he could feel his spirit still in it.

"I envy you," Sonya said, a touch of wistfulness in her voice. "It took a lot of courage to walk in here. I've never been able to go back to where my dad died—considering the city built the new ballpark and the Pavilion of Peace basically over it. Your father's cane, I guess?"

The ornate walking stick was carved out of heavy mahogany, its heavy use evident by the nicks and scratches at one end, the knob at the other worn smooth. John nodded, grasping the knob and standing up, finally leaning on it. Almost immediately, he felt stronger. "This was his favorite," he said, his voice loud in the hush of the long-unused office. "Too bad it's not a sword cane, like Geoffrey's was."

She looked at the cane. "Heavy enough to fight with."

He gripped it. "It is," he said.

Once they closed up his father's office and started down the hall, the hallways became thick with familiar faces.

"I guess Kenny sounded the alarm," Sonya murmured after John shook the fourth set of hands.

"Looks like it," he said, narrowly escaping having to shake a fifth set before arriving at Janie's offices. He waved at her secretary, who looked startled but let them through.

Janie's office was as domestic as an office could look, painted a rosy pink, with sheers drawn back by a ribbon in place of the usual heavy drapes. Her desk was, however, traditional, gleaming mahogany in the sunlight. "There you are," his older sister greeted them, not at all surprised to see them. She was surrounded—no, buried—by paper and folders, some of which he recognized from his father's areas of interest. "Care to take some of this? Neither you nor I have been around to make the big decisions."

He stared at the piles of yellowing paper and shuddered. "Not yet. I'm here because of something that happened last night."

"We were mugged," Sonya said, coming straight to the point. "By the same someone who probably mugged John at your house. Who, by the accounts of the police, made bail this morning and..."

Janie groaned. "Oh, you must be kidding. You got mugged *again*? Why didn't you tell me? What's wrong with that boy?"

That boy? She meant Jasper. John knew it. So did Sonya.

Sonya looked at his sister, and as John watched, she leaned in, her eyes intent. "You sound like you know Jasper pretty well. I thought you only saw him a couple of times."

"I'm sure Janie—" John began.

He shut up when Janie's gaze slid away. "I did," she said, clearly flustered. "I didn't think he was a bad kid."

Sonya leaned in some more. "So when did you see him last?"

"Janie, we're just trying to get some questions answered—"

His sister shook her head. "Johnny, I've got a million things to do, I have a meeting with the board of directors—"

Sonya didn't budge. "Why'd you do it?"

John felt his bearings slip away. "What are you talking about?" he asked, perplexed. "We just came to ask about—"

"I don't think your cousin stole the blueprints to the translocator. I think Janie gave them to your cousin. I think she had to leave town for a while because it got too hot for her," Sonya said, her gaze locked on the other woman. "And now she's back to finish the job. On you."

Janie recoiled. "Sonya, you don't know what you're saying."

"Sonya…" John said uneasily.

"How could your cousin sail in here and steal something that sensitive unless someone just handed it to him? Think fast, Janie," Sonya retorted. She sat on the edge of the desk.

Janie's usual easygoing manner disappeared, replaced by a flinty glare. "I don't appreciate this. John, get her out of here."

He sighed. "Can you answer the question, Janie? Please?"

"What question? All I heard were accusations. If you'll excuse me—"

"Janie. Answer Sonya's question."

"I'd be glad to pose the question to the board of directors," Sonya added. "Let me know what I should do."

John's jaw dropped. His eyes bulged as the two women stared at each other. They were playing corporate chicken, waiting to see who was going to back down first.

Janie sighed, got up and shut the door. "I'm just going to say this once." She exhaled. "I felt sorry for the kid. After all, he never had a stable home life. I thought maybe if we showed him we're all family, that might help. That's why I got him an internship here."

"When was this again?" Sonya asked.

"It was the summer before Dad died. John was taking a sabbatical—remember? In the Himalayas, with Dad? At first…" Janie faltered. "I thought Jasper was going to work out. He was bright and he asked all the right questions."

"What happened?"

Janie sighed. "One day I came in and my file on the Cycle project had been cleaned out. No physical file, nothing on my hard drive, nothing in the main server, nothing in backup. It was as though it never existed. And Jasper disappeared. He came, he saw what he wanted, and poof! He got it and left. We had to start over again."

John's rubbed his forehead. "Is that why you decided to take that offer of a fellowship?"

Janie eyes flickered and he remembered belatedly there was another reason. "Among others," she answered after a moment. "A year seemed like a good length of time. I was humiliated, I had personal reasons. Then I did the consulting job at McMurdo. But then I wasn't here when… John, I'm going to suggest you take my place as chief scientist."

"Janie, one mistake shouldn't color your decision on this," John protested. "You made a mistake, but you did it with the assumption Jasper wasn't as bad as he'd been painted to be."

"And I was wrong." Janie closed her eyes. "I don't think being related to him is going to be the best PR for Arlen Labs when the police finally catch up with him. Which is another reason I should step down."

"In that case, I should step down too. Go and talk to the board. Remember, you have as much say as they do."

"I know. I just—" Her voice broke. "Dad died because of me, Johnny. If I hadn't given Jasper that chance, he would never have found out about the alternative energy projects. And you know that's when he found out."

"You couldn't control Jasper's actions, no matter what."

He rubbed his neck. Briefly, he considered whether he should say anything, but…"I've seen Henry a couple of times."

Introducing Sonika

Janie flinched. He felt sorry for his sister. This couldn't be easy on her. "How is he?"

"Looked okay. He asked after you."

His sister's mouth set. "What did you say?"

He shrugged. "I'm not your go-between, Janie. This is between him and you."

Janie didn't look happy, but she piled the folders in front of her into a loose stack. "Did you need anything else? Otherwise, I'll see you later."

Before he forgot. "The range for the translocator. Do you remember what it is?"

The answer, promptly given, was anticlimactic after all that confrontation. After that, they were out in the hallway.

Being back at Arlen Labs had lost its charms. "Let's go."

Sonya shrugged. "We need to go back to Mercy." She paused. "Is your sister going to be all right?"

"She'll be fine." He scratched his head. "She had—has—some things she's got to work out on her own."

In the light of the day, the Mission Mercy neighborhood did not look threatening, only desolate. They found the alley from the night before.

John looked around. "This looked a lot worse last night," he said. The alley was empty, of course. It smelled of things best not considered and there was a skittering toward the back. The battered and dented trash cans were on their sides, their openings gaping sadly, the result, no doubt, from their activities the night before. Amazing what daylight would do.

"Did your father ever mention—you know, what Janie did?" Sonya asked out of nowhere. "After you and he got back from your sabbatical and found out about it?"

He shrugged. "Dad had a soft, mushy heart. He would have given Jasper the same chance, and if Janie thought about it, she would have realized that. But it's going to be a while."

"That must have been a horrible year for her, as much as for you."

"She'll get over it. But we're going to have to convince her to stay at your place tonight," he added. "She won't want to."

"I'll take one arm and you can take the other one and we can drag her," Sonya told him and he knew she wasn't kidding.

They continued to walk until they arrived at the police station. "From what Janie said, we should be able to get some idea of where those thugs went—and maybe where my cousin hangs out—by simple triangulation," John explained. "All we have to do is take into account where that alley is and then the police station."

"We need to figure out where the third point is."

He nodded, taking out his PDA. He brought up a map of the neighborhood. He pointed to the two points they knew. "We can estimate the third."

It took a few seconds to come up with three possibilities. "Can we find out what's supposed to be at those places?" Sonya asked.

"We just did," he said after a pause. "Let's take a look."

He recognized the first address. "This one's a warehouse owned by Arlen Industries. Actually, they all are."

"You guys own a lot, don't you?"

"The corporation does." The last one rang a bell. "This one has to be it. It's leased to a Rivers Corporation. Jasper's father operated under the name Rivers."

"And Jasper decided to keep the name? Wouldn't he have branched off and gone for his own?"

"I would have, but I'm not my cousin."

"I think we're all grateful for that."

He glanced at her. She smiled. "Which way?" she asked.

"Why?"

"Research," she said. She smiled again, but this one seemed a little more feral.

It wasn't far. The property in question was on the edge of the warehouse district, an area that saw a bustle of activity in broad daylight but little in the evening. Amid the activity, the warehouse leased by Rivers and owned by Arlen was ominously silent. "Arlen Industries owns that? You're a slumlord, John," she commented as they surveyed the place. "Looks like crap."

He had to agree. The windows had been blacked out and the external appearance of the warehouse was, in a word, decrepit. "I'm pretty sure it looked better when we originally leased it."

"Maybe the lessee's spiffed the place up inside."

"Maybe, considering it's got a guard at the entrance," John answered, gesturing at the sleeping man stretched across the entrance. "I'm surprised it's only one."

She looked. "How'd you know he's not just sleeping there?"

"I didn't. That was a joke."

"No, you're right. Don't look now, but there's someone on the roof," she said. "I'll bet if we made a tour of the perimeter, we'd see more than one guard."

He tried to look up without looking up. He didn't see anything, but that didn't mean anything. "No bet." He shook his head.

She looked at the place, her expression thoughtful. "Let's find out what they do with all that space."

* * * * *

"I don't care if it *is* Arlen property. This is still breaking and entering!"

His pronouncement didn't seem to faze her. She continued to double-check her equipment. They had gone back to her place and, in front of his appalled gaze, she had quickly changed from a law-biding citizen to someone who was equipped to commit crime. Worse, she expected him to help. "You've got your rope. Your grappling hooks are on securely, right?" She adjusted her black turtleneck and pulled on the edge of her black, form-fitting jeans. "Good thing that T-shirt's black," she said, looking at him critically. "Otherwise, we would have had to waste time getting you something appropriate for this."

He looked down at his garb. His black T-shirt and worn jeans looked as though he were lounging at home. Her outfit, on the other hand... "This is against everything I've been taught, you realize?"

"We're not really breaking and entering," Sonya told him, sounding very reasonable. He knew better. "We're just checking on Arlen property."

"Are you feeling guilty about doing this at all?"

She stared at him. "No. Should I?"

"What do you plan on telling the police if they catch us?"

"I dunno. Why don't we call that cop friend of yours to bail us out?"

"What cop friend?"

"The one who was at your place when you got mugged, and the one last night. The one who calls you Johnny."

"Who? Oh," he paused. He wasn't sure how to explain Henry.

"Yeah, the baby-faced one. His showing up last night was kind of suspicious."

He shrugged. "It's not." But he hesitated, saying no more.

She rolled her eyes. "Fine," she bit out. "Let's get going. It's dark enough." She pushed him out of her apartment.

"Baby-faced—Henry." He opened his mouth, then closed it. "He's not really my friend," he mumbled. "He's Janie's—" He stopped.

She gave him a hard glance. "Then the attorneys you have on retainer are going to get a workout. And I'll get by. It wouldn't be my first offense, but I'll—"

"What?"

She shrugged as she started her SUV. "I got caught when I went with Dad and Mom on a mission. It was my first time out, I was twelve. I got off easy because it was my first offense."

"At least I've got the Arlen sharks," he protested. "What would you do?"

She shrugged again, a habit that was starting to annoy him. "Put me on the payroll and the sharks can represent us both."

It occurred to him the life of a superhero was not without its drawbacks. "Fine. Welcome to Arlen Industries. You start out with two weeks' vacation. We offer full medical, including dental. You have off all major federal, regional and city holidays and also your birthday off. That was my contribution," he added modestly.

"You should be proud. I want three weeks' vacation."

"Two weeks is standard."

"Yeah, but I want three." She parked on the opposite edge of the warehouse district, he noticed, a few blocks away from the building in question. "Put on your harness now so you don't have to do it later." Without waiting for him, she strapped on hers and started to walk. He followed, fumbling with his rig. He was going to tire easily, without crutches or even his cane. They had discussed it and she had capitulated. Better to know where he was, she had told him.

He wasn't sure whether or not that was a compliment.

In any case, she was fast. "I'll give you an extra day off," he wheedled, limping, breathing harder than he would have liked to admit. She stopped short. He looked up and realized they must have been nearer than he thought, because they were at the building.

"How's an extra day as good as an extra week?" She glanced at the rope in his hand and tilted her head. "If I can't have more vacation time, I want more money. Let's go over there."

He did, following her down the alley next to the building. "You drive a hard bargain," he gasped. "You win. Three weeks it is."

She looked up and bit her lip. "No, two should be fine with more money. Here," She pointed. He looked.

It was a rusty emergency ladder that snaked down the building, ending about six feet above the ground. "Is that a ladder? Too bad," he said, trying to joke. "I was looking forward to watching you use those grappling hooks."

"Oh, I'm using mine," she said. "But not you. You're going up the ladder and I'll meet you up there."

"You're sure you don't want me to check it out first?"

She made a noise that sounded like a snort. "I should have it checked out by the time you get up there." She jerked at the ladder and it didn't collapse, which John figured was all he could hope for. It slid down into place with minimal screeching. "Be careful climbing—it's going to squeak, and we have to minimize the noise we make. Now up."

Thankfully the ladder, though rusted, was solid. He watched Sonya as she took a running start and jumped, scaling the wall using the grappling hooks. Moreover, she was almost noiseless, whereas he made more noise on the ladder.

Need more practice, my ass, he mused, gripping the ladder. She was doing just fine. He took another rung and this time the ladder trembled. One rung at a time, he reminded himself.

By the time he was at the top, his arms were quaking with the stress of unaccustomed exercise. He reached for the last rung—and found himself pulled up. "Took you long enough," Sonya said, giving him a tug to get him off the ladder, and then she sat, looking as though she were ready for a picnic.

He sprawled on the roof, getting his bearings. "Not all of us trained for this kind of thing."

She tucked her grappling hooks back into her harness. "This is why you have to do your exercises. From what I can tell, there are only three guys in the main section of the building," she told him. She glanced at her watch.

In the time it had taken him to climb the side of the building, she had scaled it, surveyed the lay of the land, taken a quick look at what she could see inside and still been ready at the top of the ladder for him. He shook his head. She noticed it. "Something wrong?"

He shook his head again. She went on. "There's another guy at the main entrance, and one at the side entrance. And check it out—half a dozen guys are coming from different directions heading this way. I'm going to assume they're going to gather," and she glanced at her watch again, "here."

His stomach sank. This was turning out to be more than he expected. He shouldn't have done this. "I can't even run—"

She looked at him, her mind clearly on more important matters than his ego. "John, you're my lookout. If anything needs to be done, I'll do it."

"This is just reconnaissance," he was quick to remind her. "We have to know what we're up against."

She didn't reply, tugging at her harness.

"Wait," he heard himself saying.

She stopped and turned. "What?"

He didn't know what he was doing, but he did it anyway. He reached over and kissed her on the lips. "Good luck."

She smiled, as sweet as the kiss itself. "Thanks." She spun and started off across the rooftop, her footsteps noiseless. In the dusk, she looked like a panther stalking her prey as she disappeared into the darkness.

Right now, he wouldn't want to cross her.

He made his way along to the corner of the rooftop and looked down at the ground, where a man was approaching the entrance. He was stopped by the goon at the door, where there appeared to be a conversation, and then he entered.

Arlen heard a scurry and saw Sonya shinny down the side of the building, hanging by her rope. He watched her pause at a window.

Ordinarily, that wouldn't have made him nervous. What did put him on edge was the fact she was hanging upside down as she did it.

More practice, my ass, he mused again. *He* could barely walk and *she* didn't find it unusual to be walking upside down the side of a building.

More and more men approached the entrance as he watched, and more and more were allowed in. Only twice were those who approached turned away. From the gestures he saw, he concluded they didn't have the ID the goon at the gate was looking for—was it an invitation? But they went away without a word.

Thieves had better manners than football fans.

Something moved at the edge of his vision and he looked in that direction. Sonya had apparently gotten tired of hanging upside down. She was now walking on the side of the building, looking like a Native American traversing a path in the woods. Welcome to the *Leatherstocking Tales*, modern version.

The trickle of visitors to the warehouse eventually slowed as the hum of activity rose to a dull roar inside. He lost sight of his partner in trespass, first with the deepening darkness and then when she turned the corner. She still had the rope, though it was unfurling, little by little, as she went farther from the spot where it was anchored.

What lesson was that from her parents? Rule One Thousand Five Hundred Thirty-Four, How to Perform Reconnaissance. Had she ever learned whatever it was that little girls learned from their mothers—knitting or sewing or cooking or whatever? He couldn't imagine it. That would have been too surreal. Superhero by night, happy homemaker by day.

The roar got louder. As he watched, the doors down below burst open and the attendees poured out, weapons drawn, shouting.

"Who was that?" he made out. "The guards up on the roof! Where are the guards up on the roof?"

John withdrew hastily, looking around. This was not good. "Sonya! Sonya?"

No answer. He heard the clang of the ladder, the shriek of rusted metal grinding against itself. That had to be the attendees, and it wasn't that far up to the top. "Sone!" he finally called out. *Where was she?*

He heard, "What the hell?" Then a shout. Then many shouts.

"We're getting out of here!" rang out a familiar voice.

Her silhouette appeared at the top of the ladder. She was kicking down, one by one, whoever came up the ladder, almost daintily. But she couldn't keep it up forever.

He looked around. The ladder was the only way down, except for the locked exit leading down to the warehouse itself. There wasn't anything on the rooftop to jam the door closed—

Yes! It was a cylinder of what looked like tarpaper, probably left there by roofers to ready the surface for the coming winter, along with a pile of roofing equipment. He hurried over and tried to pull it. It didn't budge. Finally, he began to push it toward the door, trying to block the entrance.

He heard the rattle of keys on the other side of the locked door. He had to hurry. He gritted his teeth as he pushed, ignoring the pain shooting up his leg and then the twinge when he stumbled. Finally, the cylinder of tarpaper rolled and hit just as the door was cracking open, and he guessed by the shouts their would-be pursuers were knocked off their feet.

That wouldn't hold them for long. Sonya was going to tire. She wasn't used to holding off scores of thugs, no matter how much she could do. Once he was satisfied the cylinder wasn't going to move and the door was wedged closed, he ran to Sonya and looked down.

Even thugs knew when to go around. She was fending them off, but he guessed by the way they were running they had figured out another way.

He heard the clang of metal again, but this one was new. What was it? He limped to the blind side of the building, the side he had assumed was safe because it was smooth, without a ladder.

No, not safe. It was too close to the building next door, which had an emergency ladder. They were scrambling up that ladder, and would, sooner or later, try to jump across.

Some of them wouldn't make it. But some of them would.

"Got any ideas?" he shouted to Sonya. They were surrounded and sooner or later they would have guests. He had his own rope and he had grappling hooks—they could be used as weapons if need be—but that was all, since Sonya had persuaded him not to carry his grandfather's Enfield.

Five minutes, tops, that was about all they had. That was his estimate for himself but Sonya could beat them off longer, though she too would tire eventually.

But she didn't seem concerned. She kicked off one last attacker and then turned to him. "Get ready to do what I tell you."

"What do you have in mind?"

"I'm waiting for one of the idiots across the way to start shooting," she answered calmly.

The banging had stopped on the exit door. He didn't like that. "What are you talking about?"

"I just need—"

A shot rang out.

Chapter Twelve

ಬ

She grinned at the sound of the shot. "C'mon," she whispered. "Something more. Something big, guys. I just need—"

She got a barrage of gunfire from two different sources. One was from a pair who had managed to get up to the rooftop next door, and one from the other side of the door leading to the warehouse. The door was going to be steel Swiss cheese within a minute.

Got it! "C'mon, Robin, to the Sound-Carpet!"

John Arlen had no sense of humor under stress, Sonya noted. His head whipped around. "What the hell are you talking about?"

"Watch."

The gunfire continued, the noise filling the air. That was going to bring the cops. The echo of the cacophony fed on itself and the sound of the gunfire.

When the air was bursting with the clamor, she reached out. The languor washed over her as she grasped the volley of noise and spread it out with her hand. In front of them appeared a shimmering carpet—floating, moving a little with the wind.

She'd always loved this effect.

She looked up at the sky. The wind was kicking up.

Sonya climbed on. *This* she knew how to deal with. *This* was who she was! "Get on," she urged, her excitement bubbling over, making her feel as buoyant as the board of sound she was balancing on. She reached out, gesturing toward John, who stood there, his mouth open. "Come on!"

she urged. "Hold onto me—and don't forget to hold your breath, it'll help. Remember what happened at the deli."

She pulled him aboard and arranged his arms around her. The carpet didn't buckle, didn't sway—it was as rock-solid as if it had been terra firma, and she balanced on it as though she had been born on it. John didn't say anything. She twisted around and saw the outlines of his face, frozen.

"It's going to be fun," she assured him. "Don't let go of me—you won't remember anything otherwise!"

She covered his arms with hers. He might have been thin, but he covered her, and the sensation was part of the magic of the evening. The carpet nearly pranced, as though it were eager to be off, because in this case, sound truly traveled.

"This is the easiest way to make sure you don't have that much contact with the board," she told him, turning her head. She laughed out loud at his shell-shocked expression.

His heart beat rapid-fire and his pulse alone could have turned her on. But not his breath. He was still holding it.

"It's okay," she whispered. "Watch!"

She raised her hands, taking his along. As if the carpet had a mind of its own, it rose and flew with the wind. Taking a deep breath, she laughed again. How she had missed this. *This* was what she had trained for. *This* was what she had been denying herself, all those years.

"Isn't this wonderful?" she called out as the carpet rode the wind. Out of the corner of her eye, she watched as the door leading to the rooftop was blasted into bits and men spilled onto the surface, looking for them. But they weren't there, and they were getting farther away with every gust and breeze.

The wind caressed her face, cool and intoxicating, enveloping her. "Isn't the view great? John?" She glanced at him.

His eyes were bulging and it wasn't necessarily because he was on a carpet soaring above the city. "Oh, I'm so sorry!" she exclaimed. It was a lot to ask—hold his breath, float in the air, plaster his body against hers and control that erection. But he was trying—and succeeding in some things better than others.

"Just a few more seconds," she said over her shoulder. "You should be able to take a breath in just a few seconds."

She pushed his hands gently away from her, missing his touch already. But they only had precious few seconds before the carpet unraveled beneath them, and they had to be closer to the ground by the time it happened.

Manipulating the carpet to glide closer and closer to the ground, she felt John jerk behind her. "John?" she called behind her. "Are you all right?" she looked over her shoulder.

"No, I'm not!" he burst out, but he shut up after that. It was like riding a mechanical bull, she realized, and try as he might, he couldn't get his balance. Finally, she felt behind her until he took her hand, enjoying his touch, together with the ability she loved most from her youth. "Hold tight," she urged. "Look. Isn't this wonderful? Just a few more seconds."

She could feel him steady now, looking around, but keeping a firm grip on her hand. "I've never seen the city like this," he whispered, wonder in his voice.

She squeezed his hand. It was good to share this with somebody, someone who could appreciate it. But it was almost over.

The carpet was starting to dissipate, shredding into nothingness. Her SUV was finally within sight. She had parked far enough away so they would be safe—even if their pursuers knew what to look for, they wouldn't recognize them, certainly not once they drove away. They would simply be a couple in an SUV.

They were close enough to the car now. They could hop off before the carpet melted away completely. "Ready?" she asked. He nodded, eyeing the distance to the ground. "Hold on tight and we'll just step off," she told him.

They were less than ten feet off the ground when the carpet misted away completely. "Bend your knees when you hit the ground," she called out. She held onto him as they dropped. She was pleased to see he rolled onto the ground as the carpet wisped away in the wind.

She jumped up and pulled him to his feet. "Okay?"

"Yeah," he said, looking dazed. "That was amazing," he said, shaking his head. "I don't know if I want to remember that."

She pulled at his hand. "You will, but vaguely, like a dream," she said. "Let's go."

Fortunately, he didn't need much coaxing. He followed her limping, but that was to be expected. She'd give him a massage after they got home. He didn't say another word as she unlocked her car.

The tires screeched as she drove off. She paused at stop signs, obeyed traffic signals and paid attention to most traffic laws. No small talk.

Finally, she stopped at yet another red light—there seemed to be an inordinate number of them all of a sudden—before she turned to him. "Are you all right? John?"

He was staring off into space, his mouth open. She reached out and touched his shoulder. "John? Answer me!"

He twitched. Her fingers were moist. There was blood on them. Oh, crap. "Did you get hit? John?"

To her relief, he shook his head. "I landed on my shoulder and ripped my damn T-shirt. I was—trying to absorb what we just did. I still can't believe it. You seem to be very comfortable with it all."

She shrugged. "That was the first time I've done it on my own. I shouldn't have taken you."

"It was dangerous! I thought it was just supposed to be a recon mission—"

"It was, but then it wasn't."

"So what happened?"

She stopped at another light. Only one more before she hit the highway, and then home. "Well, I was hanging there—"

"I remember," he said, and she could have sworn he shuddered.

"Again, something I was trained to do," she reminded him, her glow diminishing as she started to examine what exactly she'd done. "I'd forgotten how much Mom and Dad taught me."

"You were hanging upside down," he prompted her.

"I wasn't getting a clear view from the window I was at, so I walked around until I found one," she said, hoping she sounded as rational and reasonable as she thought she did.

"What were you looking for, a completely open window so that you could stick your head in?"

"Well, not quite."

"*How* not quite?"

This wasn't going the way she thought it would. "I just wanted a view of what was going on."

"And did you find it?"

In retrospect, she should have realized his voice was getting oddly modulated. "Yeah. I found one that was open just enough for a clear view. Across from the podium."

"There was a podium?"

"You would not have believed it!" She smiled, remembering. "It looked like a really big Weight Watchers meeting for thugs!"

"And how many did you estimate were there?"

She could have sworn he was gritting his teeth. "About a hundred. I recognized a few from the FBI's Most Wanted list."

"Oh, great."

"I didn't see the Engineer, though," she added. "Of course, I've only seen him on news clips. Do you have any photos?"

"No. Nobody was at the podium?"

She shook her head. "They were all waiting for someone."

"So what happened? They decided to come after us for no good reason?"

"Well, it was a combination of events."

"Like what?"

"Like they finally realized the guards from the roof hadn't checked in."

"What happened to them? You said when we were there before that you saw guards. But there wasn't anything when—"

"I got rid of them when I first got up there."

"Just like that?"

"It doesn't take long if you know what you're doing. Anyway, when I heard they were going to check, I paid them a visit."

"What did you do?"

If he weren't in decent shape, she would worry about him having a stroke. "Gave us enough time to get away, didn't it?"

"We could have gotten away if you hadn't done it!"

"I left my calling card." She took a quick look at him. He was beet-red, but didn't seem to have anything else to say.

They were on the highway now, five minutes to home. "Are you all right? Did you hear me?"

"I heard you," he finally said. His teeth were still clenched. Not good. "Please tell me you don't have cards for the occasion."

She laughed. Really, someday he'd see the humor in all this. "I popped in, told them the Engineer's days were numbered, and if they had any sense, they'd turn themselves in now." She giggled. This had to be the rush her parents told her about.

The rush they had warned her about, come to think about it.

"And do you think they were all running out to surrender?"

Definitely sarcasm. It was a bit of a downer. "No, but they're on alert now. They know someone's gunning for them."

He leaned against the headrest and closed his eyes.

"What's wrong?" she asked.

"I can't think of where to start."

Well, he had managed to thoroughly dampen her mood. "They're going to report back to your cousin and then he's going to know someone's gunning for him."

"And how do you figure that?"

They were off the highway. Her apartment wasn't far. Once they were back there, they couldn't talk about this—not in front of Janie, anyway. "Well—"

"Pull over," he said suddenly.

"What?"

"Pull over. We have to talk about this before we get back to your place, but we're not going to do it in front of Janie."

Sonya parked in front of Bob's Deli, closed and shuttered for the evening. The only store open was at the end of the block, the Polokoffs' all-night grocery. "Okay, I've pulled over a block from home. What did you want to talk about?"

He didn't look apoplectic anymore, which was good. Instead, he looked wary—and she didn't want him to look like that. What was he looking so wary about? There shouldn't have been anything. But clearly there was.

"You think I should apologize, right?" she said, trying to preempt whatever he was going to say next.

"Sonya—" He stopped, breathing through his nostrils.

"What?" She braced herself.

He rubbed his jaw. "We're not going about this the right way. Throwing the gauntlet in Jasper's face is going to make things worse. He's got a temper."

"I want to flush him out," she exclaimed. "Isn't that obvious? I want him to come out of his hidey-hole."

"Listen." His voice was serious now. "He's an overgrown, spoiled brat who wants to be a master criminal, but right now, he's just a vicious thug. He's going to retaliate if he figures out who you are. And he *will* make the connection."

"Good." She was serious about this. "I'm tired of the pussyfooting." She put the car back into drive.

He sighed. "You are exasperating, you know that?"

"Why, because I'm direct and you're not? I deal with things better out in the open, not slithering in the dark."

"Fine," he said as she pulled the SUV into her space. "I can take care of myself, but how do we protect my sister?"

That was the question she'd been chewing on. "I don't know." She switched the car off and turned to him. "All I know is this. First of all, she doesn't know about me. I need it that way. Second, she tried to help him. I'm betting he'll go easy on her. You, he doesn't have any problem trying to kill. Janie? No."

"He doesn't know she's back in town."

"Are you crazy? Of course he does. By now, at least."

"And you think he's not going to make the connection about you? He's not stupid!"

She opened the car door. "We'll talk about this later. Let's make sure your sister is all right." She shucked the harness and tossed it into the back of the SUV.

He followed suit and persisted. "Talk about it when?"

"Lower your voice," she whispered. "This is a family neighborhood, and it's late." She started toward her building, hopping over the cracks, still feeling lighter than air.

But he would not be deterred. He slammed the passenger door and followed, his voice still louder than she would have preferred. "When are we going to talk about it?"

She stopped at the front door and looked at him. "When we get in. Now come on."

Ordinarily, she would have run up the stairs, but she suspected John would have insisted on continuing the conversation, even if he had to yell. So she started up the stairs, one step at a time, waiting for Arlen. She stopped to greet her landlady, who popped her curly gray-haired head out her door.

"Good evening, Mrs. Mensch," Sonya said pleasantly. She continued to climb, followed closely by John Arlen. She turned around, caught the eye of her landlady — who was eyeing John dubiously — and smiled again. "Good night," Sonya said.

Mrs. Mensch disappeared from view when they turned the corner. John still looked unhappy.

"How are we going to protect Janie?" he asked again.

Sonya sighed. "I don't know. We have to get him first. And we're not going to if this is going to be your attitude!"

Finally, they were at her door. "Damn it," she muttered. "I was in such a good mood, too."

"That's because you've done some amazingly stupid things tonight and I'm trying to remind you of that."

She opened the door and stepped in. "Go to hell," she said sweetly. And slammed the door in his face.

Home. After the grimy, gritty rooftop... After the sour, vomit-inducing smells of unwashed criminals... After the depressing and dismaying sights of the warehouse district after dark, home was a cozy little haven, smelling of cinnamon and fresh bread and lemon. Which was odd, because it had never smelled like that before.

And coffee. The living room was dimmed, but the couch was made up for bed. She could hear the coffeepot dripping, and the light was on in the kitchen. "Janie? Are you home?" she called out, ignoring the pounding at the door.

"I'm in here," came Janie's voice. Kitchen. Janie must have turned a page of the newspaper, Sonya heard it crinkle right then.

Sonya turned the doorknob and grudgingly gave John Arlen entry, then ignored him as she sailed on to the kitchen.

"What was that about?" he demanded as he shut the door behind him.

She walked into the kitchen, where Janie was drinking tea at the kitchen table and reading the newspaper. But she was taking notes, which Sonya didn't expect.

Janie looked up and smiled. "I poked my nose into your cabinets and decided to do something I haven't done in ages."

Sonya sniffed. "You baked. I had something you could bake?"

"I baked cinnamon muffins. When I was a kid, our housekeeper made them every week. You wouldn't believe how homey that big ol' place could feel when I'd come home and smell the muffins baking."

John followed Sonya into the kitchen and stopped right behind her. "Making yourself at home, Janie?"

In response, his sister gestured to the plate spilling over with baked goods. "Help yourself, Johnny. By the time you were in school, we had a new housekeeper who didn't bake, if I recall."

Sonya watched as John, sniffing, moved toward the plate as if he had been pulled there. "No, but I remember when you'd bake and it would always smell so good," he said. Deliberating, he chose a muffin. "I'm starving." He bit in, steam rising.

Sonya poured herself a cup of coffee and sat down, straddling a chair. "Thank you, Janie," she said, sipping, the hot liquid coursing through her. She needed that too. "How was your day?"

Innocuous conversation. Maybe that would help John calm down and let him remember his original goal of getting his cousin, which he seemed to have temporarily forgotten.

John's attitude was going to irritate her unless he remembered. And even if he had forgotten his goal, she hadn't. Even if he had forgotten, she couldn't.

Janie hadn't forgotten their conversation—had it been only this morning? John's sister glanced at her. "After you left, I started to hunt for anything about the original Cycle project," Janie said. "Any scraps, plans that were rejected, anything to help you find Jasper, misfiled somewhere."

"Did you find anything?"

Janie shook her head. "But I'll keep looking. Anything that could have been helpful has probably been recycled by now."

Considering the trail was what, two years old? That wasn't a surprise. Sonya nodded. "What can you tell me about him?"

Janie raised her hands. "He wasn't a bad kid. He was bright."

"I've gathered that," Sonya said, without a trace of sarcasm. She wasn't going to think about the argument with John anymore, not right now.

"He wasn't that eager to study, but he'd study something if he knew there was a payoff," Janie went on.

"Did he study the translocator? The Cycle project blueprints?"

"Not really. He loved the idea—the basic concept behind the device he had no trouble grasping—but he couldn't deal with the actual mechanics."

"Then why is he nicknamed the Engineer?"

"Because his father was originally an engineer and it was natural he take after his father," John said.

Sonya glanced at him. He was eating and drinking and he finally looked more relaxed. Good. "Makes no sense. So what is he good at?"

"He was a martial arts fanatic when he was a kid," John volunteered. "By the time we saw him again, he was a teenager, bad at math, but nobody was going to kid him because he'd kick your butt."

"So we have a thug in the making, bad at math, misnamed, who can beat the tar out of anyone who crosses him," Sonya said. "I don't know about you, but I don't like the sound of this."

"That's one of the reasons I don't want you tracking him."

Janie turned to Sonya. "Why would you track him?"

"Do you want your brother dead?"

"My God. Even I admit Jasper's dangerous," Janie exclaimed. "This is something to leave to the police."

"What are they going to do, track him down and tell him to stop? The police couldn't catch him when he killed your father. They can't catch him. I can."

"It's too dangerous." That was John, back on his diatribe.

"We're not going over this again." She stood up.

"Sonya, no. Don't." John took her by the arm. "Don't go out there again tonight. Please."

"What were you doing?" Janie asked. "Johnny, you weren't doing anything stupid, were you?"

"He thinks I did," Sonya said with heavy scorn.

"But you're a physical therapist, aren't you? Why would a physical therapist go out and track down someone if—"

"I have my reasons," Sonya interrupted. "I have my own reasons for tracking down your cousin."

"Why, for God's sake?"

"Because his father killed mine," Sonya answered. "Geez, that sounds corny, doesn't it? But that was why I agreed to help John in the first place."

Janie looked up at her brother. "Johnny, you might have mentioned that."

He put up both hands. "It's not something I was going to work into the conversation, Janie! I didn't tell you because it wasn't any of your business. I don't think Sonya should endanger herself, but I can't stop her."

"Sonya, you should listen to him. You shouldn't do this."

Sonya sighed. She had been so pleased with herself, too. Trust John—and his sister—to bring her down.

He leaned in and lowered his voice. "Remember how you felt last night? Now you're overconfident. You've swung too far in the other direction."

"What do you know?" She didn't know which irritated her more, the fact that he might be right or the fact that her high was now completely gone. "I trained to do this."

"And you stopped training what, more than a decade ago? That's not going to come back just because you say so."

Sonya shook her head. "Never mind. I'm going for a walk. I can enjoy a walk in my neighborhood, can't I?"

John looked at her, mute. Whatever he wanted to say, he wasn't going to say it in front of Janie. Sonya was grateful for that.

"In that case, I'll see you later *sweetheart*," she said.

She donned a light jacket on her way out. The evening had deepened into a cool night. The stars were out tonight, perfect weather for a ride on the sound wave they had been on.

She kicked a pebble out of her way. Magical. That ride had been magical. It had been mystical and magical and other words she didn't know and hadn't even been invented yet.

Being back on the ground was considerably less so.

The neighborhood was quiet this time of night. The Polokoffs' grocery was bustling with late-nighters who need a fix of ice cream, or toothpaste, or milk for their cereal in the morning.

Inside, Sonya could see Mrs. Polokoff ringing someone up at the cash register. By the looks of him, he was a young punk, probably out for cigarettes and beer. For a moment she was tempted to linger and make sure the little old lady was safe, that the trusty sawed-off shotgun didn't get used. Sonya's training went deep. She flinched when she saw someone using a gun instead of superpower.

But not everyone had the power.

Not everyone had the training, either.

The punk finished his transaction without producing a weapon, only a few crumpled bills. Sonya watched as Mrs. Polokoff closed the cash register and, catching a glimpse of Sonya, waved.

Sonya waved back and waited for a moment until the punk, who by the looks of him was older than she thought he was, turned and left, disappearing into the night.

Mrs. Polokoff waved again and again Sonya did the same. Using that as a cue, she continued on her walk.

Quiet neighborhood, quiet night. One by one, the lights in the windows of the brownstones winked out. Families turned in for the night, putting their trust in others to protect them.

Sonya paused on the edge of the neighborhood's tiny park, sitting down on one of the iron benches and looked up at the stars.

Her parents had friends who had come from some of those stars, electing to remain on Earth. Even now, they dropped her a line from time to time, making sure she was okay, though they were themselves busy, having sworn to protect and serve.

She was okay. She should have been there alongside them all this time, but she hadn't been. She had been okay all this time, but that's all she had been. She could be better.

The Little Dipper twinkled, reminding her of the bedtime stories her mother and father had told her after they had come home from an evening of crimefighting, just in time to tuck her in. She remembered the stories of children being shot to Earth from exploding planets, of liquid entities solidifying into humanoid life after coming to Earth, of other forms of life crystallizing for decades-long trips to their native planets. She had thought they were all wonderful stories. It was only later she realized they were simply telling her the origin stories of their friends.

She closed her eyes, willing away the tears.

She heard the distinctive *tap-tap-tap* of the footsteps approaching her, but after her initial alert, she paid no attention. Whoever it was stopped in front of her. She opened her eyes.

She knew that face. And those eyes.

"You must be the Engineer," Sonya said.

Chapter Thirteen

"You have your cousins' eyes," Sonya said.

"They can't have them back," he shot at her.

She blinked. He didn't look as though he was kidding.

There was a family resemblance, and not just the darkly fringed gray eyes. The pinched look around his mouth, as if he'd spent too many years not saying something he wanted to. John had that, but not Janie. Sonya suspected Janie pretty much said anything that came to her mind. But the cheekbones, the pointed chin with that odd cleft—those were Arlen features.

He looked enough like John for her to look again. The big difference was the floppy Gilligan hat the Engineer wore and the vacant look in his eyes, as though original thought was beyond him.

"Get away from him," he demanded. "I'm going to kill him. Or it's lights out for you too."

It wasn't the hat that made him look stupid. "Why are you trying to kill him?"

He stuck his thumb at his chest. "It should be me in that house," he snarled. "With that house and that money, I could do serious damage."

She shifted on the bench. She patted the seat next to her. She wasn't going to get this bozo upset. If he got upset, he might try to attack John in her apartment—and she didn't have enough renter's insurance. "Why do you want to cause damage?"

Not unlike a puppy, he sank onto the bench, folding his frame onto the iron seat. "Because I want people to respect me."

Great. Now she had to play social worker. "There are easier ways to make a splash, Jasper — it's Jasper, right?"

"Yeah. I don't get how you knew it was me," he said, with a baffled look.

A brainchild, this one. "It was your spectacular good looks," she said, with only a trace of irony.

Much to her further surprise — and she shouldn't have been by now — he preened. "Gets you every time, doesn't it?"

Sonya suppressed a giggle. "You look like your cousins."

He looked disappointed. "I don't think so. Least, I never thought about it."

"So besides trying to come into the money and the house, is there a purpose in trying to organize all those thugs?" she asked as gently as she could.

He shrugged. "Well, my dad did it, so I figured I oughta."

"That's it? Because your father was a criminal mastermind, you think you should do the same thing?"

"Why not? It can't be that hard. I got all those guys to come, didn't I?"

She remembered a small detail she saw. "Didn't you pay them?"

"Yeah," Jasper said. "Why else would they come?"

"Maybe because they were scared of you? Maybe because you promised them unlimited power?"

"Nah," he said confidently. "I don't need to do all that."

Cheapskate. "What happens when you stop paying them?"

That seemed to stump him. She tried another tactic. "To get control of the corporation and the house — " She thought it best to mention the house, since he seemed to be fixated on it.

"You would have to get rid of Janie, too. Are you going for her after you kill John?" She couldn't get rid of the tremor in her voice.

He shook his head. "Janie's cool," he said confidently. "She'll go along. She likes me."

"You want to kill her brother! How much is she going to like you if you do?"

He shrugged again. "She'll get over it. She'll be back one of these days, and it'll be done by then."

Sonya froze. He didn't know Janie Arlen was home. Not much of a mastermind. "When is Janie expected?" she asked carefully.

"I dunno. Soon, I think. It's gotta be done by then because there's gonna be probate and stuff after Johnny-boy dies."

It occurred to Sonya that "probate" must be a word he had heard, but probably had little idea what it meant. At least he was using it correctly.

"Why would you want to do that to her?"

"I don't," was his response. He leaned on his elbow alongside the back of the bench, shifting a little so he was halfway turned toward her. Sonya started to shrink from him before she could control herself. "But she'll understand. She's cool."

Janie Arlen would have to be ice itself to accept the death of her brother in such cold-blooded terms. "I don't think she'll go along with your plans quite so blithely."

To her surprise, he scowled. "Quit showin' off," he ordered.

She promptly apologized when she realized what she had said. No words bigger than a syllable was among other things she had to remember. "I don't think she'll go along that fast, or be so happy about it."

He shrugged again—she could very easily get tired of his doing that. In fact, she already was. "She'll have to."

"So she'll sit back and go along with your plans to turn Arlen Manor into a rec room for killers and thieves?"

"He's not your boyfriend or anything. Why should you care?"

Sonya wasn't sure how to answer. "I care for him."

"Sorry, doll. Unless you want to join him?"

Well, this conversation was done. She stood up. "Leave him alone. Or you'll regret it."

He sneered. "Care to make a wager?"

She froze.

That phrase. Gentleman Geoffrey's trademark. That phrase had been his, right before he attacked with his sword cane. Sonya remembered the case studies from her parents' battles. He had no doubt used that very phrase, right before her mother and dad…

Unnerved by that memory, she couldn't move for a moment. But then Geoffrey's son continued. "What can you do? You don't look strong enough to take me on, let alone my guys."

That broke her concentration. She stared at him. "Don't you know what I can do?"

He shrugged. There was that shrug again, just like Janie's. "Don't know and don't care. But you're only a chick, and you probably couldn't take on my buds, let alone me."

She laughed, but it wasn't that funny. "You don't know, do you? You really don't?"

"Know what?" He looked at her. His eyes—eyes that in someone else, someone with a soul and a sweet smile, could melt her bones—narrowed. He looked small-hearted and mean. With a brain of petrified wood. "What can you do, bitch?"

She laughed out loud now, peals of her laughter echoing in the stillness of the night. "I'll show you. You're an idiot, Jasper. Nobody's ever told you that, have they?"

No one must have, because he turned red. "You're gonna be sorry," he snarled. "You can't talk to me like that."

She crooked her finger. "I just did."

He stood up. He was tall, like his cousin, but unlike John, whose injuries had made him to shrink a little, Jasper Arlen stood straight and intact. He took off the leather jacket with all the bright shiny metal clasps. Glinting in the moonlight was the exoskeleton he was known for, which enhanced his martial arts skills. He put his hands on his hips and preened.

But that stupid hat didn't go with the outfit. Exoskeleton or not, Sonya could still take him on. "And you're going to pay for what you did to John," she said. Taking one step forward, she lashed out. He blocked her, then slapped her. She ducked, but not quickly enough. She reeled, taking a step back.

"Stupid bitch," he muttered.

Calm, she told herself. *Oh, forget it.* "I'm so tired of you morons calling me a 'stupid bitch'!" she spat. "You pissant, you don't know who you're dealing with." She took a step back. He approached and she backed up some more.

"If you're such hot shit, why are you backing away from me?" he sneered. "Dumb bitch." And he lunged at her.

She sidestepped him, letting him lose his balance. She kicked him down and he landed on his hands. "I'm backing away from you because you're such a fool," she answered. He tried to scramble to his feet, but she kicked him in the face. Before he could regain his balance, vainly grabbing at her foot, she kicked him again, this time landing firmly in his gut.

He was persistent, she had to say that. He tried to get up again, and she started to kick him again, but this time he was ready for her and grabbed her ankle, pulling her off-balance.

"Yeah? Who's the fool now?" he shouted.

He was sneering, and boy, was that irritating. But it meant he was overconfident.

She grabbed his foot and yanked as she hit the ground. Yelping, he crashed, missing her by an inch. She rolled away, making sure she was out of his reach as she got up.

She wasn't even breathing hard, she was pleased to note. She was embarrassed at how easily he could have taken her out, but then she hadn't had any hand-to-hand combat practice in years, except on an occasional date. She looked at him sprawled on the ground. He was going to have one humdinger of a shiner.

"You were saying?" she said. He finally opened his eyes—eye—and stared at her, wincing as he touched his jaw. "Now let me say this just one more time. Leave John alone. Leave Janie alone. Get a job. Make something respectable of yourself, unlike your late father. Got it? Now git."

She never thought she'd see hatred on a human being's face, but there it was. It was official—she now had an enemy.

"I'm going to make you sorry you did that," he said with fury, his face purple. "You're going to be so sorry."

Sonya rolled her eyes. In a flash, she grabbed Jasper's shirt by the collar and yanked him up to face level, rattling the fancy exoskeleton, which hadn't helped him. Now he looked alarmed. Good. "Grow up, Jasper," she said as gently as she could. "You don't have it in you. If your father could see you now, he'd be embarrassed."

His eyes narrowed and he could have been on the verge of tears. She let him drop back to the ground. "Now go home. Janie said you were bright. Prove her right."

He edged away, staring at her. As she watched, he got up and backed away, stumbling, before he turned and ran into the night.

She'd won. Whoopee.

She stood there until the sound of his steps melted into the evening. Then she sat back down on the cold iron bench and looked up at the heavens again.

"Being normal isn't all that it's cracked up to be, is it, Dad?" she whispered.

When she couldn't feel her toes anymore and her breath came out in little puffs, she decided to go home.

The walk back to her apartment was uneventful. But her mood was considerably changed.

She slipped in as quietly as she could—but not quietly enough, because both Arlens hurried in from the kitchen.

"Oh, Sonya, we were so worried!" Janie cried. "It's not safe at night these days."

"Didn't Johnny-boy tell you I'd be fine?" Sonya inquired as she took off her jacket. John didn't meet her gaze. Fine.

"He did, but I—" Janie stopped. "What happened to you? Were you in a fight?"

Sonya rubbed her jaw and grinned. "Sort of. I met your cousin in the park. Do I have ice?"

She was in the kitchen before the Arlens caught up with her. Sonya took a detour to the refrigerator by way of a brand-new plate of goodies. She hadn't even used her abilities—the Engineer had been butt-kicked the old-fashioned way—but she was suddenly, voraciously, hungry. She took a big, satisfying bite. Hmm.

There was fire in John's eye. "You met Jasper in the park? Did you arrange that? Do you know how dangerous that was?"

Sonya dropped a few ice cubes into a paper towel and pressed it against her jaw before she answered. "No, I didn't arrange it. I know it could have been dangerous. But we had a nice talk."

"And that's why you have a mark on your face that's going to be a bruise tomorrow?"

She finished her chocolate-chip cookie—she hadn't had a home-baked one in years—before she looked around. "Do we have milk or coffee to wash this down with?"

Wordlessly he poured her a cup of coffee and she gulped it down, wincing as the scalding liquid hit her palate. It was bitter and too hot, but for now, it did the trick.

She knew he was concerned, she knew he wanted to ask questions, but he could only ask a few of them in Janie's presence. She reached out and stroked his cheek, trying to tell him, *Later. We'll talk later.*

"What did he say?" Janie demanded. "Have another cookie."

Sonya looked at what she was eating. "Didn't you bake muffins before?" she inquired, her mouth full. "But these are good too."

"I got bored waiting for you to come home, so I baked again," Janie said with a shrug. That shrug again.

Janie Arlen—physicist, Arlen Labs chief scientist, and compulsive baker. The family was filled with surprises. "That's got to be an Arlen thing," Sonya remarked.

John stared at her. "What? Sonya, what did he say?"

"That shrug." She helped herself to another cookie and another swig of coffee. She should have eaten dinner, but she'd been preoccupied. Bite, chew, swallow. "That shrug. Your entire family does that annoying shrug."

"Sonya, what happened, besides him beating you up?" John growled.

She smiled and patted his cheek. "You oughta see the other guy. Really."

"*Sonya.*"

That wasn't going to do for him. She met his eyes.

Jasper could have been his younger brother. She hadn't realized until she saw Jasper how much John's injuries must have aged him. She winced when she thought about how much pain John must have been in during the healing process.

"I told him to leave you alone. Or he'd regret it," she said. She didn't know how to interpret that look.

"And what did he say?" he asked after a moment.

"He begged to differ."

"And you expected him to agree with you?"

"Janie said he was bright," Sonya said. "Wrongo."

To that, Janie chewed on her lip. "You'd be surprised at how fast he can pick up concepts. I was surprised, too."

"Well, he certainly didn't pick up the concept of 'Leave John alone or you're going to be sorry'. He came right back and told me to leave *him* alone or I'd be sorry."

John sat down. There was a cup of coffee in front of him, but it looked tepid. He must have poured it while he and his sister waited for her to return.

"He's fixated on the house," Sonya said. She bit into a cinnamon muffin.

"What do you mean, 'fixated'?"

"Basically, he wants to make it a clubhouse for his criminal pals. Probably wants to put up a sign that says 'No girls allowed', from the sound of it. He's also got it in his head that he is taking his father's place, and he also has his sights on Janie."

Janie choked on her own coffee. "He *what?*"

"He thinks, and I quote, you're 'cool'."

Sonya had never seen John's sister's eyes widen like that. "So what makes you think he's got his, uh, 'sights' on me?"

"Because he thinks it would be fine by you if he killed your brother and moved his thug pals into Arlen Manor."

Janie sputtered. "He thinks I wouldn't have a complaint about him knocking off my brother? Is he insane?"

"He was pretty confident, in his own numbskull way."

"I take back what I said about him. He's out to lunch!"

Sonya watched her. "You sure?"

"Yes, I'm sure!"

Janie was telling the truth, Sonya was sure of it.

"Why would my sister want me dead?"

"I dunno. Tell me about your will, John. Does everything go to your sister in case of your untimely death?"

He shrugged—she wished he wouldn't do that. He looked like an older version of Jasper who'd actually grown up. "Of course. Who else would I leave anything to?"

"No progeny, no bequests to an ex-wife, no bequests to a society to prevent harm to kitties?"

"No children, my ex-wife's been remarried for the past five years and she lives a thousand miles away, and I don't like cats. Except Rover," he added. "Everything goes to Janie. There's something small in there for Jasper, I think, but that's all."

"If Janie were to predecease you?"

"Everything goes to the Arlen Foundation. The nonprofit arm of Arlen Industries," he added.

Sonya rubbed her neck. The events of the evening was catching up to her and she was tired and stiff. She decided to relax with a bath before she went to sleep. But first... "What about you, Janie? What's your will say?"

The older woman shrugged the Arlen shrug, her cornrowed hair bouncing. "Everything goes to Johnny. I have a bequest to my late husband's sister, another one to my alma mater, one to Greenpeace, one to the National Organization of Women, one—"

Sonya put her hand up. "No bequests to Jasper?"

"Sonya, I barely know him. I certainly wouldn't leave a bequest to someone who stole from me. Even if he is a relative."

"He has a soft spot for you."

"He's an idiot," Janie exclaimed. "He deserves what he gets. And since his father was disowned by our grandfather, he would inherit only if the Foundation lost that court battle."

Sonya didn't know whether to believe her, but it didn't matter, she couldn't do anything about it right now. Janie was going to stay under her roof and drink her coffee and bake muffins and cookies. Sonya could live with that.

"Did I have a cookie mix around or something?" she inquired as she bit into another cookie. "Tastes good."

"You actually had flour and sugar."

"Is that how you make cookies?" Sonya took another bite, watching Janie. "Amazing."

In the end, there wasn't much else to say. She threatened Jasper. Jasper had threatened her. She suspected Janie. Janie had protested her innocence. And John was in the middle.

Sonya got up. "I'm taking a bath," she announced. "And then I'm going to sleep. I'm beat. Good night." Finishing her last cookie, she sailed out of the kitchen.

Ignoring the protests of both Arlens, she made her way to her bathroom and locked the door. A steamy tiled room filled with the scent of roses would do the trick, she decided. Her muscles needed some pampering. She opened the tap and watched as the hot water gushed into the bathtub and then she took the crystal, stoppered vase on the counter and dumped its contents into the slowly filling tub.

She had just kicked butt, damn it. She deserved downtime.

She ignored the soft knocking. The apartment had a powder room. They didn't need the facilities here. And she was going to ignore any other reason they might be knocking.

The piping-hot water, the seldom-used sleep mask, and sheer exhaustion all combined to send her into a doze. She was startled awake when the soft knocking became a pounding.

Sonya's eyes popped open. She shoved the mask up on her forehead. "What? John? Janie?"

No answer, but then she heard something crash against the wall. The little flowered clock on the bathroom wall shivered and crashed to the floor.

"Ah, for goodness' sake," Sonya grumbled. She scrambled out of the tub, nearly losing her balance for a moment when her foot slipped on the slick floor. She righted herself and grabbed a towel from the rack. She hurriedly unlocked the door and burst out.

She stopped short.

John was standing there, holding a chair and rubbing his shoulder. Janie was peering from around the corner to the living room, looking alarmed.

"Did something actually happen, or was that a cheap ruse to get me out of my tub?"

"Don't look at me. It wasn't my idea," Janie said as she disappeared into the kitchen.

Sonya rearranged her towel and glared at John. "I wanted to be alone. I went out to be alone, but your idiot cousin had to find me. Can't I just have some time to myself?"

"Sure, but we have to talk about what happened," he insisted.

She rolled her eyes. "You know how to ruin a good bubble bath, don't you?" She stalked back into the bathroom.

John was right behind her. "You're not going back into the tub, are you?"

She shot him a dirty look. "I'm not that lucky. And neither are you." Bending, she yanked the plug. She watched as the cooling water gurgled and swirled down the drain.

Sonya sighed. It had been so nice and cozy.

She put down the toilet lid and sat down.

"You wanted to talk, now talk," she said. "I don't understand you," she went on, not giving him a chance to reply. "First you want to get back at your cousin for killing your father, but then you pull back. You bring me in on your plan, disrupting my life. You get cold feet and you pull me back after I've already made a commitment to it. I was on a real high, back at that warehouse. It wasn't anything big, but I didn't think I could do it after what happened to Mom and Dad, but I did! And—"

He reached out and put his hand over her mouth. "Shut up," he said, not unkindly.

His hand was warm. It was barely touching her lips. She didn't move her face away from his touch. Instead, she moved toward him and caressed his palm with her lips. "Okay. Now what?" She breathed deep. "You smell good," she murmured into his skin.

Sonya heard him jerk in response. "What are you doing?"

His heart was pounding. His breathing was erratic. "Finding myself," she said. This feels so good. She kissed the tips of his fingers. "No matter how your plans may have changed, mine have not. I'm going to bring your cousin to justice," she whispered. "That's what I was trained to do and that's what I'm going to do. And I'll even save you along the way."

Now he stepped back. He looked at her as though she'd slipped a cog or two. "Then why are you doing that?" But he wasn't moving away.

She leaned forward. The towel around her slipped a little. He looked away, but she didn't care. She let it slip some more. The bathroom was cooling and the change in room temperature made her shiver, but she didn't care about that either.

"Because I'm tired of being normal," she said, enunciating clearly. "You awakened the beast within, Johnny. It felt good. You awakened the true me. Now you've got to live with it."

He looked at her in a way she'd never seen someone look who wasn't about to be beaten up. "You're scaring me, Sone."

She leaned forward again. This time she felt the towel fall, puddling at her hips—about time, she thought idly. The cooling air of the bathroom touched her breasts, and that felt good too. "What's the matter?" she whispered. "Dr.

Frankenstein not like how his monster's turning out? Well, I have news for you Doc."

She was mere inches away, and all of a sudden, he was staring into her eyes, riveted. She knew he was acutely aware of her exposed breasts, beckoning him. "You have to think about the consequences of what you're planning when you start, Johnny-boy. You have to think about how it might turn out—or not. You have to assess whether it's worth the risk." She paused.

The room was chilly and she could feel her nipples tighten. He drew a shaky breath. "And then what?" he whispered.

She licked her lips. "You make a decision—and you live with it," she whispered.

Her words seemed to fill the room. "Can you do that, John? Can you?" She leaned her face up to his.

Suddenly, the room was filled with the sound of their breathing within the confines of the small, mist-filled room.

The temperature of the room was dropping, but the heat was rising between them.

Her eyes had drifted shut when she heard him speak. "Have you thought about the consequences of what you're doing now?"

Chapter Fourteen

He cursed to himself. One minute her eyes had been molten with desire. Now they were filled with fury. She was half-naked, he was hard, and he was actually trying to hold a conversation. Son of a bitch. He might as well wear a bra.

She was half-naked—no, she was naked—and those were magnificent breasts. And right now they were heaving.

Wow.

Focus, damn it. "I brought you into this," he said, staring into her eyes. Her *eyes,* damn it. "You were living a normal life, but you were following the oath you took with your mother and father, to protect and serve. The farther you got sucked in, the farther you were from the life you chose. And I'm sorry. But you're getting too far from where you started. I don't think it's healthy for you."

If her eyes got any colder, he'd have to wear long underwear. And an athletic cup.

Although he really should be wearing that cup now.

"So you interrupted a perfectly good bubble bath because you were feeling guilty." She had bundled her hair on top of her head for her bath. Whatever she had done to keep it up was coming undone, because now there were curls sliding down to her shoulders. Her *shoulders,* damn it. Eyes up.

She rubbed her jaw, which by the looks of it was going to be black and blue tomorrow, thanks to Jasper. Another thing John was responsible for. "I'm sorry. I needed to speak to you."

"So you pretended there was a fight?" She flashed a smile that almost dazzled him, and it was only a little strained. "You should be careful. If I'd been really ticked off, you wouldn't have been happy about how I reacted."

The smile was dazzling. She'd forgiven him? How could he *not* have noticed that smile when they first met? It lit up the room—granted, it was the bathroom, but it was as spectacular as the rest of her he was avoiding looking at. He expelled the breath he had been holding. It was just as well, because he took another breath when she stood up, not bothering with the towel.

He stopped breathing. She smiled again and said, "I don't have to remind you that superheroes aren't body-conscious, do I? Can't be, not with those uniforms."

She sauntered over to the bathrobe hanging on the back of the door. He had no choice, he looked.

He couldn't breathe. He bit his knuckles instead.

The back view was at odds with the pink fluffy bathrobe she pulled down from its hook. It was almost disturbingly girlish. It was certainly at odds with the smoldering glance she sent him over her shoulder—and the smile.

Dear God, that smile. He couldn't move.

"Well, I've had a long day," she announced, her voice husky, hand on the door. "I'm turning in. What about you?"

He followed so fast that he didn't have a chance to slip on the slightly wet floor, limp or no limp.

The apartment was dark. Janie had clearly decided to turn in for the evening. John followed Sonya straight to the bedroom.

The lamp next to the bed was lit, casting an eerie light. He hadn't looked at the room last night. He'd been too busy avoiding looking at Sonya but trying not to be overcurious, which had led him to look at the floor mostly.

Tonight all he wanted to do was look at Sonya, but he was pacing himself. So he looked at the room, rewarding himself with a glance at her on occasion.

The sound of the door closing behind them echoed like a gunshot through the apartment. Then she hung up her bathrobe again and now gloriously nude, proceeded to the dressing table, where she sat—there was that breathtaking view again—and stroked something on her face, smoothing it over her cheeks and jaw.

He looked around to give himself a diversion. The room was creamy gold and pink, with its wallpaper of roses and striped satin, resplendent with stained-glass overhead lights and lamps with matching shades. It was at odds with Sonya the practical physical therapist, even the secret would-be superheroine. The room was lush and romantic, nothing like her bland living room.

"Aren't you going to get ready for bed?"

Startled, he looked in Sonya's direction. He met her gaze in the reflection of her oval gilt mirror.

"You're not going to be that comfortable sleeping in those things," she said, referring to the ripped T-shirt and jeans he was still wearing. "I'd suggest a bubble bath to relax, but that may not be to your taste."

She smoothed a slick, rich cream with the scent of roses up her throat in a single movement, then stroke by stroke she slowly worked it into her skin until she had covered her entire neck. She then started on her breasts and his mouth went dry.

"No thank you," he babbled as he watched her massage the cream into her skin. Shaking, he drew the T-shirt over his head, dropping it on the floor.

It was her turn to stop what she was doing. He watched as her hand paused in mid-stroke and she watched him in the mirror.

His hand went to his zipper and drew it down. When it couldn't go any farther, he tucked his thumbs in and started to push down, but oh so slowly.

He could see her breasts flush. Her breath sped up.

His jeans were at his ankles now. He kicked them off.

He wasn't wearing underwear. And he was happy he wasn't.

John turned back the covers. He didn't get in—not yet. He watched, his mouth watering, as she resumed stroking her neck. He watched as she replaced the lid on the jar, turned off the Tiffany lamp on the dressing table and stood up to face him.

She was smaller than he had thought but perfectly formed, a tiny waist flaring out to hips that melted into nothingness when she dressed in the simple jeans and shirt she seemed to favor. Her breasts were magnificent on their own.

And she was a natural strawberry-blonde.

With a tiny tattoo of a star in the hollow of her hip.

He stared at it. "That's the sexiest thing I've ever seen," he told her. His voice was ragged and he had to force it out. He wasn't sure it made sense. Sense was beyond him now.

She flashed a smile that served as a welcoming beacon in the golden dimness of the room. "Why haven't you gotten in bed?"

"Because it's not real unless you're there first," he said hoarsely. "Unless you're in there first, it could still be a joke. I have to see it to believe it."

In response, she strolled across the room. He watched, unable to shift his gaze anywhere else, as her breasts swayed. She paused at the side of the bed, her gaze fixed on his. Not shifting her eyes away from him, she rested a leg on the edge of the mattress—and stopped there.

He couldn't breathe. He couldn't look away. The lamplight gleamed on her breasts, making her nipples look as though they were glowing. If he thought they looked good before, they looked better now. He wanted a taste. He wanted a taste *now*.

As though she read his mind, she raised her arms above her head and linked her fingers together, stretching so her breasts reached for him. Then, rolling her shoulders as though she was getting ready for an athletic event—she slipped between the sheets.

He was going to embarrass himself if he wasn't careful.

Sonya settled in, cradling her head in her arms. Her eyes were half-closed. Her breasts beckoned him.

"I can't believe I'm going to bed with a superhero," John burst out.

Even before the sound of the hushed words died away, he saw her eyes turn to ice. He watched in horror as her mouth, so lush and inviting before, pressed together into a thin line. *Uh-oh.*

"Have I told you you're beautiful?" he babbled, hoping to put that sex-goddess look back on her face.

It didn't work. "Screw you," she finally said, her jaw set. She grabbed a pillow and threw it at him. Then she sat up, bent over—there was that mouth-watering, heaven-inspiring view of those breasts again—and grabbed the blanket from the foot of her bed. She threw that at him too.

"Enjoy the carpet."

And with that, she turned out the light.

* * * * *

John didn't sleep much.

The cold shower he opted for in the middle of the night helped. By the time he was ready to come back into the bedroom, he was freezing and not looking forward to the inadequate blanket Sonya had thoughtfully supplied.

He came back in anyway, shivering. He watched her sleep, half uncovered, sprawled on her stomach, her back bare with a tiny freckle. The idea of another shower flitted through his mind but hypothermia was a possibility, so he toughed it out.

Stupid, stupid, stupid! He couldn't keep his mouth shut. He could have died happy, but no. He had to open his mouth.

By the time he woke up, it was late morning. He could barely move, thanks to his screaming muscles. "Exercise," he muttered to himself. He rolled into a sitting position after a couple of minutes and listened hard. Janie had probably gone to work, he guessed. He heard the ceramic *clink* of a cup hitting a saucer and knew Sonya was in the kitchen.

He wished Janie was still in the apartment.

Sighing, he leaned on the edge of the bed—where he could have slept but for his big mouth—and pushed himself to his feet. He pulled on a fresh pair of jeans and a T-shirt. His leg was stiffest of all, but that was no surprise. Yesterday had been the most activity it had had in almost a year. Yes, he needed physical therapy.

Zipping up reminded him of the previous night, but thinking of it wasn't going to help him any. He wasn't even sure apologizing would.

Barefoot, he padded into the living room. As he suspected, his sister was long gone—blankets folded, the pillows plumped.

If he'd kept his mouth shut, he could have...*Stupid, stupid.*

He stopped at the kitchen door. *Be a man,* he jeered at himself. Still he paused.

Sonya sat at the kitchen table, her back to the door, hand wrapped around a mug, the heat of the coffee rising invitingly. She was reading the newspaper. Then he saw her hand tremble around the mug and he knew she had been waiting for him.

"Good morning," he said as cheerfully as he could. He poured himself some coffee, avoiding her gaze. Thank God for coffee. After the night he had had, he needed to mainline caffeine.

Then his eye lit on the newest plate of something that hadn't been there the night before, covered with Saran Wrap. Coffee and something sweet for breakfast sounded right up his alley.

"Janie made it," Sonya said, though he had guessed. "She was already baking when I got up."

"Muffins again?" he asked, lifting the plastic gingerly and drawing one out. He didn't recognize the smell, but whatever it was, it smelled good and promised to be better.

"Tired of your sister's cooking already?"

She sounded surly. She sounded the way he felt. "No. But I never even knew she knew how to bake. This is a surprise."

"Physicist, sister, do-gooder, baker. Who knew?"

He looked around to see if sarcasm could actually drip. "Yeah, well, it was a surprise for me, too. Have you tried one yet?"

"Yeah, I did. It's chocolate and raspberry. I'm amazed at what she finds in my kitchen."

John bit down and relished it while sipping at his coffee. Then steeling himself, he sat down, inches away from her.

She was in a white shirt and jeans. She was wearing a bra. If he stared, he could make out the pattern and style of the bra.

If he stared, he could be on the receiving end of a slap.

He wanted to stare. He really did, considering he saw the sum of all dreams last night, but he wasn't going to. He was going to apologize like a civilized man.

Her eyes were as stormy as they had been the night before. He knew he had a chance, though. The look in her eyes wasn't cold enough to give him frostbite, the way it had been last night.

The bruise on her face wasn't bad. It ended up looking like a slight discoloration along her jawline, which simply accentuated the fine lines of her face.

"I'm sorry," he burst out, with no preliminary conversation. "That was stupid. Please forgive me."

She blinked and took another sip. But her expression didn't change. "That's all right. I came on pretty strong. I should have made it clear who was trying to seduce you."

Ouch. "Listen," he said urgently, "I knew it was you. Who you are and what you can do are integrally related. There is no Sonya Penn without the other part of you. I followed a beautiful woman who invited me into her bedroom, not a superheroine who—I don't know, took leave of her senses."

She took another sip before she answered. "It was a mistake." His heart plunged to his stomach. "I was overstimulated and you calmed me down. Thank you. It's good for us to air our opinions, so we can get back to our goals. Do you still want revenge?"

Back to business. "I want him to pay for what he's done."

"Do you want my help without getting killed in the process?"

"Yes. I couldn't do it without you," he answered, surprised at the question.

"I think you're right. Will you let me do what needs to be done?"

He snorted, not letting her finish. "As though I could stop you."

She shot him a glance that was still cool. "You're right, it's not as though you could stop me. Can you do it without arguing with me every step of the way?"

"Yes."

"Good. Let's forget last night ever happened." She took another sip. He realized, uneasily, her eyes seemed to get cooler and cooler with each sip. "More precisely, everything from the time you walked into my bathroom, interrupting what had been a very nice bubble bath."

"I'll make it up to you," he said impulsively. "I'll scrub your back next time." *Please,* he added to himself.

Nope. Her next sip seemed to send the temperature in the cozy kitchen plummeting. "I can scrub my own back. And there won't be a next time until you and your sister are safe in your own home."

He knew that tone of voice, having heard it from any other number of women before, including his ex-wife. She meant it. Meaning he'd missed the express. *Moron.*

"So are we straight on this?"

He nodded. "I'm sorry."

"I heard you the first time." She bit into her muffin. She didn't look happy about it, though.

He rubbed his jaw. "I suppose there's no way…"

"Nope. I still don't trust your sister." Sonya placed her hands flat on the table and leaned forward.

"I know." Change of topic. He couldn't blame her.

"She keeps claiming your cousin's a bright boy. He ain't."

"He's a year younger than I am."

"In that case, he ain't a bright man. But he sort of looks like you," she added.

"We looked like twins when we were kids."

"Did that get either of you in trouble?"

"No. Why should it?"

"In case he tried to pull stunts that got you in trouble instead of him."

He shook his head. "He wasn't that imaginative. I felt sorry for him a lot of the time, because he got into trouble for the stupidest things he'd get goaded into."

"By whom, you?"

"I don't pick on anybody who's down."

"Then whom?"

He shrugged, then stopped. "I think it was his father. I didn't see Jas that often. Dad didn't think he was a good influence and his father sure wasn't. But I remember his father would tell him he had to learn to do things—what that was I don't remember, except one time Jasper got caught pickpocketing."

"He wasn't very good at it."

"No. Another time it was shoplifting."

"A ritual? His father dared him to do something, so he did it? Did your cousin resent it?"

He shook his head. "I asked him once why he thought doing something stupid was fun, but he punched me and I never followed up on the question."

"What was he like then?"

"He wasn't the quickest pickup on the block, but he wasn't that bad. He just wasn't ever going to be chief scientist for Arlen Labs, you know? A lot of people aren't."

"Then why does Janie keep insisting he's bright?"

"I don't know. Why don't you ask her?"

Sonya glared at him. "If you haven't noticed, I have been. So far, all I've gotten is he's the not-so-bright version of you, in the larcenous branch of the Arlen family."

"Who wants to kill me."

"On occasion I have the same urge, so I can sympathize."

She wasn't looking at him when she said it. Again, he didn't know if that was good or bad. "Thanks for your restraint."

"I've been working at it. Especially in the last few hours."

"Sonya—"

"We're not going to talk about it," she cut in. "We're not going to talk about last night until we resolve some things. And I'm sorry I tried to seduce you."

He scratched his forehead. This time, he couldn't meet her gaze. "Actually, I wasn't going to mention last night. I was going to say I can't understand how Janie can keep insisting our dear cuz is so brilliant."

With that, he glanced at her out of the corner of his eye. He stifled a smile, because she actually turned pink.

Which was a mistake, because he remembered she blushed all the way down her body. Maybe next time he could use that cream on her, all the way down, nice and smooth.

Focus, Arlen, focus.

"Shall we go down there again?"

He looked up, startled. "What?"

She smirked. "Arlen Labs. Shall we go talk to Janie?"

It was his turn to blush. "Today's not good. She's going to be in meetings all day again."

She stood up. "Then we're going back to the warehouse to see if there's anything left for us to look at."

He groaned. "Sonya—"

"What?"

He knew that tone. He shut up.

"Are you coming with me?"

He shook his head. He didn't want to, but he had to. "I have to go to the house. I want to make sure Gloria's all right."

"You're not going alone."

"Well, I'm not going to the warehouse right now."

"Why, bad memories?"

"I have a right to have bad memories, Sone."

She leaned in, her breasts quivering under the shirt. "Chicken?"

He focused on her face. She was trying to get a rise out of him. It wasn't going to work. She was in a reckless mood and he wasn't going to play into it. "Maybe. I have to check out—"

"Your antigrav unit. What is it, your substitute for a woman?"

Goaded, he said, "I can do anything I want to her and she doesn't say a word."

Instantly he knew he'd gone too far. Her eyes flared with fury, but she didn't say a word. Instead she straightened, and he congratulated himself for not looking farther south than her eyes. "You're not going to have any protection for a while."

"I can take care of myself."

"What, you're going to hit him with your cane if you run into your cousin?"

She was practically sneering. "Are you decaffeinating?"

"You won't be able to defend yourself. He almost beat me up."

Enough. He stood. He had to move, do something, or he was going to...do something at least one of them would regret. "I'm going home. After you get through poking around the warehouse, come on over. You know where I'll be."

"Should I go in through the window or do you have a spare key I could use?"

"I'll leave the garden door unlocked, how about that?"

"No service entrance? Gee, thanks."

He didn't want her to leave. He didn't want to leave without her. He didn't want to go without working this out between them. "Sonya, I—"

She cut him off abruptly. "I'll see you later." She took another sip and went back to the newspaper. Her hand trembled.

There were too many things he wanted to say, but he couldn't say any of them. Not right now.

"Fine," he said. "Later."

He had to try hard not to slam the front door.

Chapter Fifteen

The coffee was eating away at Sonya's stomach.

She'd drunk more coffee in the past few days than she had in the past year. Not that she didn't like coffee. She did. But not this much. There was a reason she had switched to tea.

She dumped the rest of her coffee down the drain and placed the mug in her dishwasher. Then she carefully folded the newspaper and threw it across the kitchen.

She felt something at her feet. She looked down. A pair of imperious round eyes stared back at her. "Rover, I haven't seen you in a while," she exclaimed.

Sonya picked up the cat and stroked her head. "I thought you were just going to hole up at Mrs. Mensch's until John and Janie left," she murmured. The cat had free rein between Sonya's place and the landlady's downstairs, using the fire escape stairs to travel between the two apartments.

The cat was purring up a storm. Sonya knew she had been eating. She put food down in the morning and it had disappeared by the time she came home, and Sonya knew she didn't have a rodent problem. Human intruders, apparently, but not mice.

"I'm sorry," Sonya murmured. "All these people and you can't get a moment's peace!" She stroked her pet's nose, and Rover closed her eyes contentedly.

If only men acted like that. No, unfortunately, she had managed to find one who paid attention to his conscience.

A glance at her watch told her why the cat had appeared out of nowhere. "Time for food, I know, Rove," she said soothingly. She put the cat down and flipped open a tin of cat food.

Sonya didn't trust Janie Arlen. She liked the woman, she just didn't trust her.

Sonya put the cat's bowl on the floor and watched as Rover chowed down. Why would someone be so adamant about something that was clearly untrue? The obvious answer was that she was conspiring with the Engineer. But Janie wouldn't gain that much if she did. True, she would get the entire Arlen fortune including controlling interest in Arlen Industries, and true, if she were in collusion with her cousin they could lay waste to a good chunk of the world. But she already had most of it. There was no point in her joining forces with Jasper.

What was the answer that wasn't so obvious?

Janie *thought* it was true.

Why would she believe it was true?

Sonya reached down and petted the cat, which looked up inquiringly. "Hold the fort for a while, Rove," she whispered.

* * * * *

Arlen Industries wasn't quite as easy to check into without an Arlen in tow. "But you saw me yesterday with John," Sonya argued with the grizzled security guard at the security gate. "I need to talk to Janie Arlen. Can't you—"

Kenny shook his head. "Sorry, miss, but I can't," he said apologetically. "I got my orders. And my boss, he's got his. And until one of the Arlens or somebody on the board of directors tells one of them otherwise, I can't do much."

She looked around. Nope, nothin' and nobody who could help her. "Never mind," she said with a sigh.

She got in her car and drove around for a few minutes, trying to figure out what she could do. She could have sneaked in, but the chances of tracking down Janie without getting caught were slim. But—

She found an unprotected entrance, most likely one for employees with security cards that would let them in. There was also a security camera but unlike the one at Arlen Manor, it worked. She had to try.

And after she was escorted out, she tried again.

After being ejected for the third time, Sonya found herself in front of the Arlen Industries compound again. "This isn't going to work," she muttered to herself, uneasily aware of the guards inside the entrance now watching her. One more time and they'd call the cops.

She had wasted too much time. She needed to get to Arlen Manor. Not that John needed help. Of course not. Just in case.

Damn it. If nothing else, she should have at least shaved her legs.

She gave it one more try. She approached the security entrance. The guards had already seen her. Kenny by now had help, and his aides stood nearby, big and solid, as though they remembered playing football in their youth. And she wasn't that tall.

She smiled and tried to look as harmless as possible, although having been kicked out of the facility three times in an hour and a half didn't help matters any. "Don't worry, I won't try to get in again," she began, putting her hands up. "Kenny, I need to get Janie Arlen a message," she said directly. "What if I just want to get a message to her? An urgent message?"

Kenny shook his head. "Can't do it miss," he said. The biggest of the guards crossed his arms and looked disapproving.

"In that case, could I just leave a message?"

The biggest security guard glanced at her suspiciously and then at the others, who looked at her and then at each other. "Why didn't you do that before?" said Kenny, glancing at the others before looking at her.

"Because I wanted to see her," Sonya said.

"Then you should have brought Mr. Arlen along," Kenny said reasonably. The biggest one growled.

"He's busy. If I leave a message, when would she get it?"

Again the guards, in a cluster glance, conferred with each other—silently—and then Kenny said, "When she can."

Sonya had the feeling this had been a waste of time. Which meant John was right and she was wrong. She hated days like that.

"Let me write it and then I'll be on my way," she said.

Her note was simple. "Need answers to questions about family. ASAP." She initialed it with a flourish, folded the note and scribbled Janie's name on the front before handing it over. "Thanks."

Sonya left. "If she ever gets it," she muttered. She glanced at her watch. She could get to the house in half an hour if she got the lights. If she hadn't been in such a snit, she would have remembered to get his cell phone number, but no.

But she wasn't going to speed. He could take care of himself for—she looked at her watch again—the three hours he had been out of her sight. He wasn't a toddler with a penchant for getting in trouble, after all.

Just in case, she stepped on the gas.

Arlen Manor looked as quiet as the first time she had seen it. She decided to enter the old-fashioned way for once.

After the gates closed behind her, she looked around. The grounds were quiet and the neighborhood was too, with only an occasional gardener visible on other estates. The stone garden—the statuary—stood in the weak daylight, looking as though they were about to come alive. The lawn still looked battered from the police and the firefighters traipsing around—was that just two nights ago? Other than that, everything looked the way it—

What was that?

Sonya turned toward the house. But the windows were dark and nothing in them indicated anything out of the ordinary.

Shaking her head, she turned back to the stone garden. Then out of the corner of her eye, she saw—*something*.

There it was again—a flash of light from the house. Not just the house. Was it from the basement? What the—

She was running before she realized it. She should have asked for a key. If nothing else, she should be able to break the glass.

She changed course again. The garden door leading to the basement was around the back. Their conversation before had been rife with bitterness and she had nearly forgotten, but he had promised to keep that unlocked. If only he had meant it.

She tried the knob. It gave.

Shoving the door open, she rolled in.

Nothing. What was that burst of light? Where *was* he? He had to be here somewhere. He came back for Gloria.

Damn idiot calling a device that.

Where *was* Gloria? He hadn't had time to move it. But here it was, back in its normal corner.

"John?" she yelled. "Where are you?"

Had he gotten it to work? Dust was thick where the device had been and the blanket that had covered it lay on the concrete, abandoned.

He wasn't in the basement. Where else could he be? She ran up the stairs, her heart pounding. *Oh God I shouldn't have let him go alone.*

If he was here, he had to have a heartbeat.

Sonya reached into the silence and concentrated. Within seconds, her hand began to glow and a familiar stream of light started its hunt. She followed it.

The hallway was dark and cool, with nothing to indicate anyone or anything had been there in some time. But someone had to have been. She looked both ways, tried to remember the layout of the first floor and, failing utterly, chose a direction. It led to the kitchen. That too was dark, but the lights turned on automatically once she entered, blinding her momentarily. The stream of light from her fingertips hovered and then stopped.

She looked around. *Where?*

Bubbles.

Sonya zeroed in on the tumbler sitting on the counter. She approached it and examined it as closely as she could without touching it. It was filled with cola, bubbles still rising out of the liquid, so it had to have been poured sometime in the very recent past. Her hearing had zeroed in on the carbonation.

She gritted her teeth. It could be John's if he'd picked up soda pop. On the other hand, she'd never seen him drink soda. It might have been John's, it might not.

It disturbed her to realize how much she didn't know about him. She left the kitchen, pushing it out of her mind. She'd worry about it after she found him. And she *would* find him.

Sonya snapped her fingers. His study. If he wasn't in the basement, he'd go to his own study. Second floor, west wing.

She paused. But there had to be noise *somewhere*. Before she moved again, she listened.

After a moment, she relaxed. She recognized the rhythm of John's heart immediately and then the comforting beat of the grandfather clock in the main foyer, the hiss of the soda, the creak of the house—

Hold it. That wasn't the house.

There was someone *in* the house and it wasn't John Arlen.

She didn't know what those bursts of light had been about, but whatever they were, they hadn't come from John. She listened.

A third heartbeat. And it was familiar somehow.

Whoever else was in the house was upstairs, not far from John.

She started to climb the grand staircase as noiselessly as she could, trying to listen at the same time. As she did, she tried to piece together what was going on upstairs just by sound.

He—and it *was* a he, of that she was sure—was walking as quietly as she was. He had been in John's study, but no more. Now he was down the hallway, around the corner, down the hallway again—toward the bedrooms.

Why the bedrooms? Most of them were unused, as far as she knew, except for John's and Janie's. Maybe it was John.

No. It wasn't his heartbeat.

She arrived at the top of the staircase. She could hear the stranger's breathing stop for a second and she waited. The doors leading to the west wing were already open, so when the mystery man started breathing again, she walked through it.

The intruder stopped again, but this time in another bedroom—probably Janie's room.

He rummaged there, and not quietly. Sonya took the opportunity to walk toward the bedrooms, keeping a wary ear on the intruder.

It wasn't John. But she could hear John's heartbeat and it was a little slow—was he unconscious? Where *was* he?

She paused at the end of the hallway. The trespasser was no longer quiet. That made her all the more anxious about John's welfare.

Whoever you are, you're going to answer a few questions. She walked faster. The intruder rummaged. She heard him yank out a dresser drawer and dump it. As she paused at the door, she could hear him kicking at the contents—looking for something.

She kicked open the door and jumped the guy, landing on his shoulders. He screamed and staggered, but he didn't fall, forcing her to jump off before he threw her off. It was a man—the previous intruder to the house. And she had whupped his ass then, in John's study. Vaughn something, she remembered from the booking.

"You," she snarled. "You've got some nerve coming back here." She punched him in the stomach, knocking the wind out of him, and pinned him before he had a chance to react.

"Hey!" Vaughn choked out. "Get offa me!"

"*Where is he?* Tell me where he is or I'm going to beat it out of you!"

"Why are you always where I have to be?" Vaughn moaned. He tried to kick free, but Sonya shoved her knee in and made him screech.

"Answer my question!"

Then she heard something. A moan. *John.* Close by.

"John, are you all right?" she shouted.

There was a hesitation, then, "Sonya? Where are you?"

"I'm in Janie's room, with our usual unwanted guest," she called out. He was all right. *Thank God.*

She could hear his footsteps heading toward her, the limp and drag pronounced. "If you hurt him, I'm going to hurt you," she told Vaughn.

"Get off me," he snarled. He squeaked when she shifted her knee.

John was almost at the doorway. She turned her head toward where she knew he would appear, not letting go of Vaughn. "What happened to you?"

The sudden shift in air pressure alerted her. She recognized it from last time, realized what it was. "The translocator!" she shouted. She gripped Vaughn. "You're not getting away!"

Then she heard John's voice, hoarse with anger. She turned toward the doorway and cried out. "No John! Don't!"

John Arlen was standing in the doorway, bruised and battered, glasses askew, pointing his grandfather's Enfield at Vaughn. And because she was holding the thug down, at her. "John, you're not used to the gun. *Put it down!*"

He wasn't listening to her. Wild-eyed, he yelled, "The hell you're going to get away this time!"

Beneath her, she heard, "Too late!" She looked down and saw Vaughn surrounded by a blue spark. "See you later, lady!"

"Oh no you don't!" she shouted. Sonya flattened herself against the Engineer's sidekick, holding on tight. She looked up to see John fire the weapon, the recoil knocking him down. She felt, rather than saw, the bullet graze her shoulder and she saw red before she remembered to hang on.

The blue spark glowed and surrounded her and Vaughn and that was the last thing she knew for a long, long time.

* * * * *

Why?

He'd been hit on the back of his head. Why did he hurt in between his eyes?

Maybe he should start wearing a helmet when he was home.

His first mistake of the day had been waking up on Sonya's floor. There was a good reason why he hadn't been a Boy Scout—he wasn't cut out to sleep on the ground. Then there was that argument with Sonya. Then he had made the mistake of leaving.

Once he was out of the apartment, he had stood in front of the brownstone, cursing himself. He'd forgotten Sonya had driven, and since Janie was already gone, he had no other method of transport. So he called a taxi.

The cab driver left him at the entrance to Arlen Manor. John found himself looking up at the gates, trying to calculate how long it would take him to climb it. After depressing himself, he just let himself in by the door.

Somehow, home-sweet-home didn't seem so sweet anymore.

The garden door to the basement was easiest, since letting himself in by the front door reminded him how empty he had felt when he had come home from the hospital, crippled and grieving.

"I need a new housekeeper," he muttered aloud. If nothing else, some sign of life in the house once in a while would be comforting. A glance at Gloria assured him the device was still intact, though only a thorough examination would prove whether anything had been done to it. He remembered to unlock the door to the garden, for Sonya.

He made his way upstairs. By the time he was at the main floor, he was already winded. As opposed to Sonya, who didn't even bother to take most of the stairs going up or going down.

The first floor was as quiet as the basement had been, save for the steady *tick-tock* of the grandfather clock in the hallway. He strained to hear it. He'd heard all the noises in the house since he could remember but for once, none of it brought comfort. Instead it made him wonder if he'd misidentified any noises and would turn out to be someone, something, out to get him.

He wandered through the kitchen and poured himself a glass of soda. That was Janie's contribution. Soda pop was something he would drink if it were there, but he didn't go out of his way for it. He took a sip and he shrugged. If it contained poison, he couldn't tell.

If he wasn't careful, he was going to get paranoid.

A walk through the dining room and down the hall proved once more he was alone—at least in the rooms he had been through. There was nothing to indicate anyone had been in the house.

He wondered what she was doing right then. A trip to the warehouse? A trip to Arlen Industries, even though Janie was stuck in those meetings all day? Maybe he should have given her a pass so she could at least get onto the compound. But she wouldn't be able to talk to Janie anyway.

He glanced at his watch. Where was she?

The grand stairway beckoned to him, curving and stretching to the second floor. John hesitated.

This was his home. There was no reason he should be afraid. The house was an old one. It must have witnessed a century's worth of events, good and bad, and the recent spate of activity was a drop in the bucket of Arlen events.

Logically there wasn't anything in the house to alarm him.

When had it gotten dusty? He ran a hand up the banister, surprised to see his fingers come away dusty. When was the last time he'd bothered to check whether the place needed a good cleaning? Before last night, when had he noticed anything?

The mahogany double doors at the second story landing were equally dusty, but at least there were palmprints where somebody—he'd bet Sonya—had slapped it open. At least the doors didn't squeak. He left them open.

The motion-detector sconces didn't click on when he walked down the hall. Just to make sure, he flipped the manual override switches at the end of the hall, flooding the corridors with light.

At least the lights all seemed to work. He felt better.

A sense of dread flooded over him as he approached his study. The last time he had been in there he learned he wasn't alone in his own house. He took a deep breath and shoved open the door.

Nothing. He exhaled.

His study was a mess. There wasn't anything he wouldn't have to reorganize and refile, but at least it was empty. The drapes were still open from that day and he opted not to shut them. He closed the door as he left, leaving the cleanup for later.

Next, he went to the hallway leading to the currently used bedrooms, where he and Janie both had theirs, passing their parents' suite, still closed up. He'd meant to start sorting it out but he'd never gotten around to that either.

At least Janie had an excuse for not doing it. She'd been out of the country. He'd just been in the basement, avoiding life.

Well, he had made his return to it. His back still hurt from sleeping on the floor. *Idiot.*

The hallway sconces remained dark as he approached his bedroom. He had to remember to reprogram the motion sensors there. His was a large space, spartan and utilitarian at best. It might even be cozy if he lit a fire in the big white-stoned fireplace. He couldn't remember the last time he'd done that.

Come to think of it, he couldn't even remember the last time he'd changed the sheets. Where did his soon-to-retire housekeeper, Mrs. Locke, keep the bed linens?

What would Sonya make of it all? Would she look around disapprovingly and start to redecorate? Would she roll her eyes?

Maybe he could persuade her it was a challenge.

More likely she'd point out the Arlen family could afford an interior designer or two to spruce up the family manse. After all, if he wasn't interested in doing it, why should she?

Sonya would have ignored his suggestion. Except maybe the bedroom. He would have guessed she was supremely disinterested in decorating of any sort, except he had seen her bedroom, as lushly appointed as a Victorian bordello, as her living room was not.

He looked around his own bedroom. It was quiet, like the rest of the house. It was empty, like the rest of the house.

Janie's room was next, mainly because he knew that was the only other room in active use. But that, too, was empty and disheveled. His sister was as disorganized as he was. Her dresser drawers were open and clothing was thrown hither and yon, and he knew from experience that no, Janie's room had not been searched. Amazingly her notes and work habits were meticulous in contrast.

He had just left his sister's room when the first burst of pressurized static sent him staggering. He heard that hiss—

Somebody was using the translocation device again.

His bedroom. It had to be in his bedroom!

He limped toward the room, uneasily aware the baseball bat he had used in Little League was still in plain sight, mounted on the wall. That was the only means of defense or offense he had available until he could get to the wardrobe, where he had buried his grandfather's Enfield.

What else? He had to have something to defend himself with. His cane, maybe. If only it had been a sword cane, like the one Geoffrey carried. Whoever it was, his cousin or one of his stooges, he was going to have to stand up to—

He stopped. "Why is it always you?" he burst out.

Vaughn, the larger stooge of the Engineer's assistants, paused just as he opened the drawer with John's collection of cufflinks, a pen flashlight tucked under his chin. He groaned. "Why are you here? You're supposed to be at your girlfriend's!"

John gritted his teeth. "She's not my girlfriend, and I live here."

Introducing Sonika

"Well hell, she sure comes across like your old lady," Vaughn muttered, continuing to paw through the drawer. "Why do you guys have this many cufflinks?"

"Do you mind? They're family heirlooms. Why are you here?" John started to edge toward the mounted baseball bat.

Vaughn shrugged, not bothering to look at him. "Boss told me to look around in the bedrooms, since there's nothin' in your study. Do me a favor and get out of here, will ya? It's hard to work with you hangin' around."

"I think you should go back to your boss and tell him to leave us alone." John was in front of the bat now. It wasn't fastened to the frame, much to his relief.

Vaughn guffawed as he continued to paw and peruse. "You must be kiddin'! Where's your girlfriend, anyway?"

"The last time I saw her she was in her own apartment. Where you should be." John lifted the bat off its holder and hefted it.

"In her apartment?" Vaughn snickered at his own joke. "Sorry, guy. She'd kick my butt, and the boss can't control that people-mover thing."

"If he's so brilliant I'm surprised he hasn't figured out how." John was directly behind the big goon now.

Vaughn shook his head. "The boss? Maybe his old man. In fact—hey!"

The big man turned just as John lifted the bat over his head. "Whaddaya think you're doin'?"

The bat came down, but a split second too late. Vaughn ducked. "Is that the best you can do, man? Crap, without that bat you're toast!" He started to scramble away.

That alone made John feel better. "Maybe you shouldn't turn your back on me, you son of a bitch!"

"Be real, man! Without that chick, you're nuthin'!"

John swung the bat again, this time missing the goon by an inch. The bat hit the wall, smashing the light controls. For a moment the light wavered and then went out.

John could hear Vaughn moving and he smiled. "This is my room, you bastard," he said softly. "I grew up in it. I've walked through it and around it since I was a kid."

"Without that bat, you're nuthin'," the thug's reply floated in the darkness. John cursed himself for not opening the drapes. The slivers of daylight cast shadows across the carpeted floor.

Big shadows. Big, hulking shadows that streaked across the carpet. *Thank you very much, you —*

John swung the bat again, this time shattering a lamp.

Vaughn guffawed. "You're doin' a number on your own stuff, man."

John gritted his teeth. He stepped softly, mindful of what was on the floor.

"C'mon man, just give it up," Vaughn's voice came drifting across the room again. "You get close enough to me, I'm gonna take the bat away from you. You get me pissed, I'm gonna use that bat on you. Give it up and you're not gonna get hurt. That bitch of yours is gonna break my arm if she thinks I hurt you."

John shook his head. *When did I become the one nobody worries about because I can't hurt anyone? I could make their lives miserable. I can pay off politicians. Well, I know* people who can pay off politicians.

But it was Sonya they were afraid of.

He held his breath as he approached Vaughn noiselessly. *You lay a hand on her or me, you're going to be sorry,* John thought.

"It ain't personal, man," Vaughn went on, sounding almost reasonable. "But the boss says you gotta be taken care of."

Well I'm going to make sure you go, jerk, John thought. Once again, he was behind Vaughn. He raised the bat.

He stepped on a shard of porcelain, of what used to be the lamp. The crack reverberated through the room. *Shit!*

Vaughn turned around, stepping out of the way. "You know your room, all right," he mocked. "You broke your own lamp, you step on your mess and you miss out on brainin' me. Good goin'."

Infuriated, John swung the bat but Vaughn dodged it and grabbed hold of it. For a second they fought for control but Vaughn wrested it away. "Hey hey, Mr. Arlen, if you keep wrecking your room, I'm gonna take the bat from you." He hefted it, peering at it. "Hey, you did Little League, huh? So did the boss."

"We played together," John muttered. There had to be something he could use as a weapon—something that could take out the thug until he could get at the Enfield.

He cursed silently. There wasn't anything. Apart from throwing another lamp at the guy, trying to smother him with a comforter or a pillow, or cutting him with a shard of porcelain from what used to be a lamp, there was nothing unless he got to the Enfield. He jumped Vaughn, punching at him desperately, trying to throw him off-balance.

Vaughn, however, wasn't buying it. "C'mon Mr. Arlen, is that the best you can do? Just gimme what I want and I'll get out of your way," he said, sounding appallingly reasonable. He pushed John away, sending him to the floor.

"Screw you," John said, panting. He grabbed the largest shard of porcelain he could and lashed out at the goon.

It got caught in the thug's pants, ripping the fabric. Vaughn finally noticed. "Hey, son of a bitch! Watch what you're doin'!"

John knew he didn't have much time—Vaughn was going to overpower him in a second—so he tackled him at the knees, sending the large man down. He slugged the man once, twice.

It didn't work. "Aw, c'mon man, you can't be serious!" Vaughn sat up, throwing John back as though he weighed nothing backslapping him and sending him back to the floor.

John blacked out. The next thing he knew, he heard shouts and the walls shook. As soon as he could stand, he did, leaning against the dresser.

For a moment he couldn't remember what had happened, but then he did. *Vaughn. Damn it!* John crawled to the wardrobe and opened it. He started to dig, shoving aside years of sweaters and outdated ties before he came up with the Enfield, rolled up in a moth-eaten argyle vest.

He heard shouts again and this time, the furniture sounded as though it were being moved the hard way.

Sonya. That had to be Sonya. Despite his aching head, he stumbled to the door but the shouts stopped. Then he heard, "John? Is that you?"

She sounded as if she might have been glad to see him. Rubbing the back of his head, he called out, "Sonya? Where are you?"

"I'm in Janie's room with our usual unwanted guest."

The big thug wasn't going to get away with it. Not this time. He heard a groan—that had to be Vaughn—and hurried. If he had a chance to see the goon at Sonya's mercy, he was all for it.

The Enfield firmly in hand, John stumbled down the hallway to Janie's room, the pain splitting his head. With each step he took the angrier he became. He had been insulted, assaulted and worst of all, ignored. *Enough.*

The sight when John finally got there did him good. Sonya sat on the thug, one of his beefy arms twisted around his back.

But then he felt the drop in air pressure again. For a moment, he reeled, afraid he was going to pass out. Then he realized what it was. *The translocator!*

Sonya said something but he wasn't listening anymore. "No!" he shouted, raising the Enfield and aiming at Vaughn. "The hell you're going to get away this time!" He heard Vaughn shout and then Sonya shouted something back.

That hiss…that pressure…that light…

Vaughn started to buck and Sonya grabbed at him.

"Sonya!" John shouted. She looked at him, and for a moment, he saw fear in her eyes for the first time since they had met. Even as he was processing that look, he pulled the trigger, realizing too late that Sonya was too close.

For the first time in his life, for all dozen times he had ever fired the weapon in his hands, he prayed to miss. But no. Her eyes widened and then they glazed and he knew he had hit her. "*Sonya!*" he screamed.

Too late. As he watched in horror, she and Vaughn disappeared in a burst of blue light.

Chapter Sixteen

The air pressure normalized and that was the only way John knew anything had happened there at all.

In a flash of light, she was gone. With Vaughn, of all people. Which meant straight to his cousin.

John sank to his knees. "Damn it," he whispered.

It was his fault. He shouldn't have let himself get drawn into that argument this morning. He should have convinced her to go with him. Why did he think he knew how to handle the Enfield?

He slapped himself on the forehead. "Idiot," he said aloud. Then, louder and angrier, "Damn it!" Sonya was gone, hurt by his own hand because he had convinced her to join him in his crusade. Never mind he could barely walk. Never mind he couldn't defend himself and needed her to be his muscle. Never mind she did everything he had asked her to do except once, standing up for herself—and that had gotten her a trip to hell.

His cell phone trilled, breaking into his regrets. He froze. Was it Jasper already? To do what, gloat?

He flicked the phone open. "Yes," he said, and held his breath.

"Little brother! What's this all about?"

Janie. It was just Janie.

"She's gone."

Janie was instantly sympathetic. "Oh, I'm sorry, Johnny. You weren't together that long, were you? Although I didn't think she was your type."

That woke him up from his daze. "What?"

"Weren't you talking about Sonya?"

"Yeah. But you thought—no," he said, recognition dawning. "We didn't break up. We weren't together to break up. No, Janie—"

"Oh. It was a physical thing? She didn't look like the type."

"Jasper got her," John told her, exasperated. "She was fighting with one of his stooges and he used the translocator and she got in the way. And I shot her with Grandfather's Enfield."

John could go to the warehouse and confront his cousin. Would he be in the warehouse? He would have to take backup. The police? Who could he trust? Not Malone, that was for sure.

"You did *what?* She got in the way of what, the translocator? She rode along? Oh, my God."

This wasn't like Janie. "What?"

"Johnny, the translocator has to be set for mass! Oh, my—and you *shot* her? You still have that old thing?" Janie, usually the most positive of souls, sounded— They were in trouble. "Remember the Beasley experiments? Matter destroyed on one end and recreated on the other? The same size, weight, density? It wasn't meant for changing the object being transferred in the middle of transfer. Oh John. You didn't miss?"

His stomach twisted. "I think I grazed her, but I don't know."

"Where are you?"

"I'm home."

"Why are you there? Didn't Sonya say that was dangerous?"

"I had to check up on Gloria," he said. The numbness was setting in.

"That antigrav thing of yours. I'll be right there."

He pulled himself up by the doorframe, pushing his glasses up his nose. Where was his cane? He could have tried to beat the thug with it. It didn't matter. He needed to sit down. But he was going to do it somewhere he could do some good.

But first, he had to do something with that damned gun. He stopped. *No. Not yet.*

John was sitting on the floor in the basement, Gloria in pieces in front of him, when Janie found him.

He looked up, his jaw set. "I'm going to find him, get her and kill him." His tone brooked no argument.

"Is that how you're going to do it, taking apart that thing? Is it still methane powered?"

He looked up. "No. And it's going to come in handy. Don't fight me on this."

Janie didn't. He watched as his sister rubbed her temples. She looked tired. He knew how draining those directors' meetings were. During her fellowship in Paris and then her time in Antarctica, he had sat in on those board meetings if need be, but generally he had let the chief operating officer of Arlen Industries do the honors.

As if she knew what he was thinking, Janie commented, "I want to get back to R&D soon. Then it'll be your turn at the reins."

He turned back to Gloria. "After we get Sonya back and take care of Jasper."

Janie waved a sheet of paper in his face. "Hey, can you answer a few questions? Starting with this note Lina gave me when I took a break from the inquisition? And I was thinking. I don't know what the result would be with an unbalanced transfer. We never got that far in the trials. That's why I'm worried."

"I didn't leave you a note." He turned back to Gloria's guts.

"But Sonya—" Janie stopped talking for a second. "I know you didn't send the message, because according to my secretary, who got it from the security head, he got it from a casually dressed woman they had to eject from the compound. Several times. Finally, she wrote a note and told them to give it to me, which they did after they disinfected it, examined it and judged it was safe."

He looked up at her. "That must have been Sonya." He grabbed the note. The surge of hope died when he scanned it. "This is nothing," he said, disappointed.

"She knew it was going to be passed from hand to hand before I got it, Johnny—she couldn't say anything. So what did she want to ask about that she kept getting kicked off the compound for?"

He stared at the note. "Questions about family."

"I've told you everything I can remember, Johnny. I'd be glad to answer anything else, but—"

"Why do you insist Jasper's bright?" he asked suddenly.

Janie stopped. "Because he seemed to be."

"You said that," John said. "Why? Give me examples, not a generalized conclusion."

She laughed, but not very certainly. "You sound like Dad."

"Thank you. Answer, please."

"Why do I think he's bright?" Janie paused. "Okay. I think he's bright because when he was working for me at Arlen, he seemed interested, but not having an engineering, math, or physics background, he couldn't grasp the concepts. We'd explain a problem we were trying to solve and he'd be frustrated."

"Do you know how many generalizations you just used?"

She shrugged. "If you want examples, you'll have to give me a few hours to remember. It's been a while."

"So he got frustrated when he couldn't understand."

"He'd get frustrated, he'd stomp away, then he'd come back and have an ingenious solution to the problem. He was a natural. It would have been easier for him if he'd had the schooling or the temperament, but it just seemed to come a step later for him. I was so disappointed when he stole those blueprints."

John glared at her. "Don't tell me you've been harboring the hope it wasn't him all this time."

"I'd rather not make any unfounded accusations."

"They'd all be founded, believe me," he muttered. "So that's why you assumed he was that bright."

"I like to think he had the right instincts. They just got twisted," she added sadly.

He rubbed the side of his neck. "Something's not adding up."

"What are you thinking?"

"Is it possible someone was feeding him the answers?"

"Maybe. What would be the point?"

He shrugged. "Why do kids copy answers from each other on a test? Because they want a better grade."

"Isn't it easier to just study?"

"Janie, that's not the point. Is it possible?"

"It's possible," his sister admitted. "That would require some sort of surveillance..."

John looked at her. "What?"

"We had to turn off the detection system for a while that year. I told Dad when you two got back but I don't know if I told you."

He stared at his sister. "In the research & development wing? Why would we turn it off? It's there to make sure—"

"To deter industrial espionage. I know, I know. Something was wacky with the wiring. The alarms kept going off and we weren't getting any work done that summer. It was happening all over the complex. So we turned it off in a few rooms so we could concentrate and tripled the manned security." She winced. "Which didn't help, as it turned out."

"Did it occur to you the alarms were going off because of Jasper?"

She looked away and he immediately felt guilty. "The day after he disappeared. I felt like such a fool. The alarms — we never had a problem with them after that."

"He must have been wired," John concluded.

Janie nodded, her head drooping. "I felt like an idiot."

"Then why did you keep insisting he was a bright boy?"

"It didn't occur to me he'd go to those lengths to make me believe he could do the work!"

"What did you have him do?"

She sat down on the floor. "He did mostly filing and a lot of copying. He didn't have the background — "

"To do more than that. You told me."

"Why would he do that? He didn't sell the blueprints. We would have heard about it."

"How did he know how to use those prints to build one?"

"No," she said unexpectedly. "He couldn't. Especially since the thing didn't work well at that stage. And from what you told me, it doesn't work in a predictable fashion now."

John looked at her. He knew what she was thinking. Together they said, "Who?"

"Maybe somebody on the inside," she said. She stood up. "I'll look through the personnel files."

"Must be nice to be the boss. You can rifle through whatever you want."

She grinned but her eyelids drooped. "The perks can't make up for sitting through those budget meetings. I'll let you know what I find." She started to leave but stopped.

John knew that hesitation. "What?"

"I know you don't want to talk about it, but that translocator imbalance—"

He shook his head. "We'll deal with that when we get her back."

"John—"

"I *know* we might not get her back," he said explosively. "But right now, all I want to figure out is *how*. I'm not going to accept that we can't until— I'm just not."

Janie took a deep breath. "Okay. Later."

He glanced at the door as she closed it.

It wasn't anyone at the company. But he wasn't going to tell her that.

He stared at the parts of the antigrav device spread out on the floor. Suddenly, the pieces of Gloria weren't important anymore, not in the way he had put them together originally.

Painfully, he stood up.

* * * * *

Nothing.

The room was white, infinite white.

No floor, no walls, no ceiling…nothing.

No light, no dark…nothing.

She screamed but she couldn't hear herself.

No light, no dark, no sound.

Nothing. Nothing. Nothing.

She hit something—it had to be the wall.

She hammered at it but there was nothing.

She opened her mouth and screamed again, screamed until her throat hurt, but there was nothing.

There had to be something. She could feel her hands— that was something. She reached down and touched her feet— that too was something. But there was nothing.

How? How was she here? *Why?*

She slid down what she thought was the wall. If there was gravity, it would be a wall. But she couldn't be sure anymore. She wrapped her arms around her legs and tried to make herself as small as possible. Maybe she did.

She tried to piece together what had happened. She remembered going to Arlen Industries and getting kicked out. She remembered writing a note for Janie. She remembered going to Arlen Manor, looking for John and finding that thug Vaughn instead. She remembered that surge of fury when she realized the Engineer's stooge would pop out of there, leaving her with questions and a whole load of frustration. She remembered John pointing his weapon at Vaughn, grazing her. She remembered hanging on—

Then that dizzying ride that felt like all the roller-coaster rides anyone had ever taken, on equipment that was about to fall apart, on tracks that had fallen off. The ride was enough to loosen her fillings and she had stopped thinking. She'd never liked roller-coaster rides and now she'd have a good reason why.

Then it had all stopped. All the noise had stopped. All the color. Everything.

Somebody had pushed her to her knees. Something helmet-like was clamped on her head and it wouldn't come off. It blocked her vision and her hearing. She couldn't see and she couldn't hear.

She had screamed and screamed until her throat was raw but she could hear none of it. She scratched and clawed at what she thought might be the wall but she couldn't be sure. Her fingertips felt damp and dimly, she realized it was blood.

Finally, huddled in the corner, she started to whistle a tune. At least she thought it was a tune. She couldn't hear it so she couldn't be sure. She licked her lips—that, at least, she could feel and do—and pursed her lips and she blew, but she couldn't hear it.

Nothing. Nothing. Nothing.

She gritted her teeth. Her fingers were stiff and slick but she started to claw at the thing on her head again.

Where was John? Was he all right? She could remember hearing his voice right before the burst of energy, but he sounded hurt.

Vaughn must have hurt him. But he could walk, so the damage couldn't have been too much. Then he had shot her. He had to learn how to use that weapon if he wanted to keep it.

She should have stayed with him. She shouldn't have let him go to the house alone.

He had to learn self-defense. She couldn't be there all the time to protect him.

Did Jasper have him? Was he already dead?

He was okay. He had to be.

Then she could have sworn she heard her mother's voice say, *Check out the room.*

Mom? Is that what I should do? I can't tell where I am. I'm lost in a sea of nothing and nothing makes sense.

But the rules made sense, the ones her mother and father had drummed into her. How many times had she heard them say that? She could have sworn her parents had made them up randomly, choosing a good idea and pairing it with a rule number.

Don't panic—Rule Three.

That was one of those easy-to-say rules. She hated that one, but she needed to remember it. Sonya couldn't hear or see, but she could still feel the room. Rule Seventeen, Check out the perimeter. She couldn't hear or see, but she could do Rules Three and Seventeen.

The wall was flat. No, it wasn't flat. It was padded. The padding was thick. It was strong. She had scratched and clawed at it but she hadn't been able to make a mark on it—at least she didn't think so. She couldn't tell.

Think. How big was the room? She knew she was in a corner, she could feel that. Measure off the inches, measure off the feet, the way her father had taught her.

Just pretend your eyes are closed, sweetheart. Start measuring, hand by hand. It's a quiet night. Not even the crooks are afoot. The stars are twinkling up above and the mist is rising—

No, she said, or at least thought she said. Not the stars. She couldn't see the stars.

Five feet, five and a half, six feet, six and a half, seven—seven—

You can count. You know what comes after seven. It's—

It's seven and a half. Eight. Eight and a half.

She hit another corner and she stopped. She didn't think it was the same corner. So the room was nine feet in length.

Nine feet. Nine feet.

Next wall. Think.

Why was she doing this? She didn't know. It might come in handy. More important, it might keep her from going crazy.

Think.

Okay. First wall nine feet. Second wall. One. One and a half. Two. Two and a half. Three.

Was he all right? He had to be.

Three and a half. Four.

He had to be all right. He must have figured out what had happened. He had to know she hadn't abandoned him. He had to.

Are you all right? You are, aren't you? I should have invited you into my bath.

Four and a half. Five.

How was she going to get out of this?

Five and a half. Six.

She touched another corner. It was a small room. Six by nine.

What would Sounder do? What would Velocity do?

Velocity would have figured out how to get out of here. But Velocity's daughter needed to hear and at the moment, Sonya couldn't. If she could see, she could at least posit the presence of sound. But whoever had put this thing on her head had made sure she had neither sense available.

Who had it been? Jasper? Not likely. He had never seen her use her powers. He couldn't know what she could do.

But the house was bugged. Her apartment might be bugged. He could have found out that way. But this thing on her head was too well-designed. Who could it have been? Someone with designing and engineering abilities.

Think. A vague possibility came to her. She had never tried it. Her mother had told her to try it but they'd never gotten around to experimenting — *Later sweetheart, after you're introduced officially, when you turn sixteen.*

Couldn't I come out before? Please? You know I can do it. Just a couple nights with you and Daddy?

Too late.

She should have taken more psych classes. If she could believe there was sound, maybe she could —

Think. Believe.

No. She couldn't do it. Even as a child, she hadn't been fanciful. She'd never had any imaginary playmates, never played any games. Instead, she had spent a chunk of her childhood studying to be a superhero.

Big fat waste of her time that had been.

Nine-feet-by — What had it been? Six feet. Nine-by-six. It was practically a box. A padded box.

Think. How high would the ceiling be?

She pushed herself to a standing position. She didn't want to stand because she felt so dizzy. But that was the only way she could gauge ceiling height.

Okay. Now she was standing. *Close your eyes, sweetheart,* she heard her father instructing her. *Close your eyes and stretch your arms up. You know how long your arms are. If you can't touch the ceiling, you start estimating.*

Jumping jacks, Daddy?

Jumping jacks, kiddo.

Was there someone behind her?

Just then, she felt hands around her shoulders. She twisted and elbowed something solid. She lashed out with more strength than she would have thought possible in this state of senseless limbo. Whoever it was didn't take no for an answer. She was thrown against the wall and she felt herself grabbed again.

Hell, no! She fumbled for her attacker and shoved him as hard as she could so she could get her bearings.

This would be a lot easier if she could actually see her attacker but she had to make do with what she had—her wits and precious little else.

She felt herself grabbed from behind and her arms bound. *No! No you're not!* Frantically, she kicked—she still had her legs. She connected with something solid, and with a furious jerk, she threw someone aside. Then she felt first one leg and then the other being grabbed, until she was held fast.

She opened her mouth and started screaming. It didn't matter she couldn't hear it. She was screaming even though her throat was raw. She struggled and screamed even as she felt herself being picked up.

The next thing she knew, she was put on her feet and against the wall. Then all of a sudden, she could see and hear again.

"Hi," said John Arlen.

Chapter Seventeen

John had never seen her like this.

He had seen her confident and purposeful, even when she didn't know what she was doing. He had seen her angry. He had seen her cry. He had seen her irritated, happy, laughing, even pouting—but he had never seen her like this.

Sonya huddled in the passenger seat on the way back to her apartment. John took the time to call Janie to tell her he had retrieved Sonya, declining to go into details. It was the first time he had been the driver and she the passenger, and it felt odd. She was responsive, but she really wasn't there.

She said little, had barely moved after he slipped her into his car. She kept her eyes closed, although it was clear she was awake. Lucid was another matter. He didn't know.

He couldn't carry her in. He could barely walk himself, so he settled on helping her in with his arm around her as he leaned heavily on his cane.

"Sonya, you're home," he whispered as he shut the door behind them. As he watched, she stood in her living room, not moving. Did she recognize it? She started to tremble. "Sonya? Why don't you sit down."

He didn't want to raise his voice—he sensed he could scare her so easily right now—so he whispered as he led her over to the sofa and sat her down like a living doll. He grabbed the patchwork quilt that was folded over the back and wrapped it around her. "It's okay," he said. "You're home."

Her eyes were still closed. At least she wasn't trembling anymore. "Coffee?" he asked desperately.

She reacted to that. She shook her head so sharply he was afraid she would hurt herself. "No coffee," she said, her voice not quite audible. Belatedly he realized she was hoarse.

"Okay." She was sweating. He reached out and checked the pulse in her throat. Too fast and thready. "Why don't you lie down."

Sonya nodded and rested her head on the arm of the couch, her eyes still closed.

Rummaging around her kitchen produced a can of cocoa powder in the back of a cupboard. John sniffed it, dumped some of the powder into a mug, boiled some water and poured it in. It didn't look right, but maybe it had to settle. He hurried out to the living room.

"Maybe this is more your style, if you don't want coffee," he said soothingly. "It's hot cocoa." He gently placed the mug on the curve of her lips and let her smell.

He didn't get the reaction he was expecting. She wrinkled her nose, starting to turn her face away—but at least she opened her eyes. "What is that?" she whispered, her voice cracking.

"It's hot cocoa."

She shook her head. "No, it's not," she said. Her lips moved but John didn't hear anything. She closed her eyes again but she took the mug from him. She didn't drink it, though.

"Go ahead," he said encouragingly. "It's not coffee. The sugar in cocoa—"

Sonya slid open one eyelid. "Did you put sugar in it?" she said—at least that was what John thought she said.

"No. Doesn't it come with sugar?"

She started to laugh but then clapped her hand over her mouth. "Don't stop," he pleaded. "I didn't think I'd see you laugh again."

Her hand came away from her mouth and she showed him her palm. There was a smear of blood on it. "My lip split," she whispered and her voice was stronger. She sipped at the drink and blanched. "Did you use milk?"

"Was I supposed to?"

She started to laugh in earnest, her movement splashing hot liquid out of the mug. "Oh," she exclaimed, her voice a mere thread of what it was usually. "My throat is killing me." She started to sit up but he wouldn't let her. He took the mug from her hand and set it aside.

"Just relax, Sonya. Lie down. Please."

She did. John was horrified to realize her obeying him scared him more than anything else. "What can I do for you, since obviously I'm no better than you in the kitchen?"

She smiled again. He was relieved to see her split lip wasn't bleeding anymore. "Don't insult me," she said almost inaudibly. "Even I know the stuff you just gave me needs to be prepared."

He couldn't stand it anymore. He took her hand and kissed it. "I was so worried about you—what happened?" He investigated her fingers. He touched the tips but steered clear of the torn, bloody fingernails, wondering what had happened.

She must have known his unspoken question because she whispered, "I couldn't see anything or hear anything, so I made sure I could feel something."

He covered his fingers over hers. "You can see, you can hear, you can feel now."

"I can," she said, and this time he couldn't hear her at all. She squeezed his hands and he squeezed back.

"I was so worried about you," he whispered. "When I realized what happened, I was—"

"I was afraid he'd get you," she broke in, her voice still weak. "I was so worried if I wasn't there you'd start looking for me instead of coming back here."

John stroked her cheek. "Janie said the translocator wasn't designed for what happened."

"I shouldn't have let you go to your house alone," she lipped, her voice so faint it was hard to hear. "I couldn't get in to talk to your sister."

"She got the message anyway."

"And if I'd just paid attention to what you said, I would have gone with you. Are you all right?" She stroked his hair and he knew she was checking for an injury. "I heard you groan and I knew that big lug must have hurt you—"

"My room looks worse," he said with a smile.

"I'll beat the tar out of him the next time I see him, just for you." At least that was what he thought she had said. Or he hoped she said.

She stroked his head and this time he caught her hand and kissed it again. "How do you feel?"

"Better than before," she whispered.

"No to the cocoa, huh?"

She laughed but stopped abruptly and touched her lip. "No."

"Why don't we put you to bed?"

She shook her head. "I want to stay awake." She stopped. "How long was I—?"

Carefully he asked, "How long were you in that room or in the helmet?"

She looked away. "Both."

John glanced at his watch. "It's been four hours since I...shot you." Her arm had a bandage on it, he was gratified to see. At least they had taken care of her. "Sonya, I'm sorry I—"

"Never mind. Where?" She was almost audible.

"I don't know. I went down to Mercy and looked for Vaughn and Lon. I found them, but they put a blindfold on me after that." He prayed she wouldn't ask for details, not now. "I don't know how long you were in the room or in the helmet. But they put a bandage on your arm, at least." He squeezed her hands again. He was gratified when she squeezed back.

"To keep from going crazy, I measured the room," she said, her voice coming back but still husky. "It was nine-by-six. I don't know how high."

"Is that what your mother and father taught you to do?"

She nodded. "I figured I'd do something constructive and I was talking to my folks a little too much. So I measured the room."

He rubbed his eyes—they weren't tearing, he was just tired—and couldn't look at her. Talking to her dead parents. He could sympathize. "You never know when it's going to come in handy."

In response, Sonya sat up and tugged at his hand. "I want to take a bubble bath," she said, starting to look better already. She struggled to her feet. He slipped his arms around her and she felt small and so fragile. He could barely stand but he wanted to protect her.

Wondrous and unexpected, the bathtub—which he had been afraid he would never see filled again—brimmed with foam and scent in short order. His better instincts warred with his lesser ones and the better half won. He left her contemplating the bubbles.

His cell phone trilled and he answered it, smiling. "Hey, Janie."

"Did you forget about me?"

John closed his eyes. *Not Janie.* "No. I told you twelve hours. It's barely been three." He closed the phone.

He knocked on the door once he was sure he heard splashing. The image of her in the tub, running a languid hand through the bubbles, came into mind. "Sonya? Are you okay?"

"C'mon in," he heard her say. She had to repeat it before he was sure she had said it.

His palms started sweating. All of a sudden, the doorknob got slick.

The room was thick with clouds of steam. His glasses fogged instantly. He sniffed. "What's that?"

"Lavender and rosemary," came the response, her voice gravelly and hoarse but stronger. "Smells wonderful, doesn't it?"

"Sure," he said, swallowing. "What can I do for you?" He stood near the door, and he was going to stand there, not even trying to wipe off his spectacles. He'd gotten into too much trouble the last time he'd walked into a bathroom with Sonya Penn in it.

"Come on over and talk to me," she rasped. "We both got into too much trouble the last time we split up."

"I wasn't going far." He wasn't going to move, either farther into the room or out of it, unless he had to.

"Come on over," she insisted. She coughed and he immediately felt a pang of guilt for making her raise her voice. "I need to see you. Or at least hear you if I close my eyes."

"I can sit outside. You can hear me there."

"You can sit inside too. Besides, you've seen me naked. At least if I'm in the tub, some of me's going to be covered."

"Is this necessary?"

"C'mon Johnny," she wheedled. That voice, never hard on the ears to start with, kissed him with its current rough edges. John took a deep breath and stepped forward. He wiped off his lenses.

Her head was propped by one of those plastic pillows for the bath and her hair was pinned onto the top of her head again. The curls fell over her face. The pillow was almost as pink as her cheeks. But not as pink, as it turned out, as her nipples.

There wasn't enough bubble to cover her.

Her feet were propped up on the end of the tub. She wiggled her toes. "You always look so tense, John," she murmured, dreams drifting by in her voice. "You should try a bubble bath."

She grabbed his sleeve. She caught him off-balance and he stumbled into the tub. Water exploded everywhere, a miniature tsunami. The bubbles hit the walls and splattered, running down in rivulets. She took the opportunity to unhook his glasses and hold them over the side of the tub.

He spouted water and tried to wipe his eyes clear. "What are you doing?" he tried to yell, but he was laughing too hard.

"Trying to get you to relax. Why don't you join me?"

"Has anyone ever told you you're subtle?" He tried to regain his balance, but no luck. He was pressed against her breasts. He had to look her straight in the eye, because otherwise—

She leaned forward and kissed him.

After the shock, the sensations washed over him. He could feel his heart thundering, his pulse racing, his nerve endings on fire. A sense of wonder filled him. After a day filled with pain and terror and worry, this was the unexpected sweet ending.

The kiss was almost a caress. Her lips meandered, stroking his temples, the sides of his nose—he was gratified to learn they were an erogenous zone—before lighting on the tips of his ears, working down to his earlobes and finally his jaw.

He gripped the sides of the bathtub, not letting himself slide any farther. He arched his neck and she used the tip of her tongue to trace a lingering line down the tendon before she arrived at the base of his throat and she started to nibble.

John closed his eyes, his skin sensitized. But he kept his grip on the sides of the bathtub.

Her hand trailed down his sodden shirt, slipping the buttons out of their holes. Then she scooped a handful of water and drizzled it down his chest. The heat of the room wasn't enough. He could feel the drenched shirt cooling almost immediately and the T-shirt he wore beneath was no insulate. He shivered.

"Are you chilly?" Her voice was barely there.

"No. In fact, the water feels good."

She smiled. "Take a bubble bath with me." She rested a finger at the pulse of his throat. Just rested it there, not moving it up toward his lips, nor moving it down.

His pulse started to jackhammer. "I'm halfway there," he said. His arms were starting to tremble but he kept himself propped up.

"Then slip all the way in." Her finger trailed north, stopping at his Adam's apple. He swallowed. He couldn't help it.

He opened his eyes. As he watched, her tongue snaked out and wet her lips. He swallowed again and this time her finger drew languid circles on his throat. "I don't want to wet my pants," he croaked. "Hold it. That didn't sound right, did it?"

Sonya didn't answer. She licked her lips. "When I was trapped, I promised myself I wasn't going to let you go next time."

John flexed his arms—which was good, because they were quaking by then—and managed to right himself without getting his pants any wetter than they would have been in a spring downpour. He stood and unbuckled, but stopped halfway. "This isn't a gag, is it?"

"Why would it be?"

He took a deep breath. He released the catch on his watch and placed it on the counter. Then he took his glasses from Sonya's fingers, placing them on the counter. "Just making sure."

The water was hot, but it must have been hotter before. Her breasts had been a rosy pink when he had first entered the bathroom but now they were simply enticing.

Finally nude, John stepped in. He slid his legs around her, skimming his feet along her thighs before settling on the curve of her hips. He had the faucet at his back but he didn't care.

"Bubbles are gone," he remarked. He rested his arms on the shelf of the tub and took breathed deep. "Water feels good."

"It was a little hot before." She settled back, a smile curling around her mouth. "Now, it's just right." She wiggled her toes. She wasn't touching him—yet.

"You have little feet," he remarked, for lack of anything else to say to someone who had just invited him to share a tub. After the previous night, he was keeping his mouth shut.

"I think they're the right size," she responded, and she stretched her feet to touch him. His eyes rolled up for a second.

"You're suffering from post-traumatic stress," he gasped when he could sound coherent again. That didn't stop him from running his hands along her calves and ankles and insteps.

"Maybe. But no." She wiggled her toes again, but this time he backed up—just a little—digging the faucet a little more into his spine. "Being trapped in that helmet makes you think, because you can't do anything else," she said. Her voice was husky, getting stronger. "I figured if I didn't get around to inviting you into my bubble bath at least once before I died, I would regret it."

She had slender ankles he could circle with his hands. The tendons flexed and he traced them with his fingers. Her toes were wiggling again. She laughed softly. "You are determined to distract me, aren't you?" he asked.

"You're easily distracted." She took aim again, but this time he lifted her feet and nestled them on either side of his thighs.

The bubbles had dissipated completely by now, leaving a view. "Seriously, how do you feel?" He stroked her calves and massaged her feet. The graze on her arm was healing.

"Surprisingly good," she replied, her voice dreamy. "I could be suffering from post-traumatic stress but I don't think so. This time I wasn't going to get irritated at any fool thing you said."

"Gee, thanks. Whoa!" She had decided to prop her feet on his thighs, wiggling her toes again.

"Foot fetish?" he gasped as she grazed his stomach.

"Just you."

He stroked her feet. Impulsively, he kissed her instep.

She almost purred. "Thank you."

Emboldened, he tucked his feet under her butt. She didn't seem to mind. "Did you miss me?" she asked tranquilly.

"Would saying yes emasculate me?"

"Saying yes would make me happy."

"In that case, yes." He stroked her ankles. "I worried about you, I regretted not touching you in the way you should be touched. I shouldn't have been a pain in the ass."

She leaned forward. "Tonight's your night," she whispered, the lingering rasps of her voice trembling through the last of the steam. "You could get your wish, but only if you respond to our exciting offer."

"In the next thirty minutes?"

"No," Sonya said. "Right now."

Fortunately, she was more limber than he was. She had already clambered out while he was still working his way up. She pulled his arm. "Slowpoke. Last one to the bedroom—"

John laughed. "How fair is that?" He held onto her arm as he steadied himself on his feet.

Her eyes were warm. Funny. He'd always thought eyes had no emotion, but hers were definitely warm. For once, he gave into impulse—and why not now, of all times?—and kissed her.

When he could think again, he knew he should have done this the minute he had met her. She was the moon and the stars, and he knew he had been waiting for her.

Hell of a time to find out.

"Bedroom," she whispered when he took a breath. She started to pull him but he stopped her. He touched his finger to her lips when she opened her mouth and instead of speaking she kissed him.

"Where have you been all my life?" he murmured.

Her eyes shone in the dim light. "I'm here now."

He closed his eyes and kissed her. "I love you, Sonya." He caressed her cheek. He wrapped his arms around her. "If something had happened to you—"

"But nothing did, and you came to get me."

He paused. She still hadn't asked him how. He wasn't going to volunteer. He reached down to kiss her again and this time he didn't stop. He backed her down the hall into the bedroom.

Not for the first time, he cursed himself for not having healed as quickly as he should have. If he had, he could have carried her to the bed, sweeping her off her feet. But as it was, he could only pull her into her bedroom and watch as she fell back onto the thick, luxurious comforter.

She bounced, her arms spread, her hair gleaming like burnished gold in the light of her cream-colored lampshades, her breasts glowing like champagne. Her delighted laughter filled his heart.

She leaned back on her elbows and crooked her finger. "Will you keep your mouth shut if I make advances to you?"

"Haven't I so far?"

"Close enough," she whispered. He landed between her legs and she rolled them to their sides. She parted her legs and bent one to cradle him closer.

She was warm and the pearl of his world. She thrust with an exploratory welcome with her hips. He hissed. "How long did you want me to last?" he exclaimed.

He thrust back. She whimpered—she, who could flatten menacing thugs and create magic out of thin air—and wrapped one of her legs around his waist. She even did it with grace, with a kick and a stretch that would have done a yogi master proud.

"Doesn't have to be that long the first time," she whispered. She gasped as he finally thrust into her. She was primed.

Sonya. He closed his eyes. "That's what you think," he whispered when he finally opened them again.

She was glowing. "I dare you," she rasped with a grin. She teased his flat nipple with a fingernail.

He laughed. "Cut it out. I can't concentrate."

"How are you going to stop me?"

"Is that a challenge?" He reached down and began lapping at her breast, suckling at the erect nipple. She cried out. He stroked her abdomen until her skin twitched and yearned and she murmured, tilted her hips and then—

He stopped thrusting. For a minute, the world stood still. Even if he never came he could die happy.

Sonya noticed. "Something wrong?" she rasped, caressing his cheek before she reached down and pinched his cheek.

He barked a laugh, willing himself to breathe again. "No," he said, using the edge of his incisors on the edge of her nipple. "Just remembering this moment. Not good at multitasking."

"Then don't. Don't worry about more than one thing at a time." His eyes rolled back again when he felt her fingers. He couldn't stop himself, not now. The world started to spin and he knew that once more, she had been right. "I love you," he whispered, and he reached down to kiss her, barely touching her lips before the world went black.

John awoke with his arms wrapped around her, the comforter askew. She was asleep, her face nestled into the curve of his neck. She could kick butt, but she could curl up like a kitten.

And snore. She must have been exhausted. He smoothed the curls off her face and kissed her on her temple. He eased away from her, covering her again with the comforter.

He peered at the alarm clock. He had slept for a while, a fact he rued, when he could have been touching her and committing her scent to memory. He stroked her arm from shoulder to fingertip, lingering around the sweet crook of her elbow, circling around the mole on her inner wrist.

He was tempted to throw caution to the wind, forget what he had promised and hold her until morning, but no. One hour left.

A kiss, and then he touched her cheek and stood up.

Too much to do, too little time. There was the additional challenge of doing everything quietly, but he was aided in that by the thick carpet throughout the apartment muffling his uneven steps. After he slipped on his trousers, he sat down with a pen and paper in hand. Fifteen minutes left.

What could he say? Could he tell her in cold words and flat paper that knowing her had been a rare triumph in his life? That this was for the best, because there had been no way to tell what Jasper would have done to her if he discovered what she could do?

He could always renege on the deal—but he wanted to make sure she was safe. If he kept his side of the bargain, she would be.

In the end, he kept the note fairly simple. He explained the whys and wherefores, and he tried to keep it as emotionless as possible—and failed utterly.

He sealed it in an envelope when he felt, more than heard, her steps behind him.

Then he felt the heat of her lips on the tip of his ear. He closed his eyes so he could remember her caress and her scent.

"I missed you," she breathed into his ear, massaging his shoulders. Her touch was fire. It was heaven and it was agony because he knew he couldn't stay. "I woke up and you were gone," she whispered. She blew, ever so gently. He could feel the blood rising and his breath became labored. He could sense her smile as she asked in a husky voice, "Why are you dressed?"

He caressed her and opened his eyes. "Because it's almost time. And I had to leave you a note."

Her hand curled almost imperceptibly. "Time for what?"

"We made a deal. He let you go so I'm giving myself up."

"You *what?*"

She gripped his shoulder as she turned him around. He stumbled since he didn't have that much dexterity. Not that it would matter. "I didn't want him to hurt you. I was afraid if he started getting curious, he'd find out about what you could do." John stopped.

Sonya's face was ashen. "He's going to hurt you, to do whatever he can to get that formula from you. And then he's going to kill you when he's gotten everything he can from you."

"Maybe," John said, trying to sound confident, "but I'm going to make damn sure I take him with me."

She stared at him, her eyes so wide he could see the whites around her pupils. "What did you do, plant on a bomb on yourself?"

"I didn't think Gloria would mind. I wasn't getting anywhere on making her more efficient."

"You cannibalized Gloria to make yourself into a living bomb?"

"I can do what I need to do before I go down."

"No. We can figure out a way around this." He was shocked to hear her pleading. "Let me go instead. You know I can fight them. You don't have to do this. *Please.*"

Just then, a tiny alarm shrilled. He looked at his watch.

Time.

He gave her a kiss, hard, the way she deserved. Her lips were warm and they were utter pleasure, and he hoped that would be how she remembered him. "Don't come after me," he whispered. "Just check the news. With any luck, I'll take them both with me."

The air pressure around him dropped. The remote signal on his watchband tingled. He stepped away, making sure she wouldn't be in the power surge this time. "I love you, Sonya," he said as the blue halo swallowed him. "Remember me."

Chapter Eighteen

ಬ

"What do you think you're doing?" Sonya shouted into thin air. She threw the envelope with his note and watched in fury as it fluttered. For good measure, she jumped up and down on it. And felt absolutely, one hundred percent no better.

She was going to kill him.

No, she had to rescue him. *Then* she was going to kill him.

She had to go after him. Where? Maybe that same warehouse. No, there was—

Wait. Could she use her tracking instinct over that broad a space? She'd never done it. That didn't mean she couldn't.

The phone rang. She stiffened. Was it the Engineer already?

"Sonya? It's Janie. I'm so glad you're all right! What happened? How do you feel? John said something about shooting you? Is my brother around? He's not answering his cell phone."

"Janie, he's gone," Sonya burst out.

She heard a deep sigh. "Is he out on an errand? Why isn't he answering his phone? Do you remember what happened?"

"Janie, he made a deal with your damn cousin," Sonya said. "He offered an exchange, him for me, but I didn't realize it until he disappeared in front of me."

Dead silence on the other end. Then, "The police," Janie finally said, her voice thick. "We've got to call the police!"

Sonya took a breath. "You do that. But be careful who you tell. Some of the cops on the force are dirty. I'm going to see what I can do on my end."

"Then who? Who should I tell?"

Sonya shook her head. "I don't know. Maybe your friend."

"Friend? You mean," Janie faltered, "has Johnny mentioned anything about Henry to you?"

This was not the time for tiptoeing around what she knew and what she wasn't supposed to know. "I figured it out. Later."

Sonya hung up. "No," she said aloud.

She swore she would never do it. She swore the day of her father's funeral and swore it again when her mother died. She had lived by it all these years. She wore her mother's ring to remind herself of it.

Well, she wasn't wearing her mother's ring now. In fact, she wasn't wearing anything. That was fitting.

It was time.

Naked, she padded back into her bedroom. She should have known this day would come.

It had to be in the bottom drawer of her dresser, nestled amid her heavy sweaters. It had to be toward the back, next to the lavender sachet. It was in a tiny red silk pouch, hidden in a tiny jeweled box, where she had placed it the night her father died—it had been a birthday gift, appropriately enough. It represented her hopes and her dreams, and it represented the life she would have had, hidden away all these years.

She rummaged until she closed her fingers around the box. Then she opened the box and pulled out the pouch...still bright red silk, unfaded by the years.

The pouch in hand, she turned it upside down to shake its contents out onto her palm. She stared.

Her father's ring. And—

Her own ring. It was heavy and made of gold, wrought with a subtle design. It was a little smaller, a little more petite than her mother's. It should have been hers to wear the day she joined her parents in the family business, on her sixteenth birthday.

The "S" that made up the design of her father's ring stood for "Sounder" and the similar, interlaced "V" in her mother's stood for "Velocity". In her own, the design was a combination of both letters, because as late as the day she would have put it on, she still hadn't picked out her code name. But it didn't matter now.

She slipped it on. It fit comfortably, though the ring had been sized for her twelve years ago. She twisted the ring on her finger and felt under the band. Yep, there it was.

She took a deep breath. She pressed the trigger.

A blur of gold shot out of the ring, with a tiny hiss as the fabric met air for the first time in twelve years. Sonya reached out and grabbed the cloth, shaking it free of the wrinkles.

It had been a long time.

* * * * *

John wished he were dead.

At least then he wouldn't want to rap them over their heads. The Three Stooges had to be smarter than these three.

"If we just kill him, it would be fast," Lon argued. He scratched his head as he pondered the question.

"But the boss wants it to look more like an accident. If we shoot him, it don't look like an accident," Vaughn countered. The wild look in his eye and the white streak in his hair was the result of his own ride with the translocator with Sonya.

The head stooge—the Engineer, better known as Jasper—didn't say anything. He paced, occasionally shooting murderous glances at his cousin John.

He was getting tired of being discussed like a side of beef. "You have me where you want me. Why don't you just get it over with?" John asked pleasantly. Preferably with a bullet through his chest, so the explosion that ensued would take care of everything once and for all, but he chose not to mention that. "You won't get the formula from me, but hey, at least Janie might be nice to you."

"She would anyway. And I can't. That is, I haven't decided what to do with you yet," Jasper amended quickly. "I have to make it look like an accident. I have to make it look like suicide. Yeah, suicide."

"I don't understand why you're going to that much effort. Wouldn't it be more efficient if you just knocked me off?"

"Shut up! If it weren't for you I wouldn't have to do all this!" Jasper screamed. "If it weren't for you I could have everything I want!"

John reared back. His cousin was on a tether wire. It wouldn't take much to set him off. Not that it would matter. John just had to have the right circumstances once the last of the participants arrived. And he knew there would be just the right time.

He just hoped Sonya wouldn't try to find him before then.

The hours after she had disappeared with the translocator surge had been nightmarish. Figuring out what happened had taken time. Then it had taken a few hours more to find out where she could be. He had done his own research into Arlen Industries archives and discovered that Rivers Enterprises, which leased the warehouse from Arlen, also leased other Arlen properties all over town. Not only that, Rivers in turn subleased half those properties to a Jasper Properties. His cousin had dealings all over town.

Then he had discovered something interesting. Arlen Industries owned property near the Pavilion of Peace. The Pavilion was built over the old Wasserman mines. John had guessed that would be where Jasper would be holed up—and sure enough, there was a Rivers Enterprises lease on that piece of Arlen property too. That wasn't something John was going to mention to Sonya.

Introducing Sonika

Good of his uncle and his cousin to keep it all in the family.

But he still had to find them, without wandering around the Pavilion of Peace, waiting to be kidnapped. He had found two of the stooges in the Mission Mercy district—the bars in Mercy, it turned out, were the best dives around. John hadn't even had to persuade them to take him to his cousin. Even before he had the opportunity to offer them money to do so, they had put a blindfold on him.

He had struck his deal with Jasper. It wasn't a logical deal, but then John wasn't dealing with the most logical of individuals. There hadn't been anything to prevent Jasper from keeping them both prisoners, but John had told him the exchange was the gentlemanly thing to do, a family thing to do, considering he had approached him, and it was something Gentleman Geoffrey would have approved of. And that had done it.

Of course, that was a lie. From everything John had read about Geoffrey, the exchange would have driven the master villain crazy.

"Are we waiting for something?" John asked, and not for the first time. "If we are, could you untie me? My wrists are raw."

"Untie him," Jasper ordered. "Maybe then he'll shut up."

Vaughn did as he was told but the knots in the rope gave him some trouble, if the muttered curses were any indication. John said, "Sorry for the trouble. I figured I might as well be comfortable."

"Yeah, yeah," Vaughn muttered, using the tip of his knife to loosen the knot. John could feel the sharp tip skimming the skin of his inner arm. "Don't know why he don't just kill—"

"Shut up! Now look what you've done! You've got him talking like that!" Jasper screamed. He took a chair and threw it across the area, where it clattered against a collection of wooden crates. The noise echoed through the enormous space.

"If you don't shut up right now, I'm going to take you out and I don't care what he—" he stopped. His teeth clenched.

John was careful not to smile. "Who, Jas? Who are you talking about?"

His cousin didn't reply, instead resuming his pacing, the cumbersome exoskeleton he wore slowing him down. Vaughn and Lon glanced at each other. They too, warily watched the doors.

The space was a basic warehouse being used as storage from the looks of it. John had no doubt they were near the Pavilion of Peace. The sense of humor involved in having a hideout so close to where Sounder and Velocity's final confrontation with Geoffrey had taken place was not one he would have ascribed to Jasper, but he could understand it. And then as he thought more about it, he knew his theory was right.

His suspicions virtually confirmed, John fervently hoped Sonya wouldn't be able to find them in time. He wanted her to be able to clean up the mess afterward, not be involved.

The last thing he had seen in her apartment was her, rosy and replete—at least he hoped. But her expression had been one of confusion. He'd disappeared before the fury that he knew would replace it had dawned. He was glad he hadn't been around the few minutes afterward. Had she read his note? Or had she been too angry, electing to simply tear it up?

He closed his eyes. He was too tired to sit up straight—not that he had to worry about it for much longer. He was too tired to wonder how he had ended up in this situation, but not too tired to hope it was all going to be over soon. This soap opera was almost at its end and he was sure he knew how it would finish.

He opened his eyes when he heard footsteps and a distinctive *tap-tap-tap*, a noise he knew—from where, he couldn't remember.

A shadow fell across in the doorway at the other end of the warehouse. He couldn't discern anything other than height. Whoever it was looked tall, with his shadow distorted by the exaggerated lines of what he was carrying.

It had been almost two decades since John had seen him, but he could bet he knew who it was. Back from the dead and all.

His cousin clearly knew who it was. Jasper hurried over and spoke to whoever it was in low tones. Then they left, shutting the doors.

John twisted his mouth. No boss, huh? Of course Jasper had a boss. The same boss he'd always had. The same one who had always done his thinking for him.

"He always get like that?" John asked of Vaughn and Lon.

The two stooges glanced at each other and then stared at the floor. John surmised they had been trained and threatened, thoroughly. "He's old enough to make his own decisions," he offered, keeping an eye on the doors. "If he's going to do his own thing, why take orders from someone else?"

At first, Vaughn and Lon didn't reply and only continued to stare at their feet. With a glance at the doors, Lon ventured, "He got it in his head he don't got the juice to run the operation."

"Who told him that?"

"Who do you think?" Lon whispered, his voice carrying through the enormous space. Then to Vaughn, "I just want to make sure he's wasted so we can get going. It's gotta be soon."

John rubbed his wrists. They were tender and rubbed raw. The tight ropes around his wrists had almost interfered with his plans, which involved his wristwatch. He had to make sure when they tied him up again—and he knew they would—that there was enough give so he could reach for the controls. A direct shot would do it too, but—

The doors opened again. It was Jasper, alone. "I've got a plan," he announced to his stooges. "We're going to drown him in his car. We gotta get his car and cut the brake lines."

John sputtered. "How is that going to look like suicide?" He tried to get up, only to encounter Vaughn's heavy hand pushing him back down. His leg twinged and it wasn't a pleasant sensation.

"Most people know you haven't driven in a while, so people will think you lost control," his cousin informed him. "We have enough people who can testify to that."

Until there was an investigation. "So who have you had watching me, cuz?" John asked, keeping sarcasm to a minimum because he really did want to know. "I figured you had somebody."

Jasper snorted. "I didn't need anybody but the cops already in Dad's pocket. Once I got two or three, and then one to control the others, it went from there."

"Who, Malone?" John said incredulously.

Jasper shrugged, clearly pleased with himself. "You have one cop, it starts there. He tells the patrol cops to keep an eye out every time you stepped out of the house because you might get attacked again. Remember? You got beat to shit because of me?" he said proudly. "So they kept an eye on you because I coulda done it again. And those are the straight cops. I just needed a couple of others to make sure the straight cops do their job."

"You son of a bitch!" Angry now, John struggled as first Vaughn and then Lon worked to bind him again. "You killed my father and tried to cripple me! And Malone was in on it? You made sure even the *honest* cops kept an eye on me? Is that how you knew when to get into the house?"

Jasper rolled his eyes. "I thought you already knew, Johnny-boy. You mean you didn't?"

"What about Sonya's apartment? Did you make sure someone went in when she wasn't there to drop off those notes? Was that it?"

His cousin waved that off. "Don't blame me for that one. Your girlfriend has her own problems. All I did—"

A new voice cut in. "All you did was what?"

Sonya. John saw her silhouette in the doorway.

She entered and John tried not to let his eyes bulge. She was dressed in gold spandex, head to toe, in a skintight outfit. She was made for that outfit and it was clear that outfit had been made for her. It fit her every step, every bounce. With a pang, he knew that was the outfit she would have worn when Sounder and Velocity introduced her to the world. A matching gold belt fit around her hips and matching gold boots gave her height. *Yowza.*

Doomed or not, he appreciated just looking at her.

"Who the hell are you?" Jasper snarled.

"Sonika," she replied, without hesitation. "But it doesn't matter. What matters is that you're going to turn yourself in."

"Why the hell would I do that?"

"Because you're guilty of kidnapping, industrial espionage, grand theft auto, murder in the first degree—"

"Prove it," he sneered.

"You killed my father, you idiot," John reminded him. "And the cops want you for questioning in the death of that bookkeeper your father kept."

"If I kill you, who's going to say?"

"My sister. Remember, Jas?"

"You are wanted for so many crimes I don't have the time to tell you what they are. Are you coming quietly or not?"

"The hell with both of you!" Jasper screamed. He pointed his pistol—with all the technology at his disposal, a simple .38—at her and fired point-blank.

John shouted. Vaughn and Lon ducked for cover. Sonya—Sonika—raised a hand. Again, translucent film materialized and surrounded the bullets, and this time it formed into a bowl-like shield. The bullets slammed into the shield and careened off its surface. They hit the top part of the shield and bounced again and again, until they clattered into the translucent well, spent, just as the shield misted away.

The bullets clattered onto the ground. "Give up now before you regret it, Engineer," she rasped. "It won't be much of a battle even if you resist."

"Oh yeah?" Jasper screamed. "Oh yeah? I'll tell you what kind of a battle it's going to be!"

He fired again. The bullets veered off harmlessly, again and again, each volley meeting a quick end until the gun was empty. At one point the translucent substance covered him, only to dissipate after a few seconds, but enough to make Jasper scream in frustration. John held his breath. If Jasper had any more ammunition, it was going to take a minute for him to reload.

Jasper threw the gun at her. "Damn you bitch, I'm going to kill you! I can't kill him, but by God I can kill you!" She deflected the gun without blinking and she stopped in front of him. Jasper tensed. John wished he hadn't been tied up again because he didn't want to be in the way when his psychopath of a cousin and Sonya—Sonika—got serious in this showdown.

With a bloodcurdling scream John remembered from when his father died, Jasper ran and attacked her. She tripped him, slapping him across the head for good luck. He fell but he got up, kicking at her and missing again. John could tell he was getting frustrated and he was becoming impatient. That would be his downfall, one that a fancy exoskeleton couldn't prevent.

Jasper lashed out. Sonika grabbed his leg and shoved it away. He screamed as he fell to the ground, curling up into a fetal position. "Sorry," she said as his cries subsided. "I guess I was a little rough. So," she said, turning to John Arlen, "are you all right?"

"Can you untie me?" John asked. "I don't think you realize what's going on here."

She frowned. John hadn't realized until just then how desirable her lips were until that was about all he could see of her face; they were full and lush and red and… "Untie me," he said desperately. "I've got to tell you what's going on before anything else happens."

She shrugged. "What else could happen? Those two punks?" She gestured toward Lon and Vaughn, now scuttling toward their fallen leader. "They're not going to be much trouble."

"It's not them I'm thinking of. Please," he beseeched.

He could hear that tapping again. A feeling of doom twisting his stomach, he knew what it was now. He started to pull at his bindings.

She pulled at the knots, still unconcerned. "They're going to be fine for the next couple of minutes."

"It's not that. Hurry."

"What's wrong?"

He glanced at the two goons, who were still dealing with the whimpering Jasper. "Did you read my note?"

She looked at him and he knew he still had a lot to explain by the way her expression changed. "No, I didn't," she answered, finishing untying him. "I figured everything you needed to tell me, you told me."

"You should have read the note. Son-Sonika," he stammered, glancing at the doorway, "Jasper's not the mastermind behind all this. Not behind the planned crime wave, not behind trying to kill me, not even behind the notes at your apartment."

"How does that not come as a surprise to me? So what are you telling me? He's a puppet?"

"Worse," he said, grabbing her by the hand and pulling her toward the doorway. "We're not ready for his boss. We've been assuming Jasper's behind it all and we were all wrong."

She wasn't having any of it, standing her ground. "Then who is?"

"You're not ready for it," he said, giving up. That distinctive *tap-tap-tap* was getting louder. "We have to get out of here. We have to figure out what to do."

"You still haven't told me why."

"You just wait!" Jasper screamed. "You just wait. You're going to get your asses handed to you!"

"Is this before or after you get out of your cast?" she asked.

"You just wait!"

"Yeah, well, we'll be waiting for a while," Sonika said. John yanked at her sleeve again feeling like a child, but in this case, a child with a bad premonition.

"What you don't know's going to kill you," Jasper screeched.

"Oh yeah? What?"

The tapping stopped. Too late.

A shadow obliterated the light streaming in from the doorway with a tap. John turned his head, knowing he would regret it.

"It's not what, it's whom. And I am," said Gentleman Geoffrey.

Chapter Nineteen

༄

Sonika stared at the man in the brightly lit doorway. She gaped. "You. You're dead."

Gentleman Geoffrey strolled in. In the dim light, he looked the way he had twelve years ago, except his hair had turned white in the intervening years. He still dressed in the formal dress that had given him his moniker—the gray morning coat and tails with that distinctive top hat and sword cane that killed as easily as it tapped, the monocle covering one eye. It was the figure who had haunted her nightmares for years, the figure who she had, she realized now, searched for unconsciously over the years when she had felt frightened or uncertain.

What would she have done if she had recognized the source of that unease? She never found out. Until now.

Her first reaction was to tear him apart. Her second was to run. She did neither. She stood and stared at him.

"You died when Sounder and Velocity cornered you here, in the Wasserman mines," she said, willing her voice not to tremble. The rasp of her voice masked her uncertainty a little. Not enough.

"On the contrary. Sounder died, did he not? How tragic that must have been for you," the man purred.

He knew. Gentleman Geoffrey knew who she was. He had to have been the one who had left those notes for her, not the Engineer.

"You fell down a shaft five hundred feet deep, along with half the mine. The rocks alone should have killed you when they fell on you, let alone when you hit them down below. They built an entire complex over you. How did you survive?"

Now that he was closer, she could see he hadn't gotten away scot-free. He had incurred injuries, probably in the mine crash, that had twisted him, leaving him with livid scars snaking down half his face from forehead to jaw. Then he grinned and she had to stop herself from recoiling. "With a few scars here and there, but otherwise not bad," he mocked. "I was sorry to hear about your mother too. I thought about sending flowers but I thought that would be insensitive. You were so young."

Don't let him get to you. "Old enough to know I could get over it," she said. *Don't* –

"Of course you were. Personally I would have been hurt if my son hadn't wanted to take after me, but I'm sure you had your reasons for not taking up the cape until now."

She worked on deep breathing. "If I had known you were alive, I would have hunted you down to the ends of the Earth and beyond."

"How dramatic. But you must not have cared that much about your parents because you didn't bother to check, did you?"

"No!" John shouted as she lunged at the man. "Don't do it! That's what he wants you to do!" He pulled her back. She strained to break loose but relaxed when she felt John's grip falter. The last thing she wanted to do was to hurt John.

"Now look at what you've done," the older man went on as though she hadn't just been restrained from attacking him. "And what did you do to my son?"

"Dad, she broke my leg!" Jasper wailed from where he was curled up, surrounded by Lon and Vaughn. "Make her hurt!"

"Shut up," the man said, his voice flattening. "If you hadn't assumed you could get your way by kicking your targets into submission with that idiotic exoskeleton, you wouldn't be sitting there sniveling now."

"It worked until her!"

"It worked until you had competition. Excuse me," he said, turning his attention back to Sonika. "You've upset him because no one else has known enough self-defense to fight back."

"Including an elderly man who never hurt anyone in his life," John reminded him venomously. "Did that make you feel good, Jas? My seventy-eight-year-old father, who couldn't even stand up without a cane, tells you no, so you beat him into a pulp and watch as he dies from internal injuries. What a big man, cuz."

"Shut up!" Jasper screamed. "Shut up! He asked for it!"

"Doing what, saying no to you?"

Sonika shook her head. "I should have broken both your legs, you little pissant."

Geoffrey slapped the crate he was leaning against. "That's enough! I will not have you speak to my son that way! He may be weak and useless but that's for me to say, not you!"

"No, that's for a court of law to say. But the court's going to say he's guilty of first-degree murder. As for you—"

"You don't believe you're going to take me in, do you?" the older man sneered. "Better superheroes than you—more experienced, more dedicated superheroes—have died trying. Don't be foolish. I'm willing to make you a deal. I'll let you live, despite what you've done to my son, and I'll even let my nephew go with you without giving me the formula."

"That's not your call, Dad!" Jasper sobbed. "I want that house! I want control of Arlen Industries! It should all be mine!"

"Shut up," his father told him. "Let it go. You've lost."

"All I need is one more chance! Break her leg! See how she'd fight me then!"

"Shut him up or I'll shut you both up permanently," the older man said to Lon and Vaughn. The two stooges scuttled closer to Jasper, pawing at his shoulder. He whimpered but quieted.

"Perhaps my son is right," the older man said. "Perhaps he deserves another chance."

Sonika snorted. "If you give him nothing but do-overs, he'll expect it all his life—and I guess he does. You never let him grow up. You should have tossed him out into the world to let him make something of himself."

"I did! Do you know how long it took for me to crawl out of the mines? They were building that idiotic Pavilion of Peace on top of me when I finally made it out. What do you think he was doing?"

"He was doing five to ten and he would have been out in four for good behavior," John snarled. "Grand theft auto. A chip off the old block. He escaped during a riot."

The older man turned sharply on his heel. "Was that the best you could do? A *car*? You couldn't even stick up a bank?"

"You weren't around! You don't know!"

"I left you everything! Did you bother to check how many millions I left you and you get caught for stealing a damn car? What was it, a Yugo?"

"It was a classic Mustang. And I wanted it!"

"You could have bought one, you fool!"

"I shouldn't hafta buy one! Besides, I couldn't afford it."

Geoffrey glared at his son. "What happened to everything I left you? I left you—" He glanced at John and Sonika. "I left you enough to keep you comfortable for the rest of your life. What were you doing while I was working my way out to the surface?"

Jasper scowled. "The bookkeeper ripped me off," he snarled. "I told her to keep it safe and she ripped me off!"

"Mishandling of funds, wasn't it?" John asked ruthlessly. "She was just incompetent. And when you found out what happened, you just knocked her off, didn't you?"

Jasper stared at him. "How did you find that out?"

"The police came and told us when they were looking for you. I can't tell you how pleased I was to hear you'd been busy."

"You didn't mention that, you fool," the older man snarled. Sonika watched as his hand clenched around his cane. "Is that what happened to her? She was loyal! She would do anything for us!"

"She stole from me, Dad! People have to learn they can't steal from me!"

"He's going to start crying for you to change his diaper soon," John said.

Sonika turned to him. "Have I mentioned you have a very strange family?"

"Is this the first time that's occurred to you?"

"Enough. Get up off the floor," the older man ordered. "After that leg heals you're going back to training without that stupid exoskeleton. Fool," he muttered.

"You're not going anywhere. You're both giving yourselves up," Sonika said.

Gentleman Geoffrey laughed. "Who's going to make us, you? Young lady, the uniform notwithstanding—and you do look fetching in it—you're not going to stop me or my son. The best you can hope is that I don't kill you."

"I can do it, Dad!" Jasper yelled. "Let me!"

"Shut up. She broke your leg, remember?"

"She tricked me!"

"I also kicked your ass in the park."

Geoffrey looked hard at his son. "You didn't tell me about that."

Jasper sulked. "She tricked me."

"Look Uncle Geoffrey, you're not going to get far with Jasper," John began.

"His assistants can carry him. Young lady, don't antagonize me. I'm not my son. I can and will kill you in a second and not foul up the attempt."

"You killed my father. My mother died because of you. You killed John's father. If nothing else, I'm not going to let you go because of that."

"Then stop me if you can little girl," Geoffrey taunted. He turned back to his son and his minions. "Carry him. We're getting out of here."

"Care for a wager?"

Her voice echoed in the hall. John held his breath. He watched as Gentleman Geoffrey's own trademark phrase made him stop and turn. Behind him, Lon and Vaughn stopped mid-lift as they hoisted Jasper up on their shoulders.

Geoffrey's smile glinted in the dim light. "What a memory you have, my dear."

"Don't you think I pored over all the information I could find about you? You ruined my life. You killed my father and destroyed my mother. And I'm not going to let you walk away."

"You want to challenge me? My dear, I'm not a young man anymore. And you," he paused, running his gaze over her leisurely, making her skin crawl. "You are in the spit of youth. My successor—my son—you've already taken out of commission."

"You can still take me on. You may not be a spring chicken anymore but you still have the chops. More than your son."

He snorted delicately. "That's not difficult, as I have found."

"Maybe more than me."

He stopped eyeing her body and instead fixed his gaze on her face. "It would only be fair if you were to give yourself a handicap."

She eyed him. "What did you have in mind?"

John muttered, "No. Don't."

"My little helmet. You *do* recall it, don't you?"

She stopped breathing for a second. John could see it. "The white-out thing."

"I call it the senses-diminisher, but you get the idea. I can adjust it so you can see but you can't hear. I think that would be fair, considering I'm an old man past my prime and from what I've been able to gather, you manipulate sound."

She stared at him. "The environment has to be controlled. Like that padded room you put me in."

"Done. If you win, I'll turn myself in and my son will too."

"Dad!" Jasper yelled. "You can't make my decisions for me!"

"Why should he stop now?" John snarled, unable to stop himself.

"If you win," Sonya said, "you walk away."

"Done."

"I want John to observe. You've got an observation post, don't you? You probably had a grand old time watching me when you had me in there with that helmet, didn't you?" Sonya snarled. John could hear the venom in her voice.

"You're taking this personally," Geoffrey chided. "And I have no objection to my nephew being the observer. I trust you'll be impartial, John?"

"If you mean I'm not going to take an axe and hit you with it, yeah I'll be impartial. Otherwise? Remember she got involved in all this because of me. You hurt her and I will make sure you regret it."

"I couldn't possibly forget that. And I'll remember it," Geoffrey said, his tone not quite so gentlemanly. "Shall we?"

John glanced at her as they stood in front of the chamber. "Are you going to be all right?" Lon and Vaughn followed them, carrying Jasper between them, looking uncertain.

She glanced at the glassed-in observation window. "I'll be okay John. Just don't let them get away. And I *will* win."

"I know you will."

She smiled tightly. "Thanks for the vote of confidence."

"You could get hurt."

He didn't have to tell her she could be killed. She knew it as well as he did. Knew it better, in fact.

Sonya—Sonika—squeezed his hand. "I need you to do something for me." She grasped his hand with both of hers and kissed it, looking into his eyes.

His stomach sank. By now he knew that tone of her voice and he didn't like it. "Sone—"

"Listen." Her insistence was going to break his heart. "Nothing's going to happen to me."

"Damn right it's not."

"But you have to do something for me."

"What?" He looked at her warily. He didn't like requests before confrontations. Even confrontations that shouldn't be a problem.

"Unlike you, I don't have much of anything to leave anyone but I want you to have my ring," she said. She started to work at the one on her hand. John noticed it was smaller than the one he had first noticed. "And I want you to give a message to someone in Hamilton. Her name is in my desk at home, in the left-hand drawer, on a yellow slip of paper."

"I don't want to hear this," John interrupted. "I don't have to hear it. Because you're going to come out of there." He pushed the ring back into her palm.

"Are you ready, my dear?"

They turned around. The heavy steel door of the chamber was open. Geoffrey gestured inside. "My nephew will be the impartial observer. My son and his assistants will wait here. If I walk out, we will be on our way. If you walk out, I'll let you live."

"That wasn't the deal," she broke in. John realized she was getting aggressive. He placed a hand on her shoulder. She was tense and he could sense a frisson of energy in her. Fight or flight, he realized. In her case, it was going to be fight. "The deal was you surrender to the police."

Geoffrey smiled. "Of course. Shall we?"

She turned and glanced at John. He met her gaze but he didn't touch her. She knew.

"We'll talk later," he said.

The heavy door slammed shut behind Geoffrey and Sonika. From a speaker above the door, John heard his uncle's voice from inside. "Turn the wheel on the door and don't turn it again until one of us is down. But you must open it when one of us is."

"I hear you," John said. He climbed into the observation booth. The window gave him a view of the chamber. In this position he could see the room was padded in a white substance that looked as though it might have been wet, it was so shiny. The chamber had indirect lighting. If Sonya had tried to explore the ceiling, she would have felt the recessed light fixtures. Other than that, there was nothing except the helmet on the floor.

It was designed to block sight, that much was clear, and from the detail that John could see on its side, hearing as well. It might have been designed for Sonya. Perhaps it was.

He turned his attention to Geoffrey and Sonya, now in the small room. He watched and heard as Geoffrey instructed Sonya how to adjust the amount of sight and hearing the helmet would allow. There were toggles along the edge, John noticed. Those were what Sonya was experimenting with before the older man moved a toggle slightly and Sonya slipped it on.

Her movements changed the second the helmet clicked into place. Previously she had been bold and confident, able to vanquish criminals with ease, but now she was lost and stumbling.

"Can you hear me?" John heard Gentleman Geoffrey say. "Sonya, can you hear me?"

No answer. John winced as she walked into the wall, her arms in front of her. "She must have the sight controls up too high," he heard Geoffrey say. Geoffrey reached out, tapped Sonya on the shoulder and grabbed her arm when she lashed out. He kept hold of her arm — and backhanded her.

"Hey!" John shouted. He watched in horror as Geoffrey's blow sent her careening against the wall. John began to pound on the window, only to realize the thickness of the glass guaranteed there was no way any noise could filter into the chamber.

He stumbled out of the observation booth and to the door leading to the chamber. He started to pull at the controls to open it. No dice. He started to hammer at the door even though he knew there was no way that would help.

"Are you trying to open the door by now, John?" he heard over the speakers. "Shame on you. I thought we agreed you wouldn't open the door until one of us was on the floor."

"Damn you, you tricked her!" he shouted. The door itself was too thick. There wasn't any way he could prise it open in time and it wouldn't give.

As if he knew, Geoffrey grinned. He backhanded Sonya once more. She reeled and hit the floor again. "Did I mention I could open the door from inside? And I could make sure it couldn't be opened from the outside? But that didn't seem relevant to mention at the time," John heard over the speakers. "I'm all for a fair wager but my son needs a little headstart." Geoffrey hit her again. Too late John realized Geoffrey had his sword cane. Sonya wouldn't have a chance if he decided to use it.

Sonya stumbled to her feet but she was learning. She crouched low to avoid any forthcoming blows.

"The new deal's this," John heard over the speakers. Gripped with rage, he watched as his uncle took another swipe at Sonya but missed. She must have felt the breeze as it approached. She rolled away, edged backward until she bumped into the wall, where she crouched. She moved her head from side to side, discerning whatever she could with her limited senses.

"She's a bright little thing, isn't she? She's already figured out the new rules. As I was saying, the new deal's this—you know I can kill her sooner or later in here. Unless you let me walk out of here with my son and his stooges, I will. That's the new deal, John. Take it or leave it." Geoffrey took another swipe at her. This time the blow glanced off her head. She hit the back of her head against the wall, sending her to her knees.

"My dad means it, you know," John heard Jasper say behind him. "I told you that you shouldn't mess with me."

"Shut up you moron," John snarled, glued to the scene in the chamber. "You're a worthless leech. You can't even be bothered to think on your own. You're a lousy year younger than I am and you haven't managed to grow up. Your father's still alive and he doesn't even *like* you, but he'll protect you. Do you know what I would give to have my father in front of me?"

"Then you should have given me what I wanted in the first place!"

That was it. Enraged, John shoved Lon and Vaughn aside and grabbed Jasper by the throat. "Tell me how to open the chamber door or I'm going to finish the job on you," he said, teeth gritted and not letting go as Lon and Vaughn tried to pull him off. "Tell me now."

"What are you going to do if I don't? Lon and Vaughn can make mincemeat out of you!"

John shoved his cousin to the ground and wresting loose from the two big thugs, stepped back. He ripped open his jacket. "I can make mincemeat out of everyone, including that chamber door, if you don't do it. Get it now?"

Jasper gaped at him. Drool dribbled out of the side of his mouth. "You wouldn't do it."

"Oh yes I will. I came here to do it, to make sure you couldn't hurt anyone again. If you don't give me what I want, I'll do it."

John's chest was covered with an elaborate electronic system, complete with an LED readout that read 0:15 and a small, condensed square box marked C4.

"You're bluffing," Jasper whispered.

"I'm not, cuz. It's an explosive device and I'll blow you, me and everything around me sky-high. Now what do you say? Are you going to open that door or not?"

"If you detonate that thing, everything's going, including you!"

John rolled his eyes. "I know that. I've also indicated I don't care. Now do it."

For once, Jasper seemed to be on the ball. He scuttled to the door and started to punch at what seemed like random markings across the surface. The door seemed to give a little and the handle shifted. "There," he said, scuttling back and dragged back more by Lon and Vaughn. "Now get away from me."

Meanwhile, John saw Sonya was doing her best to adapt. When Geoffrey hit her again she grabbed his arm and twisted it, shoving him away from her—but keeping hold of him. Then she gave as good as she got and slugged him in the stomach, seeming to assess with fair accuracy where his face was and slammed her hand into his nose.

"Pleasure doing business with you," John said. He grabbed the handle but it wouldn't move.

He turned. "What the hell did you do?" he shouted at his cousin.

Jasper gaped. "I did what Dad told me to do to open it," he gasped. "It's true!" he screamed, hiding his face behind his hands as John lunged at him. "That's what he told me to do if the handle stuck from inside!"

"Jasper you idiot, what did you do?" screamed Geoffrey from inside the chamber. John stared as both Geoffrey and Sonya fell to their knees, their hands at their throats. "Did you forget? If you try to open the door without my unlocking it from the inside, the ventilation system automatically starts to drain the air from within the chamber!"

Jasper whimpered. "I forgot, Dad! Don't be mad! Johnny threatened me!"

"He can't hear you, remember? There must be some way to open it," John shouted. He started to first touch, then press the marked rivets he had seen Jasper push. There had to be another way, another pattern, Geoffrey wouldn't have told his son about.

"There isn't! He woulda told me!"

That clinched it. There had to be another way. But he didn't have the time, not anymore.

John ripped the wires connecting to the explosive from his body and shrugged out of the jacket. Gloria was going to be useful somehow, just not in the way he thought it would be. Inside the chamber, Geoffrey started hammering at the window, while Sonya was behind him, struggling with the helmet. *Helmet,* John mouthed through the window at Geoffrey, pointing. *Get it off.*

Geoffrey looked at Sonya and shook his head.

Do it, John mouthed. What did he think he was doing? The only one of the two of them who could do anything from inside was Sonya, and he wasn't going to get that thing off her?

Do it, John mouthed again. He jammed the wires he had just stripped off of himself into any crevices he could find in the doorway of the vault, though he knew it was airtight. Finally, he managed to line the wires into the indentation of the doorjamb, and stuck the explosive materials where he could.

Out of the corner of his eye, he saw movement in the chamber. Geoffrey had taken the helmet off Sonya's head. She looked out the window and she saw John. They locked gazes. She spread her hand on the glass and he did the same.

Hang on, he mouthed. *Hang on, and come back to me.*

She smiled. They could all die, the situation was dire, and she could smile?

He smiled back. And as if by mutual agreement, they both turned back to what they had to do.

Once the helmet was off, she had to control the impulse to smear Geoffrey into a pulp when she realized what was happening. She felt her heart start to work harder for oxygen and she knew there would come a point when she wouldn't be able to think anymore.

"Outsmarted yourself, didn't you Geoffrey?" she said, panting, as she assessed the situation. The vent sucking the air out of the chamber was too small for them to get out through. The observation window was most likely unbreakable without the proper tools, and she guessed John was doing what he could with the door.

"Regretting you told your son anything about the door now?" she continued, barely glancing at her nemesis and breathing as shallowly as possible. "Proud of him? For being the world's stupidest human being."

"He's not stupid!" Geoffrey screamed, and gasped. "Treat him with the respect he deserves, or by God I will make you sorry!" He choked and started to cough.

She rolled her eyes. "I'm sorry already. I'm stuck in here with you, aren't I? And you're threatening me for telling the truth instead of trying to get out of here." She looked up again at the vent, considering. There wasn't a choice. There had to be something she could do with the vent. It had a shallow lip with visible rivets, so she could try…

She jumped and tried to hit the vent. She missed. On the third try, she managed to grab onto it and she hung there, scrambling as she tried to figure out how to open the vent. She needed something to act like a screwdiver. What did she have?

"What are you doing?" she heard Geoffrey shout. She looked over. Geoffrey was at the window, hammering. For someone who designed the chamber configuration, he seemed to forget pounding at the glass was pointless. Not only that, he was wasting oxygen. "They're going to try to blow up the door! That moron son of mine is letting him blow it up! We will be pulverized if the explosive breaks it into pieces, don't they understand that? They—"

Sonika cut in, still working at the vent. "Do you want to live or not?" She was starting to gasp and she knew the air was draining quicker than she figured. "We'll suffocate if they don't or if I can't figure out how to work this vent! I need your sword cane," she decided, looking at the vent. "Give it to me."

"Not my cane!"

She went back to work, shaking her head as she used her fingers. The rivets were stiff, but she could work at them. *Pring!* The first rivet popped off. "Yes!" she exulted.

"What are you doing?" Geoffrey screamed, pounding at the window. "No! That's going to be destroy everything!"

Pring! The second rivet popped off. She grinned. She pried at the third corner and tried to measure her breaths, knowing she didn't have much time left for clarity. She watched as the third rivet popped off. Just a little more. "I need your sword cane now," she said aloud. She was feeling a little dazed but she didn't have far to go. "Hey Geoff!"

No answer. Suspicious, she looked over and yelled, "What are you doing?"

"I'm trying to get them away from the door!" Geoffrey screamed. He shoved his sword into the crack between the door and the jamb. "They're going to ruin my plans unless they get away!"

"Get away from that door!" she shouted. "If they're setting up an explosive on the other side, you have to stay away from there!"

"I'm not going to let them do it!"

She groaned and yanked at the last rivet on the corner. The cover dropped free, so she loosened her grip and flipped down to the floor. "Get away from the door! If they're setting the charge, you're not going to—"

There was a muffled burst of sound and then a loud creaking as the vault door started to quake. "Get away from there!" she shouted as she opened her arms and cleared her mind.

Sharp, jagged slivers of green mist appeared and solidified around the edges of the vault door, not shaped like much of anything—she couldn't think clearly enough for that. Geoffrey was yanking at his sword cane, which now seemed to be stuck. "The idiots!" he screamed. "I want my cane!"

"Get away!" Sonya yelled back.

Desperately, she yanked at the edges of the sonifer, trying to use it to stave off what was going to happen to the door very soon. But there wasn't enough sound for her to do more. *"Get away! Now!"*

They both saw the door start to move at the same time.

"No!" Gentleman Geoffrey yelled. "What have you done?"

She succeeded in stretching the sonifer so it acted like a diaphanous blanket—a skimpy one, but better than nothing. "Geoffrey! Get over here! Now!"

"No!"

In desperation, she worked the ring off her finger and threw it as hard as she could at the vault door. The ring hit the metal and the tiny little *ping!* seemed to reverberate through the chamber. She reached out and grabbed the sound and spread it as fast as she could. But the noise wasn't going to be enough, she realized in horror. "Geoffrey!"

Almost in slow motion, the door shuddered and creaked. She watched in horror as the door rocked, first slowly, then faster and faster. "Geoffrey!" she screamed, one last time.

He was still trying to retrieve his sword cane from the gigantic vault door when it finally broke off its hinges and flattened him.

The room itself was losing structural integrity with the vault door broken off its hinges. She glanced up at the ceiling as large cracks appeared, within seconds splitting apart chunks of the material and falling to the ground. She pulled the sonifer she had managed to create over her head and braced herself.

Huddled beneath her temporary shelter, she prayed the self-destruction of the room wouldn't last longer than the sonifer would. She could feel the floor under her buckling as the wall around the vault door crumbled, the observation window shattered and the world around her fell to pieces.

Chapter Twenty

How much was there to say?

Sonya left the courthouse after the trial. She paused at the bottom of the steps and closed her eyes, feeling the surprising warmth of the sunny spring day on her face.

It was over. She opened her eyes and looked around at the passersby and knew she would never have to wonder who it was she was looking for, not anymore. Nor did she have to hide herself from anyone because it was finally over.

Geoffrey was truly dead and his son was behind bars. Her parents could rest in peace at long last.

Not only that, Sonya's career as a physical therapist was over. With the hustle and bustle of the past few weeks, avoiding the press attention surrounding the Arlens and only managing to catch a glimpse of John and Janie from a distance, she had forgotten about her paycheck until it arrived in the mail. Along with it was a nice fat bonus check from the offices of Arlen Industries, with the subject line marked as "For services rendered." And along with that was a pink slip, since she hadn't bothered to show up at the clinic in the past few weeks when she should have reported in. Which was fine. She should have remembered to call in, but it had slipped her mind. She'd been preoccupied.

Which services was the bonus check for? Protecting John Arlen from a killer? Or the physical therapy she kept trying to get him back to? It didn't say and she wasn't going to break through the media frenzy to ask.

That check enabled her to pay off the remainder of her aunt's hospital bills. She didn't have to be a physical therapist anymore, but she liked the work. She also knew she could help people in other ways. If she wanted, she could probably get her job back with some wheedling. But did she want to?

For the first time in a long while, she didn't have any outstanding bills to worry about. She had the rest of her life to look forward to. What was she going to do with it?

She fingered her ring. Her uniform was safely back inside it. Would she ever put it back on?

Most of all, what was she going to do with John Arlen? She hadn't spoken to him since then.

They hadn't had an opportunity to talk after Geoffrey's plan had blown up in his face—so to speak. The explosive, she had learned later, brought down part of the storage space, alerting the police. Janie had called Henry, her cop friend, who had rallied the forces. In the ensuing melee, Sonya had changed clothes. All the police had found were two hostages instead of one, a crushed, dead supervillain, a escaped convict and criminal wanted by the police whining his head off about his exoskeleton being in ruins and two large hoodlums huddled nearby.

In talking to the police and getting John checked out at the hospital, Sonya had lost sight of him. Later, she had found out Janie took him home, where he was now, presumably avoiding the media until the press got bored and found another target.

Sonya was lucky. She had slipped away after being examined and since she had managed to dress in street wear before the police arrived, Sonika might never have existed at all.

She didn't know whether that was good either.

She parked and decided to take a walk through her neighborhood. Business was brisk, she was pleased to see. The Greek diner was packed with customers and the surly chef waved through the window as he harangued another pair of customers. Next door the deli guy gave her a thumbs-up as he sliced and packaged meat, safe from early-morning intruders.

Down the street, Mrs. Polokoff was handing off the store to her son as Sonya passed by. Sonya waved and Mrs. Polokoff waved back, her sawed-off shotgun in hand. With the defeat of the Engineer and the final—and actual, this time—death of Gentleman Geoffrey, maybe the little old couple wouldn't need the heavy-duty weaponry anymore. There would be no Gentleman Geoffrey crime wave revisited, not with his son Jasper in jail for a very long time.

The tiny park was filled with children and parents. Mrs. Mensch sat on the bench, watching her grandchildren. Sonya waved.

Rover came running when Sonya entered her apartment. The cat mewed and rubbed, purring demandingly. Sonya reached down and stroked her little nose. "Nobody's going to be coming in and scaring you anymore," she told the cat. "Just me."

No John Arlen, no Janie Arlen—who in the courtroom looked happy with Henry, her boy-toy boyfriend once again—to disrupt the cat's routine. It was just Rover and Sonya again, which would make the cat happy. But Sonya?

It would be nice to have some peace and quiet back.

She looked around. No, it wasn't.

Her apartment, once her cozy hideaway, now looked forlorn. Maybe she could put up some photos on the wall of her mother and father. The blankets Janie used had been put away, and Sonya knew without looking that her bedroom was straightened and her bathroom back to rights.

But no more bubble baths. She wasn't up to bubble baths yet.

Sonya sat down at her desk and stared at the bills there. Most of them she had gleefully stamped "PAID" on. The last one, the one she had just made out a check for and sealed, she held in her hand. It was the hospital bill.

An entire lifetime was based on that check. For want of payment, she had turned away from the destiny her parents had molded her for. If she had been able to afford it, would she have become Sonika to follow in her parents' footsteps back then?

She didn't know. All she knew was she had come full circle. Don the uniform or not? Did she like being a superhero? She hadn't done much as one. She'd beaten up an older man who'd died of his own vanity, she'd beaten up his son who hadn't been much of anything and she'd managed to pound a pair of thugs. She'd fallen in love—but that wasn't part of the superhero training.

She needed more training. Would she get more?

Well, she'd paid off her last bill. With the possible exception of Rover—who probably preferred Mrs. Mensch to her by now anyway—she had no more ties to worry about. No children, no husband, no parents.

But John Arlen kept popping into her thoughts.

Sonya knew why. She looked at the final hospital bill, stamped and addressed, in her hand. "I'm going out for a while," she said aloud. She petted Rover and grabbed her keys.

What was she going to say? Once she was in the SUV, she turned on the radio, not switching away from the news channel the way she had for so many years. "So Ron, Gentleman Geoffrey's finally gone," she heard as soon as the static cleared.

"That's right, Mike. Sounder and Velocity can rest in peace, knowing the master criminal who killed them finally died a few weeks ago and not twelve years ago, as was originally thought. Amazing about that son of his too."

"Like father, like son, Ron. His son, who was known as the Engineer, was sentenced to prison for two consecutive life terms this morning for the murders of Arlen Industries chairman Jonathan Arlen and bookkeeper Lydia Plumm. Dr. Jonathan Arlen was his uncle and Lydia Plumm kept his books."

"I think we've all thought about doing that to whoever does our taxes Mike," she heard. "Not only that, the Engineer was heard referring to someone named Sonika and her role in his capture. Is there a new superhero in town?"

"We won't know until we see it for ourselves, Ron. Let's hope so. I think we'll all keep an eye out for her."

Before she did anything else, she had to pay her respects. The gates leading to the cemetery were open. In the distance she could see mourners, their loss fresher than hers. Nearby she could see families paying their respects to a loss some time ago, laying bouquets of flowers on headstones.

Sonya followed the winding paths, which reminded her of the gardens at Arlen Manor. The cemetery had statues too.

She hadn't had the nerve to call him. Some superhero.

Sitting on a bench near her parents' gravesites, she surveyed the scene. The statues were just that, nothing more. And the white roses that clustered around the bench, again like the gardens around Arlen Manor, were starting to bloom.

"You can rest finally, Mom, Dad," she whispered. Her eyes misted, but just for a second this time. "Justice has finally been served."

She could stop hiding. She knew now that for the past twelve years she'd been hiding from anything that was a remnant of her former life. She had cut herself off from everything she could have been—and could be. No more.

"You know, I left the window in my lab open, just in case you wanted to drop by," she heard.

She turned.

His hair was standing up straight again and his glasses were askew, dots of moisture speckled on the lenses. He was breathing hard but he stood straight. In his hand was his father's cane but he didn't seem to be leaning on it as heavily as he used to.

"Someday, someone's going to come through it that you don't expect," she said, smiling wryly.

"In that case, should I leave the basement door open?"

"Only if you need some cross-ventilation," she answered. She stood, looking up at him.

His T-shirt was rumpled and stained, as if he had had it on far too long. He could never be accused of being overly formal.

It was time to start over.

"Hi, I'm Sonya Penn, your physical therapist," she started out, unsure of what to say. "You're John Arlen, right?"

To her surprise, he shook his head. "Nope, that's not the way it went."

She wasn't sure whether to glare or grin. "Okay hotshot, how did it go?"

"You said, 'Are you Mr. John Arlen?' I remember that clearly because of the 'Mr.' part. I was surprised at that. I thought it was clear I was a 'Mr.' without it being a question."

She chewed her lip. "Okay. Then what did you say?"

"I said yes. Is any of this coming back to you?"

"Not as clearly as you're remembering it. Go on."

"Then I asked who you were, because I had no idea who you were or why you were here, considering the gates weren't open."

"And I introduced myself?"

"That's right. And then you said, 'You know, you're mighty cute. May I invite you out for breakfast?'"

She smiled. "Are you sure you don't have me confused with someone else?"

"I don't think so." He stepped forward and kissed her, and she remembered why her current life had certain advantages.

"I don't remember this part but I like it," she said when she could breathe again. "But my memory's sort of foggy. Can you show me again?"

He obliged. "I suppose we should talk now," he said after he took an oxygen break. "Did— Is the trial over?"

Not sure of her voice, she nodded.

"So Jasper's away for life."

"And your father's death is avenged."

"Yes. Thank you," he said.

Sonya shook her head. "I did it for me as much as for you," she said. "And my parents can rest in peace, knowing they didn't die in vain."

"We can both live again."

"We can go on with our lives. And I wanted to thank you too," she said. She had found something in her car on the way over that she had forgotten about.

Clearly John had forgotten about the gift he had picked up for her too. But then it had been a while. "What?"

Sonya pulled it out of her pocket. "I never did thank you for this." She dangled the delicate piece of metal in her hand and tapped it. The triangle filled the air with its sweet, pure sound. She met his gaze and smiled. "It's beautiful."

"You know, there's an opening for a physical therapist at Arlen," John Arlen said after the sweet trill had died away.

"There is?" Then she remembered. "You went to the doctor. What did he say?"

He shrugged. "He said I may regain eighty percent mobility but I have to actually do the exercises I'm supposed to. So I told him I had a physical therapist."

"Is the job paying or nonpaying? Because I have options now," she said, not bothering to fight the smile now.

"We can negotiate. And if you want to wear an odd piece of clothing when there's a crime spree that has to be stopped, well, that's your business. It looks good on you."

She half-smiled. "I haven't decided yet."

"What about me?" he said, and she was surprised to hear the earnestness in his voice. "You know, you'd have a sure thing in me if you thought about it."

"Then why didn't you come to me after everything was done?"

"Why didn't you come see me?"

"Because I was afraid," she burst out. "We got Jasper, your uncle died—"

"And why are those good reasons?"

"Because I thought everything you wanted out of me was done."

"Listen." His eyes darkened. "I was waiting for you to come and tell me you didn't need me anymore. You didn't come, and I thought maybe that was true—"

"Idiot." She punched him in the arm before she remembered and he winced. "I'm sorry! Are you all right?"

He rubbed his arm. "I'll get over it. Have you come to a decision?"

"Yeah," she said slowly. "About some things. First of all, I need more practice before I can introduce Sonika to the public. So the city's still not going to have a superhero for a while."

He nodded. "What else?"

"While I enjoyed the work as a physical therapist, I'm not sure it's a job I need to do anymore."

"I see," he said, but after a hesitation. "Is this a runabout way of telling me it's been fun?"

"No, but if you need a physical therapist around, it's going to be me." That almost sounded aggressive. But she knew the next part wouldn't. "So what you're offering—"

"I need a physical therapist who makes me happy, and you fit the bill. We need someone around whose name doesn't start with a J. Or even a G."

"Good. I don't want to change it."

"Don't change. One way or another, you're still my own superheroine, whether you ever suit up again or not."

"Good," she said. She wasn't worried anymore about John being a groupie. "You, on the other hand, have to exercise."

"You got me started. After trying to fight those thugs, I knew I had to change my ways. Come take a look," he said, reaching out for her hand. "I have a surprise for you."

Sonya looked at him. "What is it?"

"It's not a surprise if I tell you."

"I'm not so sure I like surprises anymore considering we've just had people pop back from the dead intent on killing us. What is it?"

He hesitated. "Gloria's not in my lab anymore."

"Of course not. You took Gloria apart so you could blow yourself up," she pointed out. "Which I should kick your ass for, incidentally."

"Yeah, yeah. I have a universal gym down there instead."

Sonya stared at him. He was going to get better. She knew he would. Her throat had constricted but she managed, "You have to be careful not to overdo it."

"You have to make sure I don't do something stupid sweetheart." His eyes looked wary behind the glasses and his mouth was set. "I've got to start over, just like you are."

He kissed her again. She looked up at him, still uncertain of what to say. He added, "Although all this exercise is going to be a pain in the neck."

She laughed. "That's not where the pain's going to be. I'll be glad to nag you. We can do it together." Then she didn't know what to say, except, "I love you."

He closed his eyes and wrapped his arms around her. "Thank God for happy endings," he sighed as she kissed him. "What would we do without them?"

Also by Eilis Flynn

eBooks:
Festival of Stars
Hunters for Hire: Echoes of Passion
Introducing Sonika
The Sleeper Awakes

Print Books:
The Sleeper Awakes

About the Author

Eilis Flynn has spent a large share of her life working on Wall Street or in a Wall Street-related firm, so why should she write fiction that's any less based in our world? She spends her days aware that there is a reality beyond what we can see—and tells stories about it for Cerridwen Press. Published in other genres, she lives in verdant Washington state with her equally fantastical husband and spoiled rotten cats.

The author welcomes comments from readers. You can find her website and email address on her author bio page at www.ellorascave.com.

Tell Us What You Think

We appreciate hearing reader opinions about our books. You can email us at Comments@EllorasCave.com.

Why an electronic book?

We live in the Information Age—an exciting time in the history of human civilization, in which technology rules supreme and continues to progress in leaps and bounds every minute of every day. For a multitude of reasons, more and more avid literary fans are opting to purchase e-books instead of paper books. The question from those not yet initiated into the world of electronic reading is simply: *Why?*

1. *Price.* An electronic title at Ellora's Cave Publishing and Cerridwen Press runs anywhere from 40% to 75% less than the cover price of the exact same title in paperback format. Why? Basic mathematics and cost. It is less expensive to publish an e-book (no paper and printing, no warehousing and shipping) than it is to publish a paperback, so the savings are passed along to the consumer.
2. *Space.* Running out of room in your house for your books? That is one worry you will never have with electronic books. For a low one-time cost, you can purchase a handheld device specifically designed for e-reading. Many e-readers have large, convenient screens for viewing. Better yet, hundreds of titles can be stored within your new library—on a single microchip. There are a variety of e-readers from different manufacturers. You can also read e-books on your PC or laptop computer. (Please note that Ellora's Cave does not endorse any specific brands.

You can check our websites at www.elloracave.com or www.cerridwenpress.com for information we make available to new consumers.)

3. ***Mobility.*** Because your new e-library consists of only a microchip within a small, easily transportable e-reader, your entire cache of books can be taken with you wherever you go.

4. ***Personal Viewing Preferences.*** Are the words you are currently reading too small? Too large? Too… ANNOYING? Paperback books cannot be modified according to personal preferences, but e-books can.

5. ***Instant Gratification.*** Is it the middle of the night and all the bookstores near you are closed? Are you tired of waiting days, sometimes weeks, for bookstores to ship the novels you bought? Ellora's Cave Publishing sells instantaneous downloads twenty-four hours a day, seven days a week, every day of the year. Our webstore is never closed. Our e-book delivery system is 100% automated, meaning your order is filled as soon as you pay for it.

Those are a few of the top reasons why electronic books are replacing paperbacks for many avid readers.

As always, Ellora's Cave and Cerridwen Press welcome your questions and comments. We invite you to email us at Comments@elloracave.com or write to us directly at Ellora's Cave Publishing Inc., 1056 Home Avenue, Akron, OH 44310-3502.

Discover for yourself why readers can't get enough of the multiple award-winning publisher Ellora's Cave.

Whether you prefer e-books or paperbacks, be sure to visit EC on the web at www.ellorascave.com

for an erotic reading experience that will leave you breathless.

Lightning Source UK Ltd.
Milton Keynes UK
UKOW051539190911

178921UK00001B/89/P